LONE TREE CLAIM

On the Dakota Frontier

By
CK VAN DAM

Lone Tree Claim

This is a work of fiction. Names, characters, places and events are products of the author's imagination. Any resemblance to actual persons or events is coincidental.

Published in the United States in 2023 by Pasque Publishing

www.ckvandam.com

Cover design by Douglas Moss

Pasque
Publishing

Dedication

When I was young, my mother taught me that having girlfriends is important – more important than boyfriends. They support us when we're struggling. They celebrate when we triumph. They are a sounding board when we're choosing a path.

This book is dedicated to women who support and celebrate other women.

TABLE OF CONTENTS

Author's Note

After the Civil War, thousands of Americans journeyed west to claim 160 acres of land through the Homestead Act of 1862. The country was still healing from the devastating war that killed or maimed more than 600,000 men, and the western territories offered homesteaders a new start. Men and women who were the "head of household" could stake a claim. The land was theirs if they lived on the claim for five years, built a home, and cultivated the land.

Cultivation took many forms. Some homesteaders turned to farming. Others chose to become cattle ranchers or sheepherders. The inspiration for this story is a well-known adage in agriculture, "Go into sheep for the money, cattle for the prestige." Sheep provided two revenue streams – wool and mutton – while beef cattle were a "one and done" yield. On ranches with both sheep and cattle, it was often the women who managed the sheep. That was the inspiration for this story.

Chapter 1: The Battle of the Wilderness

May 12, 1864 – Chicago, Illinois

Katie Rose

"Katie Rose, see if Callahan needs a refill."

Brian Sullivan, proprietor of the Lucky Shamrock Pub, called out to his daughter, who was working behind the pub's brightly polished bar. The Lucky Shamrock in Chicago's South Side was a favorite watering hole for the city's growing Irish population.

Katie served a foaming draught to Aiden Callahan. He took a swig and said, "Did you see yesterday's Times?" He rattled the two-day-old Chicago Times newspaper. "There's news of a big battle over East. President Lincoln's new general is in the thick of it."

Katie was tired of hearing about the war. The only news she wanted to hear was that her husband, Pat Kelly, was safe and coming home. But, like any good bartender, she pretended interest in her customer.

"What's the news?"

Aiden Callahan, one of the regulars at the Lucky Shamrock, said, "Seems this new general might be the one to turn the tide. U.S. Grant's his name. I like the sound of that. He's taking on Lee and the Rebs on some battlefield called Spotsylvania in Virginia. The paper says that Hooker and Burnside retreated, but Grant kept fighting. You can't win a war by retreating," Callahan, a feisty Irishman, shook his head in disgust. "This could be the turning point in the war."

"I hope so, Aiden. I'm praying that the war will be over soon and that Pat and our other boys in blue will be coming home."

"That would be a grand thing, Katie Rose," Callahan agreed.

The pub was bustling that night, and Katie moved on to serve other customers.

June 3, 1864

Katie Rose's hands trembled as she opened the letter addressed to her in her husband's familiar handwriting.

Dear Katie Rose,

It is the eve of battle in Spotsylvania. Captain Brown ordered all the men in the troop to write letters home. If you are reading this letter, it means that I did not survive the battle, and one of my mates has mailed this letter to you.

I wish we'd had more time together before I left for the war. Pray for me.

Your husband,

Patrick J. Kelly

Katie looked at the letter in disbelief. He was gone? He was dead? Where were the words of endearment? Where was his apology for his temper and the angry words he spat out the morning he left to rejoin his company?

She swiped at a tear as it made its way down her cheek. The tear was not so much for grief as it was for a sense of loss.

Katie knew she should feel sorrow at Pat's death, but all she felt was relief. Theirs was a hasty marriage, like so many others during wartime. "Marry in haste, repent in leisure," her nan had said. But she didn't listen to her grandmother. She had been drawn up in the excitement of the moment, and even though Pat Kelly's hair-trigger temper was a concern, she had said 'yes' to his proposal.

She turned and saw her reflection in the window – a twenty-year-old woman, buxom but with a tiny waist that accentuated her curves even more. Katie had inherited her mother's copper-colored hair and her grandmother's green eyes. She also had her grandmother's steely determination.

And now what? Now, she was a war widow. She would continue as she had been – living in her father's house and working at her father's bar. Maybe she'd remarry someday, but that was a long time in the future.

Or, she could take control of her life and steer her own destiny. She could do what her nan and granda had done – go west and seek her fortune. Katie had heard men at the pub talk about going West. "Land fever," they called it. Land of their own was the dream of Irishmen who had left the Old Country, where every scrap of land seemed to belong to English landlords.

On the frontier, so they said, there were millions of acres of land that people could claim for free just for the asking. 'Just for living on the land,' Katie repeated in her head. It seemed too good to be true.

What's more, the Homestead Act even allowed women to claim land – if they were unmarried or widowed and twenty-one years old. And, after five years, the land would be hers, but that seemed like a lifetime to the twenty-year-old Katie. She would have to bide her time until she was twenty-one. Until then, she would plan and save.

At dinner, she showed Pat's letter to her family. Clare Sullivan watched as Katie Rose held a hankie to her face and dabbed at nonexistent tears. "My sweet girl," Clare started, "I know how much Pat meant to you. We will break the news to Pat's family tomorrow after you've had a chance to recover from the shock."

That night, after dinner, Katie went to her room to "be alone with her grief," she said. She pulled her journal from under the mattress and started a new chapter in her life.

Journal Entry – June 3, 1864

When this war is over, I'm going to start over, too. There's nothing for me here on the South Side. I do not want to wear widow's weeds. I cannot pretend to be in mourning forever.

I've determined to save money for passage to Dakota Territory. The Homestead Act says widows and unmarried women qualify to claim 160 acres. There's land to be had by anyone willing to work hard. I don't know much about farming or ranching, so I'll take a job where I can learn what I need to make a go of it.

I am going west! Da won't be happy, but I think Nan will understand. I'll talk with her in the morning.

KR

Chapter 2: The War Ends

April 10, 1865 – Lucky Shamrock Pub, South Side Chicago

Katie Rose

There was whooping and whistling outside Sullivan's home on that warm spring day in April. "The War is over. Johnny Reb turned tail and ran," the mob shouted. People flooded out of their houses into the street to join in the celebration. It had been four years of bloody fighting. Nearly all the families in South Side had suffered losses, with men of all ages dying on battlefields or in makeshift hospitals. Others returned home, some missing limbs or experiencing what the doctors called "soldier's fatigue" – mentally unable to fight any longer.

For Katie Rose, the war had ended nearly a year before when her husband died, but this signaled the end – and a new beginning – for many of her friends and neighbors.

People could get on with their lives now. The soldiers would return from the battlefields, ready to start where they left off.

Brian Sullivan opened the Lucky Shamrock early that day and tapped a new beer keg to celebrate. "First beer is on the house," he shouted above the din. Katie and Ryan eyed each other, knowing that no one would be keeping count.

Ryan, who would turn 16 in a few months, had already planned to join the Illinois 44th. The end of the war meant he would not see battle. Like all young men, Ryan wanted to test his mettle in war. But Katie and her grandmother had prayed to Saint Brigid nightly that the war would end before Ryan could enlist. Their prayers were answered in the Appomattox Court House yesterday.

"Dance with me, Katie Rose," urged one of the older men in the bar. He grabbed Katie's hands and started dancing an Irish jig. "'Tis high time this war was over. My boys will be coming home soon!"

Katie laughed – the jubilation was contagious. Her full skirt of widow's gray cotton lawn flared as she twirled to the tune of "When Johnny Comes Marching Home."

The song ended, and Katie untangled herself from her dance partner. "I'm out of breath, and your mug is empty, Colin," Katie said. She wasn't actually out of breath, but she saw the pints of beer stacked up on the Shamrock's bar and went to give her da and brother a hand.

September 1865

General Lee's surrender to General Grant at Appomattox Courthouse in April signaled the end of fighting – or most of it. Still, skirmishes continued to flare up on the lines throughout the spring and into the summer of 1865. Even so, soldiers began mustering out of the Northern Army and returning home. By that fall, many men were readjusting to civilian life.

Katie Rose was setting the table for lunch when she heard a knock at the door. She opened the door to find a large, bearded man with a cane on her father's porch. "Excuse me, ma'am. I'm looking for the Kelly house."

She shook her head. "This is the Sullivan home. I believe there is a family named Kelly two blocks over."

Then she corrected herself, "Are you looking for Patrick Kelly's family? They live on the other side of the river. I can have my brother direct you."

"Thank you, ma'am. I'm looking for Pat Kelly's widow. I served in the 44th with Pat." He pointed to the insignia on his blue jacket.

"Oh, well, you have the right house, Mr. …"

"Hughes, Harold Hughes, ma'am."

"I'm Katie Kelly. Patrick was my husband. I chose to remain with my family after Pat returned to the front."

Hughes surveyed the young woman at the door and smiled. "Uh, may I come in?"

"Where are my manners? Of course, of course. Please come in, Mr. Hughes."

Harold Hughes moved through the doorway and settled into a straight-back chair by the small fireplace in the drawing room. Having seen to her guest's comfort, Katie excused herself to get another family member to join them. Even as a married woman, etiquette prescribed that she should not be alone with a strange man.

Katie Rose returned with her father and grandmother. Mr. Hughes introduced himself.

"You said you served in the 44th Company with Pat, Mr. Hughes?" Brian began the conversation.

"Yes, sir. We was buddies. It was a sad day when that sniper took him. I mustered out a few weeks ago. I promised Pat that I would call on his wife – er, widow – if he didn't make it through the War. He promised me the same.."

"So, you have a wife, Mr. Hughes?" Clare inquired.

"Oh, yes, ma'am. Aggie – that is Mrs. Hughes – is still in Springfield with her folks. I'm headed there directly, and then we're bound for Dakota Territory. I have a hankering to live out west."

"Mr. Hughes," Katie said, "would you like to join us for lunch?"

"Oh, I don't want to trouble you any." He eyed the dinner table set for four.

"No trouble. I'll set another plate."

"We always have room for our fighting men," Brian agreed.

Over a hearty meal of meat and potatoes, Hughes outlined his plan. "I'm aiming to start a sheep ranch out in Dakota. Aggie's granddaddy brought sheep over from Scotland, and the family is famous for wool and mutton. I'm fixin' to cut out some of the best ewes and rams from her family's herd and ship them to the Territory on a barge. Should take about a month – maybe more – to move 'em up the Missouri River from St. Louis. The Missouri runs clear through Dakota Territory nearly to Canada.

"Once I'm in there, I'll stake my claim for 160 acres of that free land! 'Course I'll need more land as the herd grows, but I heard-tell there's land a-plenty out there. Lots of pasture for grazing."

Katie's brother Ryan interrupted excitedly, "I heard the same thing at the bar. Men are claiming land just by signing a paper. It's the American way!"

Katie Rose's mind was buzzing. "It sounds like a wonderful adventure, Mr. Hughes!"

9

Hughes sized up the comely young woman. "The frontier isn't for city gals like you, Mrs. Kelly. In fact, I had a devil of a time convincing Aggie to come west with me, and she's from a farm. No...I don't want two women to coddle."

"I'm not afraid of hard work, and I'm a good cook. I could be a big help to your wife, Mr. Hughes.

Hughes considered the offer and made a snap decision."Tell you what, missy. That might ease Aggie's concerns about life on the frontier. If you're up for the adventure, that is."

Her copper curls bounced as she nodded enthusiastically. "It would be a fresh start for me. I think Pat would want me to move on."

Clare coughed. Katie gave her a side glance.

"The missus is gonna need help in the house once we're settled on the land. We could send you train fare and some traveling money," Hughes suggested. "Of course, the train will get you only so far west, then it's a stagecoach ride. That is, once I find the right piece of land."

"It's a generous offer, Mr. Hughes. Thank you," she responded.

Brian Sullivan rose from the table. "T'was a pleasure to meet you, Hughes. I'd be honored to stand you a pint tonight at my pub. It's the Lucky Shamrock on Washington Street across from the river."

He turned to his son, "Ryan, we need to see to deliveries at the Shamrock." Brian shook Hughes' large, meaty hand, then he and Ryan were out the door.

"And that is my signal to leave, as well," Hughes said. He looked at Katie, "I'll talk it over with Aggie, but I think she'll be agreeable."

Katie blushed and nodded. "Thank you, Mr. Hughes."

She closed the door and turned to her grandmother. "What do you think, Nan? I saw how you looked at Mr. Hughes when he made the offer."

"I think we need to make very sure that there *is* a Mrs. Hughes and that she is planning to go west, too, Mo stór.*" Slipping into Irish, Clare used her endearment "my treasure" for her granddaughter.

Harold Hughes

Harold Hughes gathered his coat and hat and took his leave. As he sauntered down the walk, he continued to think about Katie Rose Kelly. "Yes, she's a fine figure of a woman. A fine figure."

He made a mental note to stop in the Lucky Shamrock that evening after he concluded his business. Hughes' first stop was at the telegraph office to let Aggie know he'd found a girl to help with chores. Aggie Hughes didn't share her husband's enthusiasm about starting a sheep ranch in the middle of nowhere. She preferred the comforts of home and hearth in Springfield, her hometown.

Hughes calculated that a hired girl to help around the house would quell Aggie's protests about moving to Dakota Territory. Even though she'd grown up on a farm, the idea of living on the frontier didn't sit well with her. He also knew that Aggie would like having someone to boss around.

Course, he thought to himself, *maybe she'll only live on the ranch part of the time and will go back home for winters.* He smiled at the thought.

He left the telegraph office and headed to the sheep auction. Chicago was fast becoming the meatpacking capital of the country. And in addition to bringing in livestock for the burgeoning meatpacking industry, farmers also brought livestock to the stockyards to sell to other growers. He might not be buying today, but someday he'd be selling his sheep. That's what really brought Harold Hughes to Chicago.

Katie

Harold Hughes' visit to the Sullivan house gave Katie Rose a new purpose, and her mind was spinning! She knew she didn't want to work in the pub for the rest of her life, and getting married again didn't appeal to her at all. And, while she was truly a city girl, she wasn't afraid of hard work. She already knew how to run a household, thanks to her nan. Working as a housekeeper for Mr. and Mrs. Hughes would certainly be an adventure.

Journal Entry – September 20, 1865

Dakota Territory – here I come! 'Tis a piece of good luck that Patrick's army friend came to our house today. He plans to go West, and he and his wife need help in the house. Mr. Hughes asked if I would be interested in working as a hired girl for Mrs. Hughes. This is my ticket west! I'll work for Mrs. Hughes and see if frontier life suits me.

Nan, of course, is skeptical about this scheme, so I will write to Mrs. Hughes to discuss the position and when it would commence. There are so many details to work out, but I have a grand feeling about this.

Da always says, "Life is like a cup of tea. It's all in how you make it."

KR

Chapter 3: Dakota Territory bound

April 1866 – Dakota Territory
Katie Rose

Just when she thought her bones couldn't take more rocking or rattling from the rough roads, the stagecoach stopped at a way station. She and the other four passengers climbed out of the small, cramped carriage while the driver watered the horses.

This was Katie's first real look at the frontier and its prairies. The stagecoach had departed from the Sioux City train depot in the very early hours, and they'd kept the shades down in an attempt to block some of the dust from the road.

Now, as she stepped down from the stagecoach in the bright light of the spring day, she saw a sea of green grass dotted here and there with patches of pink and yellow flowers. But, other than the way station, not a building in sight.

Taking a handkerchief from her reticule, Katie wiped the dust from her face. She gratefully accepted a dipper of water from the woman who ran the way station.

"Hank don't want to linger here, so I've packed box lunches for y'all," said the woman. Her face was weather-beaten, and her hair, coiled into a messy bun, was more gray than black. "I'm Irene. Don't see many women coming this way," she said to Katie, the only woman on the stagecoach.

Katie nodded. Irene continued, "I've been running this station since before the War. Then my man went off to fight. Now it's just me, but I like it that way."

"You're a widow?" Katie inquired.

"Not sure. Mebbe," the older woman shrugged and changed the subject. "Where you headed?"

"Somewhere near the White River, " Katie replied. "Two more days, I'm told."

Sally nodded, "Safe travels, missy," Irene called after Katie as the travelers returned to the stagecoach to continue their journey.

During the stagecoach ride, Katie alternated between uncomfortable boredom and surprised awe at the beauty of the prairie in spring.

Finally, Katie and the other passengers arrived at Ft. Randall. The army fort, located west of the Missouri River, was built as a stopping point for military expeditions. It naturally became a place for settlers heading west to rest, restock, and reassess. And, because it was located on the "Muddy Mo," Harold Hughes had chosen Ft. Randall as the final destination for the barge that had carried his sheep west last fall. Now, Katie Rose Kelly had followed the same passage in her trip west.

Stagecoach travel limited passengers' baggage since mail bags took up much of the space. Katie arrived in Dakota Territory with a carpet bag that included three dresses, some personal items, and her nan's shawl, which Clare had insisted she would need. Secreted away in the lining was the cash that Katie had received as a war widow pension. Mrs. Hughes promised that Katie would be able to purchase other "necessaries" after she settled in.

So, Katie stood alone on the dirt street outside a boarding house, just her and her suitcase. She shook her head. "Not sure what I expected," she said aloud. "Head up and back straight, Katie Rose. You wanted to be on your own, and," she laughed, "you are!"

She turned and entered the boarding house. "I'm here for Mr. and Mrs. Hughes, but they must have been delayed," she explained to the young woman inside. "I'll need a room for the night."

"Welcome, Mrs." said the young, very blonde woman at a table in what looked to be the dining room as well as the lobby. "We don't have any empty rooms, but there's a spare bed in Room Three if you don't mind sharing it with Jenny."

"That would be...." Katie started, but the young woman interrupted.

"Befores you answer, Jenny's from the colony – the colored colony over west," she nodded in that direction.

"Fine," Katie continued. Katie Rose recalled the stories her nan told about the prejudice and hate that she and Katie's grandda had encountered as Irish immigrants in the 1830s. Americans had been vocal in their hatred for the Irish and the "Irish Invasion" that was just beginning. But those same hated Irishmen volunteered in multitudes to defend their new country during the War Between the States and to free the slaves. And now that same hatred was being visited on freed slaves. Katie would have none of it.

"Coloreds are fine with me, Miss...." Katie waited for the boardinghouse clerk to introduce herself.

"Miss Baker, ma'am. Caroline Baker. My ma and pa own the place," she gestured to the establishment.

"And I'm Mrs. Kelly, but you can call me Katie, lately of Chicago, Illinois. I've been hired by the Hugheses. I understand they have a ranch near here."

"Yes, ma'am. It's a half-day's ride from here. Now, let's get you settled." She had Katie sign the ledger and pointed past the dining room table. "Room Three is just down the hall."

Katie found the room empty, although it was evident that she had a roommate. There was a small bag similar to hers in the corner. And, unlike many boarding houses that required guests to share a bed, whether or not they were acquainted, this room had two narrow cots. Katie nodded at the accommodations. "These will suffice," she said to herself. She claimed the other empty corner for her bag and then left to explore her new world.

She surveyed the stockade-enclosed garrison. There was no mercantile, no saloon, and not even a church in sight. It was clear that Ft. Randall did not cater to civilians. But, since it was also the stagecoach station nearest the Hughes' ranch, this was where Katie Rose had been instructed to meet Harold and Aggie Hughes. For now, she simply sat on the bench outside the boardinghouse and enjoyed not being jostled and jarred on a stagecoach.

She watched soldiers coming and going from the barracks, practicing on the parade ground, or cleaning cannons. All of them were enjoying the spring weather just as she was.

Caroline Baker popped her head out the door. "Mrs… er, Katie? We'll be having the evening meal now."

Katie returned inside to join the other boarders at the long table. Thinking she would finally meet her roommate, she looked for another woman at the table. Instead, she was seated across from two roughly dressed men. One of them tucked a napkin into the neck of his shirt. The other hung his large hat on the back of the chair. Then, a dark-skinned woman entered the dining room from the kitchen. She carried a large platter of sliced meat and some type of vegetable Katie didn't recognize.

The man directly across from Katie passed her the platter and asked, "And who might this tasty morsel be?"

"I am not on the menu tonight," Katie said in a honeyed voice. The voice her da would have recognized as the signal that Katie was "getting her Irish up."

"I would call you 'sir,'" she continued, "but that doesn't seem accurate."

Katie looked at the man. He was large, and she pitied his horse for having to carry his bulk. He wore a leather vest over a dirty, plaid shirt and sported a long, greasy mustache. His hat hung on the back of his chair.

Before she could hurl another insult and perhaps get herself into a peck of trouble, the other diner spoke up. "Duke, I think the lady has taken your measure. You'd best back down. The boss wouldn't want you getting into a fistfight with a girl at the Fort." He smiled at his joke.

As far as Katie could tell, the other cowboy was younger and a bit cleaner, but not by much. He wore a black leather vest, unbuttoned, over a light blue chambray shirt that looked the worse for wear. His hair was shaggy, jet-black hair, and he had the start of a thick, black beard, about a three-day growth, Katie observed.

"Thank you, *sir*," Katie emphasized the last word to contrast the men's manners.

The second cowboy snickered, tipped an imaginary hat, and then reached for a second helping of meat. Katie waited for the men to introduce themselves, but they were more interested in eating than in niceties. "Just as well," she thought.

After the meal, Katie disappeared into her room, not wanting anything more to do with the "eejits," as her father would have called the cowboys.

Just as she wondered when she'd meet her roommate, the woman who had served dinner entered the room. "Hello, Mrs. Kelly. Caroline said you didn't mind sharing the room with a colored."

"Nice to meet you. You can call me Katie if I can call you Jenny."

Jenny smiled, sat on her bed, and unwound the scarf from her mass of black curls. I work for room and board here and a little bit of change. My man is at the Fort, and this is how we can be together. It's a better life than we had before."

Katie could only imagine the horrors that Jenny and her folks had suffered before – and during – the War. "Seems that we're all starting new lives," Katie told her roommate. "My husband was in the Army, too. He died at Spotsylvania. That left me a widow. Now, I'm bound for sheep ranch as a hired girl. It's a new start for me, too." She shrugged.

Katie eyed the empty cot. "Truth be told, Jenny, I'm glad to have a roommate after meeting those fellas at dinner." She sighed. "It's been a long trip out here, and I'm exhausted. That bed is looking pretty good, so I'll bid you a good night."

But before she dropped off to sleep, Katie made a short entry in her journal.

Journal Entry – April 20, 1866

I'm finally in Dakota Territory. I expected to be met by Mr. and Mrs. Hughes, but there's no sign of them. I certainly hope that, after this planning, they've not changed their minds. They sent me travel money, but something unexpected may have happened. Did I make a mistake by leaving my home and family in Chicago? I do miss Nan and Da. I even miss Ryan!

The trip by train and stagecoach was a long one – but I have a feeling this is just the beginning of a long journey. The land is beautiful and so different from Illinois. Of course, the frontier is nothing like Chicago. It's so vast.

It feels like the stuff of dreams. I can't wait to see what tomorrow brings!

    KR

Chapter 4: The Hired Girl

Katie

The following day, Katie stretched and noticed that the other bed was already empty and made up nice as could be. The smell of coffee propelled her from the bed, and she hurriedly slipped into a fresh dress, ready to start the new life that she'd promised herself.

At the communal dining table, Katie noticed the cowboys were absent. In fact, there was only one other guest at the table, and he was buried in a newspaper. Jenny brought in a hot pot of coffee and filled Katie's cup.

"It feels odd to be waited on," Katie said with a laugh as she sipped the hot brew.

"And you're not likely to be waited on again any time soon, Missy." Katie recognized Harold Hughes' voice from behind the newspaper. He put the paper down. "I hope you're good an' rested. The missus sent me to fetch you. I got in late last night. Finish your breakfast, collect your belongin's and we'll head out."

Rather than the Union jacket he'd worn when he called on Katie and her family in Chicago, Hughes wore a gray corduroy vest over a black shirt with sleeves rolled up mid-arm. She could see suspenders under the vest. A large, floppy-brimmed hat was on the table next to his breakfast plate.

Katie was a bit taken aback by Mr. Hughes' curt greeting. She had expected that he would be happy to see

21

her. Determined to make this a good start, she smiled brightly, "Mr. Hughes, it's so good to see you. And thank you again for paying my way out here. Even though we corresponded by mail, I'm looking forward to finally meeting Mrs.Hughes and seeing the ranch." She polished off the bacon and eggs Jenny had heaped on her plate and took a final drink of coffee.

"Jenny, it was nice to get to know you," she said as Jenny cleared her place.

Katie disappeared down the hall to retrieve her carpet bag, emerging from the boarding house just minutes later.

Hughes was waiting near a buckboard wagon and helped Katie onto the bench. "It's a good three-hour ride back to the ranch. Best settle in," he said.

Katie was just as captivated with the limitless horizon of the prairie as she had been on the stagecoach. In fact, her perch on the wagon bench gave her an even better view of the undulating sea of green grasses and flowers. And now, without the enclosed stagecoach to restrict her view, she could see large birds circling overhead.

Hughes followed Katie's gaze and said, "Them's eagles. I ain't seen them carry off a lamb yet, but I've heard-tell it happens."

Katie shook her head. "I have a lot to learn."

"Gotta keep an eye on the new ones in the spring," Hughes liked to show his authority. "Between coyotes, wolves, foxes, and eagles, there's always something out there lookin' for a free meal. Sheep are pretty defenseless; that's why a good sheepdog is so important."

"I like dogs. We had a terrier in Chicago."

22

"These ain't pets, missy. They're workin' dogs. They watch the herd, protect the sheep from other animals, and help move 'em from pasture to pasture." He continued, "We just finished most of the lambing, so we're between seasons."

"Seasons? You mean spring and summer?"

"Nope. I mean lambin' and shearin'. Gotta cut the wool off the critters before the weather gets hot. I have a crew comin' in for that. You won't be expected to do any shearing, but the crew will keep you busy. Those boys eat their fill."

Katie nodded. *"This really would be a new life,"* she thought. *"I have a lot to learn."*

She kept an eye out for the predators Hughes had mentioned. Still, all she spotted were some deer and, after asking Hughes to identify the smaller animals, a herd of antelope. "Hmm, I've never seen an antelope," she mused aloud.

"They're thick out here. Not a lot of meat on 'em, but if they're cooked right, they can be tasty," he said. He took out his rifle, got a bead on one of the larger bucks, and shot it. "Might as well start your learnin' now. Climb down and watch me field dress that critter."

With the antelope gutted and cleaned, Hughes tossed it into the back of the wagon, and they were on their way again. "You can quarter it and cut it up for meals when we're home. From the look on your face, I'm guessing you don't know how to do that. Aggie will show you."

It was late morning when the wagon pulled up to a small shanty. Hughes jumped off the buckboard and went around back to shoulder the antelope. "Go on in and introduce yourself to the missus."

Katie climbed down with her bag, squared her shoulders, and entered the small house.

"Hello, Mrs. Hughes," she called.

Aggie Hughes turned from the cookstove. "You must be Katie Rose Kelly," she said. She tucked a graying strand of hair behind her ear. "Call me Aggie. It's good to have you here. I need another set of hands to keep up with all the chores."

Katie saw that the woman she had known only through letters was middle-aged. She was thin, perhaps too thin, and wore her graying hair in a long braid down her back. She had warm, brown eyes and a kind face.

Katie wanted to start on the right foot with her new employer. And, knowing that first impressions count, she gave Aggie her best smile and said, "I am so glad to be here, Aggie. Thank you for giving me this opportunity."

Aggie handed her an apron and pointed to what looked to be a bed attached to the wall. "We will build a shelf above the bed for your things. The bed folds down. We keep it up during the day to make room in this little cabin. I declare, I didn't know I would be roughing it when Harold talked me into coming west," Aggie said. "But when he promised to hire someone to help with the cooking and cleaning, I finally gave in. Don't get me wrong – I'm a farm girl – a farm woman." She laughed self-consciously and continued, "And I am not afraid of hard work, but more hands make light work.

"Still, the frontier is sooo," she paused for the right words. "So wild. I didn't expect life to be this hard out here.

24

And when Harold's out tending the flock, it is horribly lonely. It will be good to have someone to talk to."

She smiled and gave Katie an appraising look. "You're pretty, but you look sturdy. Can you cook and clean?"

"Oh, yes, ma'am. Just like I wrote in my letters to you. My nan – my grandmother – had me cooking and baking since I was a lass. Wait till you taste my soda bread."

May 1866

Over the next few days, Katie and Aggie worked side by side. Aggie Hughes was a strict but fair taskmaster. And Katie, for her part, was a quick learner. Soon, she was managing most of the meals for the three of them.

Katie learned to cook the wild game and occasional mutton filling the Hughes' larder. And she learned about sheep. She especially liked watching the new lambs as they explored their world, chased each other, and responded to their mothers' calls during playtime.

"You like watchin' them woolies?" Hughes said.

Katie, startled, had been watching the young ones with their mamas and hadn't heard Hughes approaching. "Oh, yes. It's grand to watch them play about."

"The shearing crew will be here next week. You'd best make sure there's enough food to feed 'em."

Katie and Aggie began making lists of ingredients and cooking supplies needed to feed the crew.

"We need to stock up for the week," Aggie said. "Harold and I will go into town tomorrow for supplies."

"To the Fort?" Katie said. "I didn't see a mercantile there."

"Oh, no, my girl. We'll need to go to Twin Brooks. It's nearly a day's ride by buckboard, but there's a store there. Twin Brooks is small but growing."

"And I'll be here alone?" Katie wasn't sure she was ready to be on her own on the prairie.

"We'll leave the shotgun for you. I saw you practicing. No time like the present to get your prairie feet under you." Katie agreed and knew it made sense for her to stay back since Aggie *didn't* know how to use the shotgun.

Aggie patted Katie's shoulder. "Besides, Rob and Roy will be here to watch the sheep, and they will keep watch on you, too," Aggie said, referring to the ranch's two sheepdogs.

That evening, Katie sat on the log bench outside the shanty. She started a letter to her family back in Chicago.

Dear Da, Nan and Ryan,

Life in the Dakota Territory brings something new every day. Most of the time, I do the cooking while Aggie (Mrs. Hughes) does the cleaning. There is not much firewood on the prairie, so once a week, we collect "prairie muffins" – the sun-dried droppings from buffalo – to use as fuel in the cookstove. Surprisingly, they don't smell bad when they burn, and they're nearly as good as coal for cooking.

The prairie is beautiful in the spring. It is green, just like the Ireland that Nan always tells us about. Sometimes at night I can hear animals howling in the distance. Mr. Hughes says it's coyotes. He keeps a loaded shotgun by the door in case they get too close to the flock or to us.

We have a large garden since there is not a greengrocer around the corner. I am learning to cook venison – both deer and antelope – and, of course, mutton.

Even though I miss all of you, I am learning that there is another world outside of South Chicago. Every day is a new adventure.

She put her pen down and gazed at the sunset. The horizon was filled with orange, pink, and purple to signal that the day was ending. Katie smiled and said a silent 'good night' to the prairie.

Chapter 5: Coyote Attack

May 5, 1866 - Hughes Ranch, Dakota Territory

Katie

The following day, Aggie and Harold headed west before dawn, leaving Katie with instructions to stay near the house.

Shaking her head as she swept the dirt floors in the shanty, she made quick work of cleaning the small house. There was a window on each of the four sides of the wooden shanty. Shutters were intended to keep out most of the harsh weather but were open during the warmer seasons to catch cooling breezes. A cookstove served as the only source of heat during winter.

The home was sparsely furnished. A steamer trunk did double duty as a storage chest and a bench at the kitchen table. In the corner, by Katie's fold-down bed, there was a washtub used for laundry and bathing. On the other side of the room, a large quilt had been hung to provide some privacy and sleeping quarters for Harold and Aggie. Shelves held dishes, cooking pots, and cooking ingredients.

Aggie had insisted on bringing two rocking chairs from back East. Surveying the bare furnishings, Katie understood what Aggie had said about "roughing it."

The sheep had been moved to a nearby pasture. When she couldn't actually see the sheep, Katie could certainly hear them. While the prairies were basically flat, rolling hills did break up the horizon. Still, Katie couldn't get used to the lack of trees in Dakota Territory. She missed the stately oaks, the colorful maples, and the hickory trees with their sweet nuts that thrived in Illinois.

It was promising to be a warm May day, so Katie dressed to suit the weather. Since she was alone on the ranch, she decided that her camisole top and skirt of pale green would suffice. Aggie had left a short list of chores – baking and light cleaning. She had just popped several loaves of soda bread into the cookstove when she heard the dogs barking excitedly.

Katie grabbed the shotgun and headed outside to find out what the ruckus was about.

In the distance, Katie could see both dogs snarling and barking at a pair of coyotes that were circling the flock.

"Oh, bollocks!" Katie leaned into her Irish heritage when she saw the scene unfold on the pasture. "Rob! Roy! Good boys!" she called out to the two border collies.

She tucked the shotgun under her arm, picked up her skirts, and ran toward the sheep. She raised the shotgun when she was close enough to get a "possibly accurate" shot off in the direction of the coyotes. Taking aim and making sure that the dogs were not targeted, Katie pulled the trigger. Even though she expected the kickback, the shotgun's recoil knocked Katie Rose Kelly to her bottom.

The shotgun blast did its job, though, scaring the coyotes away from the sheep.

Before she could gain her footing, she heard someone laughing behind her.

Katie Rose looked over her shoulder to see a rider dismounting from a large, black horse. She recognized the black hat, vest, and blue chambray shirt as belonging to her one-time dinner partner at the boarding house. At least it was the less disagreeable of the two cowboys, she thought.

"I do not find this amusing." Katie's eyes squinted, and she fleetingly thought about aiming the shotgun in the direction of the cowboy. "Besides, it was a good shot. I didn't hit the dogs, did I?" She rose, dusted off her behind, and smiled despite herself.

"No, ma'am. No dogs were harmed while protecting your herd – er, flock. A bunch of sheep are a 'flock,' right?"

The man laughed and gave Katie an appraising look.

He swept the dusty, wide-brimmed hat from his mop of black hair and said, "Name's Jake. Jake Riley. We didn't have a chance to introduce ourselves at the boarding house. And you…" He didn't finish his question.

"You and your friend were too busy eating to mind your manners," Katie reminded him. "I am Katie Rose Kelly."

"New to these parts, Miss, or is it Mrs. Kelly?"

"Mrs. Kelly."

Before she could ask what brought him here, he said, "Kelly? I thought this was the Hughes place."

"It is the Hughes Ranch," she confirmed. But not wanting to admit that she was alone, Katie did not mention that her employers were absent. "What is your business with them?"

"I work for the Double D – that's Dan Deacon's ranch to the north. We'll be moving our cattle soon, and I wanted to get the lay of the land."

Katie pretended to understand what he was saying.

Trying to prolong the visit, Jake said, "Say, could I trouble you for some water for me and my horse?"

"And now it's my manners that are lacking. Of course, Mr. Riley." She motioned for him to follow her to the well and saw that he drew a bucket of water for the horse before enjoying a dipper of cold well water himself. "Hits the spot, it does. And call me Jake," he said.

"You sound like you have a bit of the Irish in you, Jake," Katie said to make conversation.

"That I do, Mrs. Kelly – as do you."

She laughed. "Is it the red hair?"

"That and your," he paused and looked down into her eyes, "kelly-green eyes. Green as a shamrock, my grand da would say."

Remembering that they were alone, Katie blushed and backed away. "Well...."

Jake took the hint and said, "Well, I'd best be on my way. Keep that shotgun handy in case those coyotes return, Katie Rose Kelly."

Jake

Jake Riley mounted his stallion and loped off to the north. He looked back once to see Katie patting the two sheepdogs. One of the dogs had rolled onto its back, and Katie was rubbing his belly.

He smiled at the memory of her – a tumble of coppery, red curls that fell to the shoulders of her snowy white bit of a blouse. And her figure – a small waist with high bosoms that would haunt a man in his dreams!

"Damn," he thought. "The good ones are always taken. That is one good-looking woman." Still, the names didn't add up. If that was the Hughes' place, where were they, and why was Mrs. Kelly tending house? He'd have to do some asking around. His bunkmate Sam might know the story.

In the meantime, Jake couldn't get that red-haired gal out of his head. He patted his horse's withers and said to the animal, "I should have known better than to mess with married women after that time in Fort Smith. But who knew she'd have a husband who was also the town sheriff."

He thought about his days as a trail hand, driving cattle on the Shawnee Trail. He could laugh about the incident now. Jake was just glad that his trail boss assured the sheriff that the crew would be pulling out the next day. As a punishment, Jake had to ride "drag" – at the back of the herd in the dust. He sure didn't miss those dusty, long days and nights moving longhorns from Texas to the rail lines up north. He preferred working on the Double D, where he wasn't on the move all the time. Still, someday, he'd like to have a spread of his own.

He'd ridden about an hour when he came to "Lone Tree," a shaded oasis on the treeless prairie. The cottonwood tree stood proud and defiant on the rolling land. Its leaves rustled in the slight breeze, offering some respite from the day's heat.

"Ain't that a pretty picture, Finn?" he asked the horse. "And it serves a purpose, too. Let's stop and enjoy the view before getting back to the Double D." He dismounted and let the horse graze while he considered who might know more about that Irish girl at the Hughes place.

Katie

Katie felt pretty proud of herself for defending the flock – yes, it was a flock, she thought. Still, she needed to work on her shooting.

She didn't intend to work as the Hughes' "hired girl" forever. Now that she was 21 and single, she met the requirements to claim 160 acres through the Homestead Act. But before that, she had to be able to shoot straight, ride a horse, and figure out how she fit into this new world.

She thought about her visitor. Jake Riley was a fine-looking man; his manners were acceptable, and he seemed to be an interesting fellow. "Now don't go thinking about men, Katie Rose," she said as she rubbed Rob's belly. (Or was it Roy's belly, she wondered?) "If you want a piece of that Homestead Act land, you must be on your own. Only unmarried women can stake a claim." The dog righted himself, and she could tell from the markings that the border collie was, indeed, Rob.

She tucked an errant red curl behind her ear and thought she still had a lot to learn about life on the prairie. A lot to learn.

Knowing that Harold and Aggie wouldn't return until late the next day, Katie finished her chores. She decided to practice some of those skills she would need for life on the frontier. She saddled Sugar, the Hughes' mare, and practiced riding "Western style." She had to hike up her skirts to straddle the saddle to do that. But practicality won out, and Katie realized she was not a bad horsewoman. "I like seeing the world from this perch," she said to the horse.

She couldn't practice her shooting skills because it would scare the sheep, so she sufficed by loading and unloading the shotgun. Eventually, she felt at ease enough with the weapon that she took it apart and reassembled it.

Before the sun was too high in the sky, Katie tended the garden and saw that sprouts were appearing in the dark soil.

By evening, Katie could feel the effects of the day's activities. Her shoulder ached from the shotgun's recoil, and her backside was sore from her time in the saddle. Easing into the large tin tub filled with steaming hot water, though, Katie was content with the choices and the life that she was making.

I can do this, she thought.

The next day, Katie went about her chores, keeping an ear and, at times, an eye on the sheep. She loved to watch the mamas tend their lambs. As she made herself a plate of cold mutton and some greens for dinner, she saw the Hughes' wagon come down the dirt road toward the shanty.

She quickly prepared two more plates for her employers, then went outside to welcome them back. To her surprise, only Harold was in the wagon.

"Howdy-do, Katie girl," Harold called out. "Yep, you are seeing right. Aggie decided to go back East. Seems homesteadin' was not to her liking."

Katie's mind roiled, shocked at this turn of events. What did this mean for her? Her da and nan had agreed to her "western adventure," as they called it, on the condition that Mrs. Hughes was part of the plan. Now, Aggie Hughes had changed that plan.

Hughes continued, "She told me yesterday that life on the frontier was dirty, dusty, and disgusting." He shrugged. "We don't need her anyways."

Katie was speechless and certainly didn't like the sound of "we."

"I…I have a cold dinner ready for you, Mr. Hughes." Katie didn't want to sound too familiar with the man. He swung off the buckboard and landed a little unsteadily on his feet. Katie knew he'd been drinking and became even more wary.

"Cold dinner, you say? I was hoping for something a bit warmer," he laughed.

Calling on her skills as a barkeeper, Katie knew that the best way to handle this situation was to distract Hughes. She needed to keep her distance until he passed out or fell asleep.

"Your dinner is on the table, Mr. Hughes. While you eat, I'll unload the wagon."

Hughes laughed again, took a swig from his whiskey bottle, and headed into the shanty.

Katie slowly unloaded food supplies from the wagon and piled them outside the shanty. Rather than re-entering the small house, Katie unhitched the horse. The sun was nearly down when she fed and watered the animal. It was dark in the shanty, and she could hear snoring.

"Good," she thought. "But what about tomorrow? Maybe it was the drink talking, and it will all be forgotten," she told herself. Still, to be safe, Katie made a bed in the back of the wagon, covered herself with Nan's shawl, and laid down for the night.

But it was a sleepless night for Katie Rose. She considered her options and decided that staying at the ranch was out of the question. She would tell Harold Hughes that she was leaving the position immediately. Having made that decision, Katie needed to determine where she would go.

Thoughts tumbled around in her head. Was she ready to be a homesteader? Maybe she could get a job in town while she sorted things out. Even though she didn't know anyone in Twin Brooks, she decided that might be her next step. All she really knew was that she needed to leave the Hughes ranch.

The next morning, Katie gathered up her nan's shawl and entered the shanty, resolved to give notice that she was leaving.

Harold Hughes sat at the small kitchen table drinking a cup of coffee. "'Morning, Katie girl," he said.

"Good morning, Mr. Hughes." Katie did not join him at the table. Instead, she stood between the doorway and the table. "I'm sorry that Aggie – Mrs. Hughes – did not find homesteading to her liking. Her departure has changed the agreement we made. I will be leaving today to find employment elsewhere." Katie was proud of herself for the straightforward manner she addressed her employer.

"Now, Katie Rose," Hughes began. "If I did anything yesterday to offend you, I'm sorry for the misunderstanding. This is the busy time of year for a sheep ranch, and I need someone here to feed the shearing crew. Like you said, we *have* an agreement." He emphasized the word "have."

"Aggie's leaving doesn't change the fact that I have a ranch to run and I hired you to help with the chores. I expect you to keep your end of the bargain."

She shook her head in disagreement. "It would not be proper for me to stay here unchaperoned, Mr. Hughes. Even though I am a widow and not a young, single woman, this is highly improper."

"We're both adults, Katie. Be reasonable. You might like not having Aggie around to boss you."

"Mr. Hughes, a single woman living alone with a man just wouldn't do. If you won't bring me into town, I'm prepared to walk there."

Realizing that he was not going to change her mind immediately, Hughes took a different tact. "I had a bit too much to drink yesterday – the shock of Aggie leavin' and all – but that won't happen again. Tell you what, I'll bunk in the barn. The shearing crew should be here tomorrow. Once they're done, I'll bring you to Twin Brooks. 'Course, I'll settle up what I owe you, too."

Katie nodded in agreement. A couple more days would allow her to firm up a plan. "Thank you. I'll take you up on your offer. Now, I'd best get to work cooking and baking for the crew."

At the end of the day, Katie reviewed the menu that she and Aggie had made for the shearing crew's meals – four loaves of bread, venison stew, mutton roast, three apple pies using dried apples from last fall, plus green beans, early beets, and radishes. "That should get us through the first day," she thought.

True to his word, Harold Hughes bedded down in the ramshackle barn that was more of a storage shed than a shelter for the animals. But, the night was mild, and Katie was relieved to see him take his bedroll from the shanty.

And, given that reprieve – because Katie still didn't trust Harold Hughes – she thought about continuing her letter home. Instead, she picked up her journal.

Journal Entry – May 7, 1866

My time on the Hughes sheep ranch is ending. There's always been something about Harold Hughes that made me uneasy. But without a horse or buggy to make my "escape," I decided to stay until the shearing crew completes their work.

In the meantime, I'm keeping a shotgun by my bed, even though Mr. Hughes is sleeping in the barn. The end of the week cannot come too quickly for me.

Then what? I wish I could talk to Nan. She would know what to do.

KR

Chapter 6: The Shearing Crew

May 8, 1866 - Hughes Ranch, Dakota Territory

Katie

When Harold Hughes entered the shanty, Katie had the coffee and hot buns on the table.

"You know, I was thinkin' we should get some chickens," he said by way of a greeting. "Aggie didn't cotton to birds, but fresh eggs would be tasty in the morning. And we wouldn't need to buy them at the mercantile."

"Mmm. Good morning, Mr. Hughes." Katie Rose didn't like his use of the word "we," but she was not in a position to challenge the statement. Best to wait out her time here. "When do you expect the shearing crew here?"

"Sometime today, I reckon." He motioned for more coffee.

And, just as Harold Hughes had said, the shearing crew arrived before noon amid a jangle of clippers and knives. At first, Katie thought the crew consisted of two men, but she soon realized it was a man and a woman – even though the woman wore breeches. Harold and the shearers surveyed the flock as Katie brought out a pitcher of cold well water and a dipper. She introduced herself as the "hired girl" and said the noon meal would be served shortly.

"Yessir," the man was saying. "Me an' Lara can get these critters clean in two...mebbe three...days. You bring out the wool sacks, and we can start after eatin'."

The process fascinated Katie. She watched as the couple each wrangled a big, wooly sheep to the ground. Then, they began deftly cutting off the winter coats using sharp clippers. For the most part, the sheep didn't move during the process, but once the shearers let go of the animal, it jumped up, shook quickly, and rejoined the flock.

As she watched the crew, Harold Hughes came up behind her. "I reckon those sheep feel a heap better without that wool coat," he said as he started to put his arm around her waist. Katie saw the move coming and slid away from him. "Mr. Hughes, I will not tolerate that familiarity."

Lara gave Hughes a side glance when she heard the sharp rebuke from Katie.

The shearers – Ben and Lara Goya – finished working just as the sun set. Katie brought out bowls of stew, a loaf of bread, and some fresh vegetables for the evening meal. All four of them sat on the grass and enjoyed the meal as the evening sky deepened.

"You two can bunk in the barn tonight," Harold told the crew.

Katie's head jerked up when she heard the new sleeping arrangements.

The Goyas headed for the barn. "You can't expect me to sleep with the crew, Katie girl," Harold said.

"Very well, then. I'll make a bed in the wagon," Katie countered.

Realizing how strange that might look to the Goyas, Hughes said he would sleep in the wagon while the shearing crew was in the barn. Inwardly, Katie sighed in relief.

Two days later, the shearing crew finished the last of the sheep by late afternoon. They packed up their tools, and Hughes paid them for the work. Katie expected to serve dinner and was surprised to see the husband and wife team load their mule.

"They're not staying the night?" she asked Hughes.

"Nah, they said they wanted to get to the next job."

Katie wrapped a loaf of bread and some slices of cold meat into a napkin. She added two slices of pie to the package and brought it to the couple as they headed down the path.

"I've packed you a cold dinner for the road," she told the woman.

"Thank you kindly, miss," Lara said as she took the bread and sliced meat. "Now, you take care."

That evening, she moved uneasily about the kitchen. Then she remembered that she could leave this place tomorrow. That lifted her spirits a bit. After cleaning the kitchen, Katie packed her belongings into her traveling bag. She checked the hidden pocket in the carpet bag to ensure that the last of her money was still safe. Even though she expected Hughes to bed down in the barn, Katie opted to sleep in her camisole and skirt.

No sooner had she climbed into her narrow, fold-down bed than she saw Hughes looming over her. "Katie girl, wouldn't you be more comfortable in the big bed…with me?"

He grabbed her arm and started pulling Katie from the bed. Katie struggled. She tried to escape Hughes' grasp and fell to the floor.

Harold Hughes was on top of her in a second, his weight holding her in place. She struggled, scratched his face, and pummeled his arms. Undeterred, Hughes pulled Katie's skirts up with one hand and unbuttoned his pants with the other. When she continued to struggle, Harold Hughes punched Katie in the face. Katie screamed, but only the sheep and the dogs could hear her cries. She clawed at his face, leaving bloody trails down the side of his jaw and neck. Feeling trapped, Katie kicked and pounded at Hughes' massive arms. "Get off me," she screamed.

"Hold still and enjoy it, missy," Hughes sneered as he positioned himself over her. Katie continued to struggle, almost escaping from under his weight.

Then Harold Hughes shifted again and forced himself inside her. "Hold still, or I'll kill you when I'm done," he threatened.

After it was over and satisfied at last, Hughes rolled off Katie. Soon, he was snoring.

Katie wasn't a virgin, but Patrick Kelly had never touched her in such a manner. She felt debased. And she was in despair. Then she heard her nan's voice in her head. "Katie Rose, pull yourself together, mo stór." She didn't cry.

She inched away from the sleeping man. Gathering her bag – and her wits – Katie silently crossed the room. She was so shaken by the violent encounter that she knocked over a whiskey bottle Hughes had left on the table. The bottle broke as it hit the dirt floor, and Harold Hughes stirred in his sleep. Katie froze. She grabbed a knife to defend herself in case he came at her again. Instead, he rolled over and began snoring again.

Once clear of the house, she ran. She ran from Hughes. She ran from the degradation he had inflicted on her. She ran to be free.

Under a full moon, Katie Rose Kelly ran down the path until she could run no more. Finally, she collapsed and quietly sobbed until she couldn't cry anymore.

Then she heard something approaching. A coyote? A wolf? Something was out there. She wished she had grabbed the shotgun – or at least a knife – before she fled. She was helpless.

"Miss, are you all right? Miss, it's Lara, the sheep shearer."

The woman walked into the moonlight. Katie breathed a sigh of relief and began crying again. "He…he…he… attacked me."

"Are you hurt?"

"Bruised, but nothing is broken." She carefully touched her cheekbone to make sure the assessment was correct.

"He is a bad man. I told Ben that Mr. Hughes was a bad man. That is why we left as soon as we finished the work." She stroked Katie's hair soothingly. "Do you want to come with us? We do not have much, but we will share what we have. And we will help you if Mr. Hughes follows."

Katie relaxed and realized it was the first time she had felt safe since Hughes had returned without his wife. She and Lara walked the short distance to the couple's rough camp. There was a fire, and Lara made a cup of tea for Katie.

Katie's shoulders heaved as she sipped the dandelion tea. "It was…it was horrible. I should have left as soon as he returned from Twin Brooks without Mrs. Hughes. It's my fault." She started crying again.

"Oh, laztana." Lara reverted to her native language as she soothed Katie. "'Laztana' is 'my dear' in Basque," she explained when Katie looked up confused. Katie was curious but left the questions for another time.

"Thank you for your help. Running out to the prairie may not have been the best decision, but it seemed my only choice."

"Try to rest, Miss. We will break camp at sunrise. And the sun comes early this time of year."

Katie curled up with her nan's shawl as a pillow and drifted off to a fitful sleep.

In the morning, Ben and Lara shared a cold breakfast with Katie. It was the pie that Katie had packed for the couple before they left.

"We are headed to the Wright ranch. It is just past Twin Brooks. You could find a room in town before going back east," Ben said.

She shook her head. "I need to decide what to do next, but I'm not turning tail and going home. Someday I hope," she picked up a handful of prairie soil, "this will be home. And Harold Hughes is not going to scare me off." Katie's words were brave, but her voice shook as she made the bold statement.

She thought about the widows and fatherless children she knew back home. Families that had lost men in the war. She thought about her grandparents, who had come to America from Ireland to start a new life. She didn't see herself returning to a life in her father's house, spending her nights tending bar at the pub. And as for marriage? Maybe the right man would come along someday, but for now, she needed time to find herself and chart her own path.

Ben Goya knew better than to contradict a strong woman. "We will be in town by noon."

The town, Twin Brooks, wasn't much of a "town," in Katie's opinion. "But then," she told herself ruefully, "I can't compare it to Chicago."

She surveyed the settlement – a saloon – no, two saloons – a boarding house, a government office of some kind, and a general store. A dirt road ran lengthwise through town, ending with a corral and livery stable at the edge of the village.

She surmised that Aggie and Harold bought supplies at the general store. "That would be a good place to start," Katie thought. She also wondered if Aggie Hughes was still in town or if she had left on the first stagecoach headed east.

She thanked the Goyas, picked up her carpet bag, and made her way to the general store.

Inside, the small store was crammed with barrels of sugar, flour, and coffee. There were shelves of canned goods, some in tins and some that appeared to be local preserves. And on one wall, the store displayed bolts of fabric. It was the fabric that drew Katie's attention. A woman a little older than Katie was haggling about a bolt of pale blue wool with the storekeeper.

"Now Jim," the woman was saying, "you know this cloth is worth twice what you said."

45

That got Katie's attention. It was rare that she heard a shopper ask to pay more. Then she realized the woman was *selling* the cloth to the storekeeper.

"Times is tough, Sarah. It's a beautiful piece, I grant you. But I ain't sure I can get that much for a length of your wool."

Katie stepped up to finger the fabric in question. "It would make a beautiful shawl or a church dress," Katie said wistfully.

"You buying?" the storekeeper said eagerly.

Katie shook her head. "Not today, but I would if I could. It has a fine feel to it."

The other woman smiled and said, "Now, here's a woman who knows quality when she sees it. Would you meet me in the middle, Jim? I'll leave it on consignment, and we'll settle up after you sell it."

"I can do that, Sarah," the storekeeper agreed. "It's a deal."

Sarah turned to Katie. "Hello. You're new in town. I'm Sarah Wright. My husband and I have a ranch just north of here. Would you like a cup of tea? There aren't many women around these parts, and it's a pure pleasure to talk with another female." She paused, smiled, and said, "There I go again, bein' 'overly friendly' as my Tim would say."

The woman who addressed Katie was in her early 30s, with wisps of blond hair escaping from an untidy bun. She wasn't tall, but her bearing made her seem more authoritative than her height. Around her shoulders, she wore a beautiful lavender shawl in the same weave as the blue wool on the fabric bolt.

Overwhelmed by the woman's welcoming nature, Katie said, "I would love that. I'm Katie Rose Kelly, and I could use a friend."

"Sounds like there's a story there, Katie Rose. Let's go to Polly's Place. It's a saloon, but we can get a cup of tea there. The saloon keeper, Polly, is a friend; if she's not busy, she'll join us."

The saloon's bar wasn't as long, nor was it as polished as her da's bar at the Lucky Shamrock. But somehow, Katie felt right at home. "Oh, I've missed this," Katie said. Sarah looked curiously at her.

"My Da – my family – owns the Lucky Shamrock Pub on the South Side of Chicago, and for the first time in months, I feel at home. I used to tend bar at the pub on busy nights."

"Then you're the answer to a prayer." A middle-aged woman with salt and pepper hair approached the two women. She wore breeches and boots, but her white blouse was trimmed with fine lace and tied with a smart red bow. She was the picture of contradictions.

"Polly, this is Katie Rose Kelly. Katie, this is Polly Gibson," Sarah said by way of introduction. "Polly is the proprietor of Polly's Place."

"Howdy, Katie Rose. Did I hear you say that you're a bartender? Mine just took off for the gold fields. He heard about some strike and said he wouldn't miss the next gold rush." She waved a bar towel in the air.

Katie and Sarah laughed at Polly's gesture. "Sit down, ladies, and I'll bring out the tea."

"What a whirlwind," Katie said. "But maybe Polly is the answer to *my* prayer. It would help me get back on my feet and give me time to figure out what's next."

Sarah squeezed Katie's hand. "Do you want to talk about it?" Katie nodded.

They chose a small table in the corner and settled in as Polly brought out a tea tray complete with delicate porcelain cups and a teapot.

Katie started from the beginning when Patrick died at Spotsylvania, making her a widow. Then, she explained Harold Hughes' offer, emphasizing that she only took the job after exchanging letters with Aggie Hughes. She talked about her time on the Hughes sheep ranch, cooking and cleaning for the couple, ending with the Hughes' trip to Twin Brooks.

"And when Mrs. Hughes didn't return, I gave my notice, but Mr. Hughes asked me to stay until the sheep shearers were done. He said he needed someone to cook for the crew. He promised to bring me into town so I could return home or look for other employment. But after the shearing crew left, he...he..." her voice trailed off.

Sarah gasped. "Oh no, Katie. How horrible. Were you injured?"

Polly interrupted, "Of course, she was injured, Sarah. The damn man attacked her – she was injured whether he left marks or not. But I can see that she's got the start of 'shiner' on that left eye." She turned to Katie, "That was just last night? How did you manage to get here? You are made of sterner stuff than you seem, Katie Rose."

Katie started to cry again. Polly handed her a handkerchief. "Now, now, Katie. Have some more tea, then we'll make a nice, warm bath for you. You can wash off the filth of that man and get some sleep." Polly went behind the bar and fetched a bottle of whiskey. She added a healthy measure to Katie's teacup – and then to her and Sarah's cups. "Tomorrow, we'll decide what to do next. But tonight, you need to rest."

True to her word, Polly Gibson prepared a warm bath for Katie Rose and then tucked her into a real bed with clean sheets that smelled of lavender. Katie fell off to sleep almost immediately, but in the middle of the night, she awoke with a start. Relaxing back into the pillow, she recognized she was in Polly's guest room. Still, she couldn't sleep, so she found the journal in her bag and made a short entry.

Journal Entry – May 9, 1866

The last two days have been the worst of my life, even worse than losing Patrick in that horrible War. Harold Hughes was not the man he seemed to be – or maybe he was. But I am clear of him now. Tomorrow I will truly start a new chapter in my life.

KR

Chapter 7: Safe in Town

May 10, 1866 - Polly's Place Saloon, Twin Brooks

Katie Rose

The sun peeked through the linen curtains of Polly's guest room, and Katie realized this was the first time she'd slept past sunrise in months. Stretching, she gingerly touched her cheekbone and grimaced. She knew her black eye would undoubtedly draw attention. Still, she decided to wear it as a badge of honor rather than play the victim.

Polly had coffee going when Katie entered the kitchen. "Go ahead and pour yourself a cup. I make a mean flapjack. After breakfast, I'll show you around the saloon. You'll start tending bar tonight if you're up to it."

"I'm ready, Polly. I still can't thank you enough…"

"I recollect when I landed in the Territory. Weren't many women out here at all. Still aren't. That's why we women need to support each other, Katie Rose. And you're helping me out, too."

That afternoon, Katie tied on an apron over her light green dress and stepped behind the bar. Polly opened the saloon, and the customers came in to see the "new girl." Apparently, word had gotten around. But Katie didn't give it a second thought – she was too busy pouring beers and whiskey – just as she had in da's pub.

"How'd you git that shiner, miss," inquired a middle-aged man. "I hope the other guy looks worse." He had steely gray eyes, bushy eyebrows, and graying hair. Still, his face and posture exuded an undeniable strength. He wore the badge of a lawman on his black corduroy vest.

Katie tried to laugh off the question as Polly sat beside the gentleman. "Katie, this is Micah Brown. He's the sheriff in these parts. I told him about your troubles. I hope that was all right with you."

"I don't know much about Hughes," Brown said. "I did hear that his wife left him a few days back. He runs a sheep ranch south of here, ain't that right?" Katie nodded, and he continued, "So, you wanna tell me about that black eye?"

After Katie told the lawman about the attack, the rape, and the beating, Brown asked if there were any witnesses. "No," she said, "but the Goyas – sheep shearers – left the ranch just before nightfall. They found me on the road after I ran away. Why?"

"It's always easier to prove something if there's a witness, but if they saw you before and after the attack, that's enough for me. Any idea where they might be?"

"They were going to a ranch north of here," Katie said.

"Sarah and Tim Wright said they had a crew coming up this week," Polly offered.

"Why are you doing this?" Katie questioned.

"Well, it's my job to protect people. Also, my pa liked to beat on my ma when he had a mind to. He thought it was his right. When I was big enough, I put a stop to it. I don't cotton to seein' women abused in any manner. I'll ride up to the Wright place, then I'm gonna have a visit with Harold Hughes."

Katie shuddered. "I don't want more trouble from him."

"That won't happen, Miss – er Mrs. Kelly. Now, are you planning to go back east, or will you be stayin' in the Territory?"

"I'm not going back to Chicago," she declared. "I planned – eventually – to stake a claim for land. I guess now that will be sooner than later."

"You wanna be a farmer?" Brown asked.

"I've learned some about sheep herding, and I think I have a knack for it. I'm not sure how I'll get the sheep, but I can stake a claim and worry about the sheep after that."

"Hmmm. You best see about that claim, then," Brown said. "I'm gonna have a talk with your former employer."

Katie didn't realize it until after the sheriff had left the saloon, but she had already formed a plan for her new life. "A sheepherder! I'm going to herd sheep!" Katie said determinedly.

Polly laughed and said, "You know, you should talk with Sarah and Tim Wright. They run sheep and cattle just across the river north of here. They staked their claim right after Tim mustered out of the Army. When you're feelin' up to it, we can ride out to their place."

Katie finished her shift at the saloon and dropped into bed that night. "I should be dead tired," she thought, "but it feels so good to have a plan!"

The following day, she pulled several bills from the secret pocket of her carpet bag. The cash was part of her widow's pension from the government. She hadn't told anyone about the money, thinking it might be safer to appear penniless. The cash would be put to good use when she filed for her homestead claim.

Since the saloon opened after noon, Katie had the morning to herself. The first stop was to file a land claim.

Katie squared her shoulders and remembered her nan's words, "Chin up, Katie Rose!" She gathered her courage and stepped into the claims office. An older man hunched over a small secretary desk in a room that was a bit dark and more than a bit dusty. She cleared her throat. "Excuse me, I'd like to file a claim for land," she began.

The man squinted through spectacles at Katie. "Need to be head of household, miss. Where's your man?"

"I am head of my household, sir. Widowed."

"My mistake. Sorry for your loss. You have paperwork to prove it?"

Katie pulled out the government documents along with the ten-dollar filing fee. After Mr. Owens, the clerk, thoroughly digested the papers, he pulled out a land map and said, "You qualify. Here are the sections that are open to homestead."

Having grown up near the Chicago River, Katie understood the importance of water. "I'll need land for grazing and a creek or river nearby."

"This one," he pointed to a section southwest of Twin Brooks, "has a creek running through it." Katie nodded. "I'll take it." She paid the filing fee, and Owens stamped and dated her claim document.

Next stop, Katie thought, *is the livery to purchase a horse and wagon.* She was so engrossed in reading through the paperwork that she didn't see the pothole in the road and nearly tripped. Nearly tripped because someone behind her caught her arm before she fell.

"Better watch your step. These streets can be dangerous," she heard a man say. Katie turned to see Jake Riley holding onto her elbow.

"Well, hello, Mrs. Kelly. Fancy seeing you in Twin Brooks. You do get around. Are you in town on a shopping trip?"

"No. I am no longer employed at the Hughes ranch." Katie looked up at Riley, and the cowboy frowned when he saw her bruised face.

"Okay….," Riley drew out the word, not knowing how to respond. But recovering quickly, he said, "Well, wherever you're headed, better watch your step."

"I'm headed to the livery stable. I need to buy a horse and wagon," she paused, then continued, "and I could use some advice from someone who knows horses."

"That'd be me," Jake poked himself in the chest. "Let's do some horse tradin'."

A half-hour later, Katie made a down payment on a chestnut-colored mare, a saddle, and a reasonably sturdy wagon. Katie promised the livery owner that she would pay the balance when she collected her purchases. "But in the meantime," she said, "I'd like to stable my horse here."

"Yes, ma'am," said the short, muscled blacksmith who also ran the livery. "I'll take good care of her."

During the "horse trading," as Jake called it, he got answers to some of his questions about Katie. She told him she was a widow and had staked a claim for a section of land southwest of town.

"I like spending other people's money," said Jake. "Where to next?"

"I need to get to work," Katie answered.

"I thought you said you were 'no longer employed' at the Hughes ranch."

"I'm the new bartender at Polly's Place," she replied. "I'll buy you a beer for helping me find a good horse if you're interested."

"I never turn down a free beer," Jake declared.

He was finishing his beer when Micah Brown entered the saloon. The lawman nodded to Polly and said, "I need to speak with Mrs. Kelly."

Katie removed her apron and emerged from behind the bar. "We can talk over here, Sheriff," and they made their way to an empty table in the back.

Jake addressed Polly, "This have anything to do with her bruises?" Polly shrugged and presented her standard poker face in reply.

At the table, Sheriff Brown said, "At first, Hughes denied everything. Said you up and left in the night. He tried to accuse you of stealing." Katie's Irish temper started to flare, and Micah Brown put up his hand. "But he couldn't think of anything you'd taken. So that was his first lie. I told him that assault is a jailable offense in this Territory and that he could cool off in jail until the circuit judge heard the case – in about six weeks."

"But even with the bruises, I can't prove he hit me and … the other," she said, referring to the rape.

"He made it clear that he doesn't want to go to jail. And he doesn't want his wife or her family to know about the, er, the attack. Seems that Mrs. Hughes' family provided the sheep for Hughes' new ranch. I'm guessing that they'd come out and take back the animals. So, he offered to pay you off instead," Micah said.

"Pay me off? What do you mean?"

"It's basically 'hush money.' Even if we can't prove the extent of the attack, it's still against the law to assault someone in Dakota Territory. We have witnesses that saw you before and after the assault. If you promise not to contact his wife and not to press charges, Harold Hughes will give you a dozen ewes with lambs."

Katie was dumbfounded. "He'll *give* me part of his flock?"

The sheriff nodded. "I'm a hard bargainer, Mrs. Kelly. I was hopin' that might help you get started, and instead of paying a fine to the county, he'll pay the damages directly to you. What do you think? Is it a deal?"

"I don't know what to say!" Katie said.

"Say yes!" said Jake, who had been eavesdropping from the next table. "You've got the land; you've got the horse and wagon. Now you need the livestock. Say yes!"

Katie's green eyes twinkled. She said, "It's a deal. It's the best deal I'll get from that sleeven." Micah looked confused.

"Oh, that's Irish for scoundrel," Jake supplied.

"Did you just bargain me out of a good bartender, Micah Brown?" Polly brought a pitcher of beer and glasses to the table. "But it's a bargain worth celebrating." She poured beers for Katie, Micah, Jake, and herself. "Cheers!" they said in unison.

That night she dug out the letter home that she had started earlier in the month and finished the letter to her father, grandmother, and brother, editing out the parts about Hughes raping and attacking her.

She wrote:

Continued on May 10, 1866

So much has happened since I started this letter! I am no longer a housegirl at the Hughes Ranch. When Aggie Hughes decided to quit the frontier, I also quit my job there. I am living in Twin Brooks now. (You can send your letters to the post office here.) And da, you'll be pleased to read that my time as a bartender at the Lucky Shamrock put me in good stead. I have been working at Polly's Place, one of the two saloons in town. The proprietor, Polly Gibson, runs a proper establishment.

But I won't be here for long. I used some of the money from Patrick's pension to file a claim for 160 acres of land. A friend gave me advice on buying a good horse and wagon, and soon I'll have a flock of sheep to run on the land.

I knew I wanted my own piece of land in Dakota Territory, but I wasn't sure what I wanted to do on the frontier. Now I know. I will be a sheepherder.

I am also making new friends since I left the Hughes' place. My employer, Polly Gibson, knows the business, da. You would like her. I've also met another woman, Sarah Wright. She and her husband are ranchers (cattle and sheep) north of town.

A lot has happened since I came west. I know I will have more challenges ahead of me, but when I do, Nan, I hear you in my head saying, "Chin up, Katie Rose." That always gives me strength.

My love to all,

Katie Rose

Chapter 8: Collecting Her Due

May 10, 1866 - Double D Ranch, Dakota Territory

Jake Riley

The ride back to the Double D Ranch gave Jake time to think about that spitfire gal with hair the color of flames and eyes as green as the prairie grass in high summer. "And, Finn," he patted the withers of his black horse, "she's widowed! Now, I should be feelin' sorrow for her loss, especially since he served in the Union Army, like me. But there's no husband to show up unexpectedly." The memory still stung a bit.

He continued the one-sided conversation with the horse. "Gotta do something about that damned Hughes, though. Sheriff Brown did his best to help Katie Rose, but Hughes is a devil."

The two rode along in silence for a while as Jake considered the situation. "But dang it, Finn, why did Micah saddle her with sheep! Sheep – those shaggy, bleatin' grazers. I'm a cowboy – a cattleman – I can't be...." He thought again about Katie's green eyes, how her nose tipped up just a bit at the end, and those dimples. Oh, those dimples! And his imagination took flight considering her other attributes. "She is a looker, Finn. And she's a lady, through and through. She's gonna need help on that new spread of hers. I'll just have to make my peace with those wooly critters."

That night in the bunkhouse, Jake confided in Sam Goodman, a freedman who used to tend sheep on a plantation in Missouri before the War.

"Sheep are the most ignorant creatures that the good Lord put on earth," Sam said after Jake told him about Katie Rose Kelly. "What she needs is a good dog. I heard that Tim Wright's collie had a litter this spring."

Jake considered the suggestion.

May 15, 1866

Katie

While Katie was eager to see her new property, she enjoyed the companionship and atmosphere of Polly's Place. The saloon reminded her of da's pub and helped her "get her feet under her again," as Polly put it. Every day she found more things she would need or tasks to do when she got to the claim. Lists helped Katie plan and acclimate herself to her new life as a homesteader.

Of course, word got around that the Irish gal at Polly's Place was staking a claim near Lone Tree. Katie started getting unsolicited advice from every customer in the saloon.

"There ain't no soddy or dugout on that claim," said a customer. "Where are you gonna live?"

"I heard that a lot of sheepherders live in their wagons," said a second customer. "That's a fact," agreed a third customer at the long bar.

Katie was used to customers' bantering and usually paid little attention to talking. But, since she'd been wondering the same thing, she followed their conversation. *I could outfit that wagon for the time being,* Katie thought.

She immediately started making another list of what she would need from the general store to outfit her new home on wheels.

She also needed a way to move the sheep from Hughes' ranch to her new land. That was at the top of her list when she bumped into Sarah Wright at the store a few days later.

"I heard you're going into the sheep business. Congratulations!" Sarah said.

"Yes," Katie replied. "I have a lot to learn, though. And I still have to herd the sheep to my claim."

"We run a couple hundred on our land, but Tim mostly leaves the sheep to me. He considers himself a cattleman." She laughed. "But you know, it's the wool and the mutton that pay the bills. Folks say 'cattle are for the prestige, but sheep are for the cash.'"

"I'm starting out small, just a dozen ewes and lambs."

Sarah considered. "My sheep are in good pasture lands right now. I'll send my nephew over to help you move your flock if you'd like. Jimmy, my sister's son, works at our place. He's good with sheep."

Katie was overwhelmed by the offer. "That's so kind. I'm outfitting my sheep wagon right now. I could be ready next week." The two women discussed when and where to meet. Katie left the mercantile a bit lighter – both in cash and in her mood. Her biggest challenge now had a solution.

She told her plan to Polly and Micah that evening. "I'll ride over with you and Jimmy just in case Hughes has forgotten about our agreement," Micah said.

Katie was relieved that she wouldn't have to face Harold Hughes alone.

By the following week, Katie had outfitted the wagon with food, a cookstove, utensils, and bedding for herself. As almost an afterthought, she bought two pairs of trousers and a pair of boots just like the ones Polly wore. "Now I'm ready," she thought.

The trio set out on a warm May morning. Katie drove her wagon with Sheriff Brown and Sarah's nephew Jimmy leading the way. Jimmy Turner was a tall, lanky boy of about 15 or 16. He wore a tattered straw hat on his mop of straw-colored hair. His black and white appaloosa was outfitted with a shotgun in a scabbard, a bed roll, and a canteen. Dancing behind Jimmy was a brown and white border collie. "This here is Buddy," Jimmy said, indicating the dog. "He's one of our best herders."

They arrived at the Hughes ranch by midday. Harold Hughes met them as they neared his shanty.

"Howdy. We're here to collect the sheep that Mrs. Kelly's due," Micah said to the stone-faced Harold Hughes. "

Hughes sized up the small group and considered arguing the agreed-upon payment. Instead, he glared at Katie Rose and said, "I knew you were trouble the first time I laid eyes on you, missy. Nothin' but trouble. And now you come to steal from me – 'cept it's all legal with the sheriff here doin' your bidding."

Katie was stunned. She was still frightened of the large man, but his hostility triggered her courage – and her anger. She wasn't about to back down from this bully. This aggressor. This rapist.

Before Katie could respond, though, the sheriff spoke up. "We can do this the easy way or the hard way, Hughes. We can sort out a dozen ewes with lambs at side and be on our way, or I can haul you into jail for assault and battery. Then you'll have no one to watch your flock. I heard some coyotes on the trail here. I'm guessing they'll like that option. Now, I've got me an arrest warrant in your name, just in case you want to do it the hard way." He pulled a folded document from his breast pocket and waved it at Hughes.

"Can't fight the law," Hughes muttered as he stomped toward the nearby pasture. He started separating ewes and lambs from the flock. In a low voice, Brown said to Jimmy, "You know sheep, boy. Make sure he's not giving Katie the sickly ones."

Jimmy dismounted and started inspecting the selected animals while Katie got off the wagon to tag behind the boy. Once the small flock was assembled, Jimmy and his border collie started pushing the sheep westward, away from Hughes' ranch.

Katie and Micah followed behind the flock. "Let's get them as far from Hughes as we can before nightfall," he told Jimmy. "Then we'll make camp."

The sun set on the Dakota prairie in pastel hues. And in the morning, it rose with an orange glow. "Let's get these critters moving," Brown said to Jimmy. The boy whistled to his dog, and they continued the trek west. It was another full day before they reached what Katie determined was the boundary to her claim.

"Mr. Owens at the claims office said that Lone Tree marked the start of my land. I think we're here." Katie surveyed the claims map, found the creek that was part of her property, and jumped off the wagon bench.

"This is where we part ways, Mrs. Kelly," said the sheriff. "Jimmy, stay tonight and make sure the sheep 'settle in' or whatever these critters do."

The boy nodded and started unsaddling his horse. The dog continued walking around the flock, ensuring they all stayed together.

"I can't thank you enough, Sheriff," Katie began.

"No thanks needed, Katie. Just doin' my job. This is little enough for the beating that varmint gave you." He tipped his hat and rode toward Twin Brooks.

That night, as they ate supper around a campfire, Jimmy pointed out other landmarks and gave Katie a general sense of direction. "Due north is the Double D Ranch," he said. "They run strictly cattle. Twin Brooks is northeast of here. And our ranch – I mean Uncle Tim's ranch – is past Twin Brooks. It's less than a day's ride from your place, but it's still a far piece. Further west is Indian country."

"Should I be worried about them?" It hadn't occurred to Katie that she might face Indians alone on the prairie.

"Well, Uncle Tim says that coyotes and wolves are more worrisome. Besides, most of the Indians have moved farther west. We do see 'em from time to time, but when you do, Aunt Sarah says to treat them neighborly and fairly, and they'll do the same."

When she worked at da's pub and Polly's saloon, Katie met all sorts of people, and Sarah's advice seemed to make sense to her.

In the morning, Jimmy saddled his horse and called to Buddy. Before he left, Katie asked him about hiring a crew to help build an animal pen, a barn, and a home of some sort for her. She didn't intend to live in the wagon forever. He promised to leave word with Polly when he passed through Twin Brooks.

Katie watched as Jimmy and Buddy headed northeast, slightly into the rising sun.

Katie spent the first full day exploring her new land – but always keeping within a distance of the sheep. "My sheep," she said to herself.

Not far from Lone Tree, she found and climbed a good-sized hill that gave her a view of her claim. She decided this would be her new home – a dugout, it was called.

She curled up in her wagon and counted the twinkling stars in the velvet night sky.

Journal Entry – May 20, 1866

As I look at the stars tonight, I realize that my blessings are as plentiful as the stars above me. I couldn't have done it without help from my new "prairie family: Polly, Sarah and Tim Wright, Jimmy and Sheriff Brown.

Now, I have my own home on my own land. I have so much to learn, but I also know I can do this. I am blessed.

KR

Chapter 9: Lady Sheepherder

June 1866 - Kelly Ranch, Dakota Territory

Katie

June brought a riot of color to the prairie. Pink coneflowers, purple clover and blazing star, blue indigo, yellow black-eyed Susan, and orange-red blanket flowers seemed to compete for the sunshine. And each, in turn, drew butterflies, honey bees, and dragonflies. Katie marveled at her "prairie garden," as she called it.

Still, there was much work to do. Her main concern was to watch over the flock, keeping them safe from coyotes and other predators. And there were the daily chores that went with living on the frontier – hunting for food, cooking, laundry, and collecting fuel for her cooking fires. That last chore was her least favorite. "Prairie muffins," or "buffalo chips," as some homesteaders referred to buffalo droppings, were her main source of fuel for cooking and warmth.

She was becoming more comfortable living in her sheep wagon, which, she learned, was particularly practical for moving with her sheep when they required fresh grazing land. Come winter, though, Katie was determined to have a more substantial dwelling – probably a dugout or soddy since lumber was scarce on the prairie. But since watching the flock was a full-time job, Katie could not make a trip to Twin Brooks to hire a crew to do the work.

As she was despairing her solitary life, Katie spied two riders headed her way. She recognized Jake Riley on his huge black horse when they got close. The other rider, though, was a stranger.

"Hello, the house," the stranger yelled from a distance. Katie had never heard that greeting, but the meaning was clear.

"Hello," she called back. When they were closer, Katie said, "You're the first people I've seen since I got here two weeks ago." She smiled at Jake. "It's good to see you, Mr. Riley."

"Aw, we're on a first-name basis, aren't we, Katie?

She smiled again and nodded. "What brings you out here, Jake?"

"Introductions, first. This is my bunkmate, Sam Goodman. He knows a thing or two about sheep – even though he's seen the light and is a through-and-through cowboy these days."

Sam dismounted from his mostly white horse. He was a large man with a black, bushy beard and skin the color of coal. He removed his wide-brimmed hat and said, "Pleased to meet you, Mrs. Kelly. Jake's told me about your new spread. Beings you're a city gal, and he only understands cattle, he thought I might be able to step in and lend a hand."

Katie needed clarification. "I can't afford hired help, Sam."

"I'm not looking for a job, ma'am. Just wanted to be neighborly, beings' you're by your lonesome."

Jake stepped in to explain. "A few days ago I was riding herd on the east side of the Double D – it borders the Wright ranch. Well, Tim was riding his herd and he said

67

you were out here alone on your claim." Jake started to fidget as he continued, "Well, I thought you might appreciate having someone give you a day or so to go to town and get supplies and what-nots."

"That's so thoughtful," Katie said. "I was just thinking I need to hire a crew to build a house and a barn out here. I could use a trip to town to take care of some business – and to simply see another human being! Of course, I can't take you away from your jobs."

"We've got a couple of days to kill before we're needed back at the Double D," Jake said. "Sam, here, can babysit your critters, and I'll ride into town with you if that suits you."

"Jake, ain't you forgetting something?" Sam said.

"No, I….oh, yeah." He went back to his horse and unstrapped a covered basket. "Sam tells me that every sheep rancher needs a herding dog." He pulled a half-grown border collie out of the basket. "I got her from Tim and Sarah Wright. She's the last pup from their spring litter." He handed the mostly black-colored dog to Katie Rose.

"She's adorable." Katie put the dog on the ground and scratched it behind the dog's ears. "What's her name?"

"That's up to you. She's your dog now," Jake replied.

She assessed the dog and pondered. "Maddie…short for Madigan. That's Irish for 'little dog.' Hello, Maddie," Katie said to the pup.

"She's done some herdin', and what she doesn't know will just come natural," Sam assured her. Maddie took off on a dead run to push a wandering lamb back to the flock as if to prove his point.

The two cowboys and the lady sheepherder all laughed.

"I have venison, some biscuits, wild spinach, and berries. Who's hungry?" said Katie. "Watching the flock gives me time to forage for greens and berries. I got a late start on my garden, but I'll have squash, beans, carrots, and – of course – potatoes this fall."

They finished lunch. Katie packed an overnight bag, and she and Jake left for Twin Brooks. It was nearly dusk when the two rode into town. After stabling their horses at the livery, they went directly to Polly's Place.

"Well, look who just walked in," Polly called out. "It's 'Bo Peep' – and I mean that in the nicest way, Katie Rose." She poured draught beers for Katie and Jake. "Tell me all about your new adventure, Katie Rose. Micah said Harold Hughes tried to wriggle out of the agreement, but that badge of his makes people behave." She paused and looked at Katie quizzically, "Who's watching the flock?"

Katie sipped her beer. "Sam Goodman is on watch," Jake answered. He continued, "She's got a nice spread, Polly. It's near Lone Tree, and there's good grazing out there."

"Actually, Lone Tree borders my claim," Katie corrected him. "I'm here to hire a crew to build a dugout and a barn. Living in a sheep wagon in the winter – even with a canvas roof – doesn't seem practical. Can you please pass the word?"

"I think I know a couple of guys looking for work," Polly answered. "Do you have an account at the mercantile for supplies, lumber, and hardware?"

"That can wait till tomorrow, Katie Rose," Jake said. "Let's get a couple of steaks at the local restaurant – I'm buying."

"Anything but venison," Katie laughed. "Polly, do you have a spare bed tonight? I expect you to charge me, by the way."

"Your old room is open. Two bits a night," the bar owner said.

The diner was owned and operated by Emma Jackson. She and her husband had a claim east of Twin Brooks, but the restaurant provided the cash to keep the homestead operating. With only four tables, it offered townsfolk a welcome change from their own cooking. Most of the customers, however, were men – soldiers and miners – passing through the western town.

"I'll be right with you. Go ahead and choose a table," called a voice from behind the swinging door to what Katie assumed was the diner's kitchen.

When she emerged, Katie saw a slightly plump, middle-aged woman with walnut-colored skin. Her iron-gray hair was coiled on top of her head. She wore a white and blue apron over a blue polka-dot dress.

"Jake! It's been a while. How's life on the Double D?" Then, realizing he was accompanied by a woman, she amended her question. "Or, have you left cowboying?"

"I'm still at it. Emma, this is Katie Rose Kelly. She's got a claim over by Lone Tree. Katie, this is Emma Jackson. Best cook in the Territory."

"Nice to meet you again, Emma." Turning to Jake, Katie explained, "I used to pick up box meals for saloon customers when I worked at Polly's."

Then, addressing Emma, she said, "But I've not had the opportunity to enjoy your cooking. I'm looking forward to it!"

The meal lived up to Katie's expectations. "Thank you for the nice dinner, Jake. Can I return the favor by buying you a beer at Polly's?"

Over two draughts, Katie and Jake discussed plans for the next day. Polly joined them with some welcome news. "I spread the word about you needing workers to build a barn and a dugout. Sure enough, two likely boys on their way to Oregon stopped in, and I think they might be what you're looking for, Katie." She pointed to two young men at the end of the bar. "I'll send 'em over."

"News gets around faster in a saloon than a newspaper," Katie said.

The two men, barely in their twenties, were from Texas. "We come up through Abilene, pushing cattle for Goodnight." The shorter of the two men referred to Charlie Goodnight, who made a name for himself by moving longhorns from Texas to the rail yards in Kansas. From there, the cattle usually traveled by train to packing plants in the East, such as Chicago.

"We had our fill of eatin' dust and singing to restless longhorns," the other man said.

"The trails aren't for everyone," Jake agreed. "I'm Jake Riley. I hear you're looking for some work up here."

"That's right," said the first man. "My name's Tom Slaton and this is my brother Joe."

"Where you headed now?" Katie asked, seeing an opening in the conversation. The Slaton brothers turned to Katie. "Howdy, ma'am," Joe tipped his hat. "We're making our way to Oregon. We heard there's some work to be had, and we're running short on cash." They turned back to Jake.

"What do you know about building?" Katie inquired.

Jake smiled and said, "This is Mrs. Kelly. She's the one doing the hiring."

Confused but trying to make a good impression, Tom Slaton said, "We're not strangers around lumber and nails. Grew up on a farm and did our share of carpentering."

"Do you know what a dugout is?" Katie asked the men.

"Yes, ma'am. We've seen a few of 'em. Is that what you're looking to build?"

"That and a barn. I've staked a claim a few miles southwest of here. I want a dugout and barn before winter comes. If you're willing, you're hired."

"Thank you, ma'am," said Joe. "When do we start?"

Katie considered the question and said, "Two days should give me time to get supplies ready." She gave the brothers directions to her claim, and the Slaton brothers agreed to bring the lumber and supplies when they arrived later in the week.

That night, before putting out the lamp in her room, Katie wrote a letter home.

Dear Da, Nan and Ryan,

Where do I start? So much has happened since my last letter. I'm a true sheepherder now. It's a small flock. I have a dozen mama sheep with lambs – but that's plenty for me to take care of right now. I'll have wool and mutton to sell, and then more lambs will be on the way.

I'm writing this letter while I am in Twin Brooks. A friend is watching the sheep so I can do some business in town. I want to get a home and a barn built before winter. Today I was able to find two willing workers. The pension money from Patrick's passing is being put to good use!

Twin Brooks is a nice little town, and the people are friendly. Even though it's over, there isn't much talk of the war here. The people are more interested in talking about farming and ranching, and of course, the weather. And, although living alone on the claim can be lonely, there's so much to do that I don't have time to sit around and fret.

The prairie is beautiful. The emerald-green hills are what I imagine Ireland looks like, Nan. I wish you could see it. And when it rains, oh, the flowers bloom in explosions of color. It's truly a sight to behold.

I'd love to know what's happening at home and at the Lucky Shamrock. Ryan, even though you're now doing my work, too, I know you are up to it. You've always loved the pub. And da, say hello to Callahan, Murphy, and O'Neill for me.

The post office in Twin Brooks will hold your letters for me.

Your loving daughter, granddaughter, sister – and now a sheepherder!

Katie Rose

Chapter 10: Settling In

June 1866 - Twin Brooks to Kelly Ranch, Dakota Territory

Jake

Katie and Jake met at the general store the following day to order lumber, tools, and hardware. Jake watched as the copper-haired woman matter-of-factly discussed shovels, nails, and lumber with the storekeeper. She was dressed for business and for the ride back in a dark green skirt split. The split skirt allowed her to ride Western style, which he thought was much more practical on the frontier. He also liked that the skirt followed the curves of her figure better than those oversized dresses most women wore.

"I've got a couple of errands to see to, Katie," Jake said. "And then I'll bring the horses around." Katie nodded and continued bargaining with the shopkeeper.

At Emma's diner, Jake picked up a picnic basket filled with bread, sliced beef, some preserves, and two pieces of pie. "Looks good enough to eat, Emma. Thanks for putting this together."

Emma's eyes crinkled in a weathered smile. "If she's not charmed with you yet, this should do the trick, child."

"Let's hope so," he said as he hefted the basket and strapped it to his saddle.

The June sun beat down on the riders as Katie and Jake put Twin Brooks behind them on the road back to her claim.

Katie adjusted her wide-brimmed hat and took a sip from her canteen. "It's going to be a warm one today."

"I thought we'd stop at Lone Tree. It'll give the horses a rest, and we can have a bit to eat. Emma packed lunch for us," Jake motioned to the basket behind his saddle. He was encouraged by Katie's bright smile and began whistling.

"I recognize that tune," Katie said. "What is that song?"

"We sing to the herd at night. Singing helps keep the cattle calm. It lets 'em know someone is out there protecting them and watching over them. Sort of a lullaby for long horns." With that, Jake's strong baritone voice put words to the tune.

Beautiful dreamer, wake unto me,

Starlight and dewdrops are waiting for thee;

Sounds of the rude world, heard in the day,

Lull'd by the moonlight have all passed away!

Beautiful dreamer, queen of my song,

List while I woo thee with soft melody;

Gone are the cares of life's busy throng,

Beautiful dreamer, awake unto me!

Beautiful dreamer, awake unto me!

Katie was enthralled. "I can see why the cattle would love to be serenaded by you, Jake.

What a beautiful song."

Lone Tree, the familiar cottonwood that marked Katie's claim, was now on the horizon. Their horses sensed

75

the nearby creek, and the riders allowed the animals to break into a trot. When they arrived at the prairie oasis, Jake jumped off his horse and lifted Katie off her saddle before she could dismount. She looked at him questioningly.

Jake threw up his hands, "Didn't mean to…."

Katie stopped his apology by leaning in and kissing him. He tentatively returned the kiss at first and then, with more intensity, cupped her face in his large, calloused hands and kissed her soundly.

When they pulled apart, Jake said, "I've been thinking about that since the day at Hughes' place." And then, remembering what Harold Hughes had done to Katie, he frowned. "But, given what you've been through from that bastard, I was taking it slow. Um, sorry for the cursing," he added.

"I've heard worse; I grew up in a pub, Jake," she said, referring to his language. Then she became serious. "What Harold Hughes did to me was horrible. Awful. Degrading. And I'm grateful that Sheriff Brown took action. Most times, nothing is done, and the 'bastard' gets away with it – and maybe continues abusing women. I won't forget it, but I'll get over it."

"You're a strong woman, Katie Rose Kelly." This time, Jake kissed Katie. The kiss was longer and sweeter. He thrilled when she returned the kiss with an intensity he had only hoped for, wrapping her arms around his neck to draw him closer.

Before anything more could transpire, Katie broke off the embrace. "I don't mean to lead you on, Jake Riley. We can be friends, but I'm not ready to get 'serious.' I've been married once, and I didn't find it much to my liking."

"Whoa…we went from a kiss to a wedding way too fast for this cowboy," Jake laughed a bit in relief. "Being 'friends' is just fine with me. Let's cool off in the creek and then have some lunch."

They pulled off their boots at the bank of the creek. Katie rolled down her stockings and hiked up the hem of her split skirt. Jake appreciated a look at her ankles and longed to run his hands up her shapely calves.

Katie, for her part, playfully kicked a splash of water Jake's way. "Now we're going to have a water fight? Let's do it," he said as he sent a splash of water Katie's way.

Thoroughly soaked, the two climbed out of the creek and sat under the shade of the large cottonwood tree. Fluffy white seeds drifted lazily through the breeze.

"I could stay here forever," Katie said, leaning against the tree trunk with her eyes shut.

"We'd best be packing up soon," Jake said. "Me and Sam need to get back to the Double D tonight."

"Oh, I'd almost forgotten about Sam…and my sheep. See what you do to me, Jake Riley. You're a bad influence," she said in jest.

The ride back was filled with easy conversation, as if Katie and Jake had been friends for years.

"How did you and Sam end up in Dakota Territory," she asked.

"We hooked up on a cattle drive out of Texas. Sam came by way of a plantation in Missouri after the war. After the slaves were freed, he lit out for Texas. A lot of cowboys were slaves. They're not afraid of hard work. Heck, they knew nothing else." He considered Sam's history.

"He's a good man to have on a cattle drive – maybe that's where his name came from. I never asked him that. Sam has a knack for anticipating what the cattle will do, and he's one – or two steps – ahead of them. What I can't understand," Jake continued, "is how he can tolerate sheep." And he laughed at his own joke.

"Seriously, Katie Rose, you're in cattle country. Ranchers like Dan Deacon – he owns the Double D Ranch – don't cotton to sheep. Most cattlemen don't like sheep. Those wooly critters graze pastures right down to the ground, leaving nothing for the cattle. You'd best keep your herd – er, flock – well south of the river. That's the southern border of Deacon's land."

"I didn't know much about sheep before coming west, but I'm learning," Kate countered. "I've watched spring lambing – even nursed a sick newborn when Mr. Hughes didn't give it a chance. I was there for the shearing and did my share of watching the flock when I wasn't cooking or cleaning for Mrs. Hughes. Sarah Wright says 'cattle are for the prestige, but sheep are for the cash.' I'm not looking for prestige, Jake Riley."

"Guess you told me! And speaking of sheep, I believe that's your," he paused to make sure he used the right word, "flock…over the hill."

"It's a pretty picture, isn't it?" Katie teased, motioning to the small flock of white, cream, and even one black sheep off in the distance.

He shook his head in good-natured annoyance. "Beauty is in the eye of the beholder, they say." And his gaze moved to the copper-haired woman riding at his side.

Sam gave Katie a quick recap of the two days she'd been absent. "Nothin' much to report, Mrs."

"Please call me Katie. Can I call you Sam?"

"My pleasure, Miss Katie."

"We'd better high-tail it back to the Double D, Sam. Now, Katie, those two Slaton boys will be here day after tomorrow. I did some checking, and they appear to be straight shooters. Er, I mean, they seem to be trustworthy. But just in case, keep your shotgun with you. And if something happens or you have a bad feeling about them, make tracks to Twin Brooks."

"Thanks for checking and for worrying about me. My shotgun is loaded."

"And she's got Maddie here to watch the flock. That little dog is gonna be a right fine sheepherding dog. She's got the instincts," Sam assured her.

"It's not fair that you got to know her before I did, but we'll make up for that, won't we, Maddie?" Katie petted the bright-eyed border collie. Maddie's pink tongue hung out of her mouth at a goofy angle, making her irresistible to pat.

"You boys better get going," Katie said. "Thank you again for watching the sheep, Sam. And, Jake, thank you for helping me get a jumpstart on the building." The two cowboys started north to the Double D, but then Jake wheeled his horse around and returned. He jumped off his stallion, grabbed Katie in an embrace, and kissed her soundly. "That's until next time, Katie Rose Kelly."

Sam laughed at the spectacle, turned around, and kept riding. "Keep going. Ain't none of our business," he said to his horse.

After Jake mounted his horse, he leaned down and kissed Katie one more time. "You're really something, Katie. Don't forget me." He rode off, whistling "Beautiful Dreamer."

Katie

She watched as both cowboys disappeared into the distance. She liked both men. But she was attracted to Jake Riley. *More than attracted,* she thought. A tingle of electricity went through her when she kissed him at the creek. And she smiled to think she had taken the initiative. But, oh, she really liked his response. It felt good to be kissed by a man again. And, when she thought about it, Jake Riley was a very good kisser. She twirled a copper curl and thought about her future. Marriage? Maybe, but then she'd lose control of her claim.

Quit dreaming, girl, Katie scolded herself. *You're working too hard to lose this land now.*

And that brought Katie back to her immediate tasks, including menus to feed the work crew, ideas for her new "house," and thoughts about the barn. Now, she wished she had driven the wagon to town so she could load up on supplies. Instead, she'd make do with what she had on hand, along with some fresh meat.

My aim is getting better, she said to herself as she returned to her wagon with three prairie chickens.

Joe and Tom Slaton arrived the next day, one driving a lumber wagon with supplies and tools and the other on horseback with the second horse trailing by its reins.

"You made good time," Katie greeted the two men. "Let's unload the supplies and get started. Want some coffee?" She held out two mugs of coffee.

"Yes, ma'am. Thank you kindly," said Tom, the shorter of the two brothers, who took a steaming mug of coffee. The other brother, Joe, bobbed his head in appreciation.

Katie showed the Slatons where she wanted her dugout. "This hill has some height," she said. "I want the opening facing south to catch the summer breezes and block the winter winds." Joe nodded at the logic. "And I'd like a well between the house and the barn so I don't have to haul water from the creek every day. Oh, and an outhouse over there." She indicated a flat piece of land behind the hill."

"Now, let's talk about the barn," she continued. They "walked off" the dimensions for a small shelter for her animals. "I want a couple of horse stalls and plenty of room for the mamas to give birth when the weather is bad," Katie said. "It doesn't need to be fancy, just sturdy for now."

The brothers got to work and, by nightfall, had made good progress on the dugout. The home was constructed by scooping out the dirt from the hill. They used to lumber to close off the front of the house. Katie had decided she'd use river rocks to reinforce the front of the dugout and to help insulate it. There would be one window in the front wall, but unlike Hughes' shanty, Katie bought a glass window to keep out bugs as well as rain and snow.

The Slaton boys were able to clear an interior space about twelve feet into the hill and about eight feet wide. The room was tall enough for the Slatons to walk in. Later, Katie would whitewash the interior dirt walls to put a barrier between her home and the bugs that still lived in the hill. Finally, they would drill a hole through the top of the hill that would eventually accommodate the pipe on a cookstove.

Katie kept her shotgun within reach and kept an eye on them to make sure that they were as trustworthy as Jake had said. They made camp around the fire. Katie joined Maddie to watch over the flock. She had an uneasy feeling about the coyotes.

Under the light of the full moon, Katie made an entry in her journal.

Journal Entry – June 28, 1866

It's a quiet night with a new moon and bright stars. I don't think I ever saw the night skies this clearly in Chicago. Maybe the stars and the moon just shine brighter on the frontier. Or maybe it's just that my future seems brighter out here.

I enjoy being a single woman again. Nan was right about not marrying Patrick. He wasn't the man for me. Perhaps if the war hadn't cut our married life short, we would have gotten to know – and like – each other better. As it was, his temper was always a worry for me. But that life is behind me now.

There is another man, Jake Riley, who's caught my eye. He's a grand-looking man with coal-black hair and a ready smile. He isn't courting me, but he has become a good friend, and that's what I need right now. I made it clear that I'm not in the market for a husband – and by my estimation, he's not in the market for a wife. Fine by me.

The dugout, my new home, should be done in a week or so. With help and advice from friends, I've hired two brothers from Iowa to build the dugout and a barn. I'm looking forward to having an actual home, although the sheep wagon is very practical for following the flock.

With the new barn, this will be a working sheep ranch. I've been thinking about a name for it, like the Double D Ranch that Jake works at. Da, I'm going to call my claim the Shamrock Sheep Ranch. It seems fitting, and I hope Da will be pleased.

KR

Chapter 11: Spinning

July 1, 1866 - Shamrock Sheep Ranch, Dakota Territory

Katie

Katie carried buckets of water from her new well to the small garden she had planted. *The beans and squash would probably make it*, she thought, *if the rabbits didn't nibble them to the ground. The potatoes, thank goodness, looked healthy.*

The dozen ewes and their lambs had grazed most of the pasture east of the dugout. Today Katie would load the sheep wagon and move the flock further west. She just finished packing several days worth of food and supplies when she saw a rider in the distance.

"I was hoping I'd catch you at home," Sarah Wright called as she dismounted.

"Just barely, I'm moving the flock to greener pastures," Katie said as she motioned to the west. "But it's so good to have company. You'll be the first guest in my new home."

Sarah explained that her family had ridden into Twin Brooks for church that morning. "Tim and the children took the wagon back home. Since I was this far south, I wanted to call on you. It's been too long since we've visited." She surveyed the dugout and garden. "It looks like you're settling in nicely, Katie Rose. Polly told me about Harold Hughes. That devil. You had a rocky start to homesteading, girl. I'm glad to see that it didn't deter you."

"My nan always said 'What doesn't kill you makes you stronger.' I'm stronger." She joined Sarah at a small table in the dugout and poured tea for the two of them. "It was terrifying, and if the Goyas hadn't found me on the road, I'm not sure what would have happened. God bless Lara and Ben. They are angels."

Sarah nodded. "Lara told me about the attack when they got to our place. Your nan is right, though. And you are the stronger for it." She patted Katie's hand. "Now tell me how you like being sheepherder."

"It's a lot of work, but I love the wooly little beasties," Katie admitted. "And with Maddie to keep them in line…." Sarah looked puzzled. "Oh, that's what I named the darlin' dog that Jake Riley brought me from your dog's litter."

"She comes from good stock. Maddie will be a good herder for you. Now, for the *real* reason I'm here." This got Katie's attention. "Twin Brooks has an Independence Day celebration next Saturday. There will be a picnic lunch in the afternoon and a dance that evening. Everyone will be there. You should come."

Katie shook her head and started to beg off, but Sarah stopped her protests. "Now, before you say you can't leave the flock, I have a solution for you. Jimmy can stay with your sheep so you can have a day off. What do you think of that?"

"It's been a long time since I've danced. But won't Jimmy want to go to the dance?"

Sarah shook her head. "He's not much for people and parties. I'll send Jimmy over later this week. He can learn the ways of your animals, and the animals will get used to him."

"That is so kind, Sarah. It looks like you've thought of everything."

"No, one more thing, Katie." Sarah rose and went to her horse. She brought back a large sack and dumped a pile of raw wool on the floor. "Do you know how to spin, Katie?"

"I've seen it done, but I don't have a spinning wheel," Katie replied.

"I use a drop spindle, but first, you must prepare the wool. We'll start with the basics. Now, I've already washed some of the wool to get rid of the lanolin and the dirt that's on wool fleeces. After washing the rest of the raw wool, you can dye it if you wish. For now, we'll spin undyed wool so you can see the process.

"These are wool carders." She handed Katie two boards with short handles and sharp teeth on one side of each board. "Carding is the next step," she explained. "Carding and spinning keep my hands busy in the evening hours." Then Sarah demonstrated how to place the raw wood on the carding board and comb through the wool.

"It takes a light hand. The point of carding your wool is to separate the hairs so they're untangled and ready to spin. You're done when the wool has been combed to the other board." She loosened the separated wool from the teeth of the carder and rolled it into a sausage shape. "After you roll it into a sausage, it's ready to spin."

Katie practiced the techniques until Sarah said, "You've got it. Now on to the next step."

Sarah drew a drop spindle out of the sack and showed Katie how to attach a length of leader yarn to the wooden spool. "Next, you'll pull a section of the wool and wrap it around the leader yarn like this." Her hands moved deftly but slowly enough so that Katie could follow her movements. She held up the spindle. "Now, give it a flick from the bottom. You can see how the twist gathers the fibers and wraps them around the leader yarn." When sufficient wool had wrapped around the leader yarn, she moved the leader yarn to the spindle and began working the raw wool itself.

"I hold the spindle like this so I can get the next length of wool ready." Sarah tucked the spindle between her knees and showed Katie how to pinch the raw wool. "Then I twist the spindle again, like so. Here, try it." She handed the spindle to Katie and watched as the novice practiced twisting and spinning.

Soon Katie was handling the raw wool with confidence. "I hope I don't forget how to do this by the time my sheep are ready to be sheared next spring."

"This bag of wool and the tools are for you, Katie," said Sarah. "It's your 'starter kit.' Every sheep woman needs carding boards and a spinner. It will keep your hands occupied on those long nights in the winter."

"It certainly will. Thank you so much, Sarah."

"Now, I must get back home." Before Sarah mounted her horse, she gave Katie a hard hug. "Homesteading is hard work, but friends ease the burdens. I'm glad you're here, Katie Rose Kelly."

"I'm thankful for your friendship, Sarah. I'll see you next Saturday at the Independence Day celebration. And thanks again for sending your nephew to watch the flock so I can dance again!" Katie twirled, and Sarah laughed.

Katie and Maddie – mostly Maddie, to be honest – moved the flock further west, away from the new dugout. Maddie made sure the flock stayed together. The lambs were growing quickly and liked to explore every rock and crevice on the prairie. That night, Katie made camp on the western edge of her claim while the sheep grazed the lush, green prairie grasses.

She'd just pulled some raw wood and the carding boards out of the wagon when she heard Maddie barking and growling fiercely. Katie grabbed her shotgun and ran toward the uproar – and her flock.

When she arrived, Katie found Maddie in a stand-off with four good-sized coyotes. Maddie had already fought off at least one of the predators and was bleeding from a wound in her shoulder. This was a side of Maddie that Katie had never seen before. Even though she was outnumbered, the border collie snarled and growled fiercely at the pack. She stood between the flock and the coyotes, making it clear that they would have to get past her to reach their quarry.

The coyotes were preparing to circle around the flock when Katie joined her watchdog. Carefully, she took aim at the largest of the coyotes. Sending up a quick prayer that her aim would be better than when she'd fired off a wild shot to protect the Hughes flock, she pulled the trigger. Her prayer was answered. Her shot found its mark in the tawny fur of the animal's chest. The other three coyotes scattered, howling in unison. Katie could hear the pack long after she'd lost sight of them.

Turning to Maddie, she said, "What a brave girl! You deserve a treat. But first, let's look at that shoulder." The dog dutifully sat as Katie cleaned the wound, deciding that a bandage would be a wasted effort. "We'll keep an eye on it, though," she said as she stroked the dog's head.

Neither of the sheepherders – human nor canine – got much sleep the remainder of the night or the following night, thanks to the howling and yipping in the distance.

As good as her word, Sarah Wright's nephew rode into Katie's sheep camp mid-week. Jimmy Turner had the same blond hair as his aunt, but where her eyes were a deep shade of blue, his were a warm brown. Under his bib overalls, he wore a sleeveless union suit.

He jumped off the dappled gray mare in a fluid movement and removed his worn straw hat. "Howdy, ma'am. It's good to see you again. Your flock is looking good."

Katie suspected this might be the longest string of sentences she'd hear from the young man. "Jimmy, It's good to see you again, too. And that's Maddie," she gestured to the border collie that was pushing a stray lamb back to his mama. "She's a big help."

"Yes, ma'am."

During the next few days, Katie and Jimmy got to know each other better. He reminded Katie a bit of her younger brother, Ryan. However, her brother was much more talkative than this child of the prairie. By Friday, the two had gotten into a rhythm, with Jimmy doing most of the herding while Katie watched him work. In fact, she admitted to herself, she picked up a few pointers on sheep herding from the boy.

"I'm going back to the dugout to collect a few things for the picnic and the dance," Katie said. "I know the flock is in good hands with you and Maddie. I'll be back on Sunday."

"Yes, ma'am."

She smiled at his standard reply, saddled her horse, and headed east toward her home.

Along the way, Katie marveled at the swarms of orange, yellow, and blue butterflies that abounded on the prairie. Their brightly colored wings made her think of flying flowers.

Back at the dugout, Katie packed one of the handful of dresses she had brought from Chicago. This was a blue-and-white striped frock with elbow-length sleeves and an extra ruffle at the hemline. The square neckline was edged in white lace. Along with the dress, she packed the green shawl from Nan. And, almost an afterthought, she grabbed a red hair ribbon.

The buildings in Twin Brooks were decorated with red, white, and blue bunting, and every establishment proudly displayed Old Glory. Katie's first stop was Polly's Place to inquire about a room. She was pleased to see Polly talking with Sheriff Brown.

"Well, I was hoping you'd make it into town for our 'little' party," Polly called out when Katie entered the saloon.

"Sarah volunteered her nephew, Jimmy, to watch the flock so I could get away," Katie explained. "I'm hoping there's a room available to rent for a couple of nights."

"I kept one open with that very thought," Polly said. "Now, tell us all about the life of a lady sheepherder."

With that, Katie updated Polly and Micah on the new dugout, the barn, and her encounter with the coyotes.

"Good thing your aim is getting better. The last time I saw you shoot at coyotes, you couldn't hit the side of a barn," said a familiar male voice. Katie turned to see Jake entering the saloon.

"I'd starve if my aim hadn't improved," she countered. "Those prairie chickens don't dance into my cooking pot of their own accord."

"Don't expect they do. Sounds like you've got dancin' on your mind, Katie Rose."

"I guess I do," she laughed. "It's been way too long since I've danced."

"Smitty plays a mean fiddle. The town's gonna do it up right," said Micah. "And I heard talk about a ceremony to recognize Union soldiers." Jake looked away for a brief moment.

Polly nodded and poured beers for Katie and Jake. Together, the four chatted about events back east, the weather, and who was new in town.

"Say, I was planning to eat at Emma's tonight. Do you want to join me," Jake offered an invitation to the group.

"Count me out," Polly said sadly. "I'm on bartending duty till close."

"I've got rounds to make," said the sheriff.

"Guess that just leaves you, Katie. Care to join me?"

"Well, I have been dreaming about Emma's pot roast."

"Pot roast is an odd thing to dream about," Jake said as he led Katie from the saloon to the diner.

"Not if you've been eating venison and prairie chickens every night."

"Yup."

Dinner at Emma's Diner was as delicious as Katie had remembered – and anticipated. As they left, Jake said, "Would you care to take a stroll, or do you want to go directly back?"

"It's a nice evening. A stroll would be lovely."

The couple walked arm-in-arm down the wooden boardwalk, past the livery, until the town was behind them and a blanket of stars was the only light. They stopped, and Jake took Katie into his arms. "While you were dreaming about pot roast, I was dreaming about you," Jake murmured in Katie's ear.

"Who said pot roast was the only thing I was dreaming about, cowboy."

This time, it was Jake who initiated the kiss. It was a long kiss, filled with the hunger that parted lovers experience. Katie returned the kiss. She wrapped her arms around his neck as he ran his hands down her back, stopping at the small of her waist. He pulled her in closer to inhale her scent.

The kiss ended when Katie heard a coyote howl and stiffened at the sound. Jake held her until she relaxed again in his arms. "It's the night song of the prairie," he whispered. "But it's late. Let's get back."

In her room at Polly's Place, Katie opened the pack of letters from her family. The first letter was from her grandmother.

Katie, mo stór,

I'm reading between the lines, as they say, about your time with Harold and Aggie Hughes. I never did like the cut of that man, but I trusted that Aggie Hughes was a good woman and would do right by you. Learning that his wife left the homestead did not put me at ease. I have a sense that there is more to that tale. Maybe someday you will tell me the story you're not telling. But, as you are rid of that man, I'll leave it be.

So now you are a sheepherder, are you? I am sure I told you about my da's family back in Kilkenny. They were great sheepherders, too. Mayhaps sheepherding is in your blood, Katie girl. I'll be sending you the loom that my nan used back in the old country. She was a weaver of great renown. Mayhaps that is in your blood, too, dear girl.

I believe you made the right decision to go west, Katie Rose. You are strong and you will succeed at whatever you put your mind to.

Now, some advice from your nan: Katie Rose, you were not meant to be alone forever. I know that your marriage to Pat was not the happiest union. You deserve a man who loves and cherishes you. More than that, you deserve a man who is your friend – someone you can build a future with. Your heart and your head need time to heal, but please open the door when love comes knocking.

I send a prayer to your mother in Heaven every night that she watches over you and keeps you safe. Be happy, my darling girl.

Nan

Chapter 12: Independence Day Celebration

July 7, 1866 - Twin Brooks, Dakota Territory

Katie

Saturday morning burned bright and promised a hot, dry day on the prairie. "A scorcher," the locals called it. Rising with the sun as was now her habit, Katie washed up quickly. She looked longingly at the deep bathtub in the corner but knew there wouldn't be time for that luxury today.

"How can I help you, Polly," Katie inquired when she saw her friend behind the bar.

"The dust is everywhere," said Polly. "Let's rinse off the glassware and make sure they're all upside down."

Katie tied on an apron and got to work.

"I didn't bring any food for the picnic," Katie said. "Any suggestions?"

"I've donated a keg of beer," Polly said. "And the town council is cooking a beef. I'm guessing most of the women will bring pies and such."

"I'll make Irish soda bread," Katie decided. "Can I use your kitchen?".

"Better start before it's too hot to bake," Polly said.

With that, Katie finished her chores behind the bar and left for the general store to purchase baking ingredients.

Polly had been right about the heat. Baking bread on a hot summer day was perhaps not the best idea, but Katie proceeded to bake a dozen loaves using her nan's soda bread recipe.

Jake poked his head into the kitchen just as Katie pulled the last loaves from the oven. "Lordy, it's hot as a nickel...." He paused and searched for something more genteel, "hot as a griddle in here," he said lamely.

Not understanding the saying, Katie smiled at the cowboy as she placed the last loaves on the table to cool. "I'm done here. But I'm not ready for the picnic or the dance." She unwrapped the head scarf from her coppery hair and dabbed at the perspiration on her face.

"Here, you're just smudging the flour around," Jake said as he took the scarf and started wiping at Katie's face. "One more spot." With that, he cupped her face and gave Katie a light kiss on the lips. "I'll be back in an hour. Better have your dancing shoes on, Katie Rose Kelly."

On his way out, he stole a slice of the warm bread, tasted it, and said, "Hmmm, almost as good as your kiss."

"Be gone with you, you scallawag!" Katie waved him out the door with her scarf. Then she hurried to her room to wash up and dress up.

Less than an hour later, Katie emerged wearing her white and cobalt blue dress. The bright red ribbon secured her hair into a partial bun at the back of her head. A quick look in the mirror told her that the patriotic colors were just right for the day.

The first thing she heard upon entering the taproom was a whistle – a whistle of admiration.

"I hope you don't mind if I say you're looking as fine as Old Glory," said Sam Goodman.

"Thank you, Sam!" Katie gave a slight curtsey. "It's so good to see you. Can I buy you a beer in thanks for watching the flock?" She went behind the bar, poured a beer, and dropped a coin in the till.

"No need for that, but much appreciated, ma'am."

They chatted about the health of the sheep, how the grazing pastures were holding up, and her encounter with the pack of coyotes.

Sam laughed at the story, which Katie now retold with characteristic Irish humor.

"She's pretty *and* a good shot," said Jake as he entered the saloon. "Sorry I'm late. I ran into someone." A cloud passed his face, and then he continued, "Never you mind. It's going to be a glorious day. Who's hungry?" With Katie between the two cowboys, the trio left the saloon, walking arm-in-arm.

The picnic was set up on the main street at the far end of the livery stable. A beef was roasting on a spit. Next to the roasting meat were tables laden with baked beans, pastries and breads, fresh vegetables, and jars of preserves. Wooden tables, covered with white tablecloths, were decorated with alternating red and blue bouquets of flowers.

The delicious smell of roasting beef wafted through the air, whetting people's appetites for the feast to come. Townspeople were already lining up, plates in hand, as the cooks sliced off pieces of the roasted meat.

Katie, Jake, and Sam filled their plates and looked for an empty table. They spied Sarah and Tim Wright, along with several tow-headed youngsters, at a nearby table. Since Katie hadn't met the Wright children, Sarah made brief introductions. "The girls are Susan and Sally. The boys are Tom and Tucker." Katie smiled and greeted the younger Wrights.

"It's gonna be a hot one today," said Tim, in the time-honored tradition of starting any conversation with talk about the weather.

"Let's hope everyone can keep cooler heads," Jake said in a low voice to Sam. He nodded in the direction of the food line.

Katie heard the remark, and then she saw Harold Hughes. Immediately, she tensed up.

"How's the carding and spinning coming along, Katie?" asked Sarah. Katie realized that Sarah was probably trying to distract her.

"Oh, um. I'm getting better at it. I have several balls of yarn already," replied Katie, following Sarah's cue. Warming up to the topic, she said, "In fact, my nan is sending me a loom so I can start weaving. She wrote me that *her nan* was quite the weaver. Nan brought the loom over from the old country. I didn't even know she had it."

"Well, then I'll be able to teach you how to weave," Sarah said. The two women started discussing how to dye the wool using local flowers, nuts, and vegetables.

The men talked about their shared interest – cattle.

"We'll be rounding up the cows and their calves for branding next week, I reckon," said Jake.

"I just finished branding my beef," said Tim. 'Course my herd ain't near the size of the Double D's."

Jake frowned. "Say, how do you mark your sheep? Do you brand them like beef?"

"Nope," replied Tim. "Branding an 800- or 900-pound beef cow is one thing, but sheep are only eighty or ninety pounds. Sheepherders generally paint 'em."

"Paint 'em!" exclaimed Jake. "How does that work?"

Sam joined the conversation. "It can be just a mark on the sheep's coat, but some herders get creative."

Jake tilted his head, listening intently.

"That's right," said Tim. "We use a 'Rocking W' brand on the beef. The sheep are painted with a 'W' that looks like the Rocking W, but it's not permanent. Generally lasts for most of the grazing season, though."

"Hmmm. Learn something every day," Jake said. Turning to Katie, he said, "Have you thought about a brand for your herd? …I mean flock."

Ignoring his gaffe, she said, "I'm calling my ranch the 'Shamrock.' I guess that means my sheep will have a shamrock brand. I'd best be buying a can of green paint." They all laughed and enjoyed the good food, the good conversation, and the good fellowship.

After the meal, Jim Bowers, the general store owner, stepped up to the stage and addressed the crowd.

"We're all here to celebrate the day the United States declared independence from England. But I think it's also fittin' that we celebrate the end of the Civil War. Our country survived a terrible war. A war where brothers fought against brothers. A war that resulted in way too many of our countrymen dying or being injured. A war that has touched the lives of each and every one of us here today." He emphasized his words, like a good orator would do.

Katie thought about Patrick's death and of the deaths of the many young men who had frequented the Lucky Shamrock Pub before they marched off to fight. She also thought about the men sitting at her table. Jake had enlisted in the Kansas 3rd Infantry Regiment. Sam, an escaped slave from Missouri, had made his way to Kansas and volunteered in the 2nd Kansas Colored Infantry Regiment. After the war, they both joined cattle drives down south and ended up in Dakota Territory. She knew that Tim Wright had served in the Union Army, too, but wasn't sure which regiment – not that it mattered anymore.

She turned her attention back to Jim Bowers. "Today, we want to recognize the soldiers who valiantly served our Union." He called the names of about two dozen men, young and old, and asked them to join him on the makeshift stage. Among the men joining Tim, Jake, and Sam on the stage was Harold Hughes.

Each man received a red, white, and blue ribbon with a medal attached. The band struck up *The Battle Hymn of the Republic*. There was a moment of silence when the song was over, and then the men returned to their seats.

Now in a subdued mood, the crowd cleared tables and cleaned the area in preparation for the dance. Many of the men migrated to the town's saloons. Knowing how busy Polly's Place would be, Katie finished cleaning up and hurried to the saloon to lend a hand.

"Thank the good Lord you're here," Polly called over the din. "They're four deep in front of the bar."

Polly and Katie poured dozens of cold draught beers for their customers. When Jake made his way to the front of the bar, Katie put him to work. "We'll need more kegs brought up. Could you and Sam give us a hand?"

They disappeared in the back room at Katie's request.

"The first keg was on the house, fellas," Polly shouted. "You've done drank it dry. I still have beer, but it'll cost you now."

"I'm buying the next round for all the cattlemen here," boomed a very large man in a gray cowboy hat who had just entered the saloon.

"And I'm guessing every last man in here is a cattleman right now," Polly whispered to Katie.

"Who's that?" Katie whispered back.

"That's Dan Deacon, the 'DD' of the Double D Ranch," Polly supplied.

Katie sized him up. He stood well over six feet tall and had the imposing presence of a man used to taking charge.

Polly was right. Dozens of customers crowded the bar, waiting for a free beer from the owner of the Double D.

Jake and Sam reappeared, each hauling a keg of beer. Jake whistled when he saw the crowd at the bar. "It's busier than before."

"Your boss, Dan Deacon, is standing for the next round," explained Polly.

"For all the cattlemen," Katie added. "Which looks to be everyone in the saloon." She smiled, reminded of her days at the Lucky Shamrock.

"Riley and Goodman: I'm buying. Grab some cold ones," instructed Deacon.

Katie handed beers to the two cowboys as Deacon strode up. "Good to see you two at the festivities," Deacon said. He turned and looked Katie up and down. "And who's this pretty filly?"

Before Jake could introduce Katie, she said, "Katie Rose Kelly. I'm a friend of Polly's. I have a claim southwest of town."

"Are you running cattle or just dirt farming?" the cattleman asked.

"I have sheep," Katie replied.

A cloud crossed Deacon's face as he shook his head. "Damned sheep. They're just hooved locusts that chew the grass down to nothing."

Overhearing the conversation, Polly knew that Deacon was ready to fight. Hoping to head off a confrontation, she directed Katie to help at the other side of the bar.

Deacon moved away to gladhand a group of cowboys playing poker.

"Well, aren't we a couple of gents," said Sam. "We should've spoken up for Katie."

"You mean *I* should have defended Katie's honor," Jake countered.

"Not if you want to keep your job, buddy. You know Deacon doesn't cotton to sheepherders. Come to think of it, you didn't used to have much time for 'em either."

"That was before I met a fiery redhead with sparkling green eyes and.."

"And what? Are you boys talking about me?" Katie smiled as she approached the two. She didn't appear to be rattled by Deacon's comment.

"I've been serving beers too long to get upset by a big-talking man." She tilted her head toward the music outside. At that point, Polly joined them and said, "I can handle it from here. Go on with you. I expect to see you out on the dance floor."

Outside the saloon, Katie pulled a lacey fan from her sleeve and began fluttering it. That got Jake's attention. Sam was already talking with a couple of cowboys from the Double D.

"Thank you for helping out at Polly's," Katie said as they made their way to the tables by the dance floor.

"Glad to lend a hand. You ladies were plum busy. Are you too tired to dance now?" he teased.

"Never!" Katie snapped her fan shut, and the couple made their way to the dance floor – an area of main street near the stage where the musicians started with a lively rendition of *Jeff in Petticoats*. The song, about Confederate President Jefferson Davis' attempt to escape capture, was a hit with Union soldiers.

After several more turns around the dance floor, they claimed two chairs at a nearby table. "I had no idea that Mr. Bowers had such a good singing voice," Katie said as she fanned herself.

102

"He does, indeed," Jake agreed. "Say, can I get you a glass of lemonade?"

"I'd love one, thank you."

As Jake headed over to the refreshment table, Harold Hughes took his opportunity to confront Katie. "I hear your ranch is up and running, missy. With MY sheep."

Katie's eyes flew wide in surprise. "A woman on her own," he sneered. "You're gonna need a man at your place to make a go of it."

Hughes's words would have intimidated or even frightened Katie two months ago. But Hughes was addressing a new Katie Rose Kelly. She thought of herself as a phoenix, the mythical bird that rose from its ashes to start over again. She was stronger. She had survived his brutal attack. She was building a new life for herself. And she couldn't resist provoking him – just a bit.

"Oh, I am 'making a go of it,' Harold." She used his first name to show they were equals. "*My flock* is doing very well on *my pastures*. Thank you for asking."

He reached out to shake her. Katie used her folded fan as a small baton and struck him on the face. Jake, seeing the confrontation, ran back to the table to protect Katie.

"I warned you earlier today, Hughes," Jake shouted.

This brought the attention of Sheriff Brown. "Boys, there'll be no brawlin' here tonight. Would you both like to cool off in the jail?"

"Harold was just inquiring as to how I was 'making out' on my claim, Sheriff," Katie said sweetly.

"She hit me!" Hughes said as he tenderly touched his left cheek.

Brown looked at Hughes. "Unprovoked?" asked the lawmen. Hughes shrugged.

"It's best you two men steer clear of each other for the rest of the night." He paused and said, "And Hughes, if there's any trouble on Mrs. Kelly's ranch, I'll be looking at you first."

Hughes beat a hasty retreat. "Looks like you handled yourself just fine, Katie," said Brown.

"He got my Irish up," she said, referring to her temper.

"I wouldn't want to be on the other side of that fan," he laughed. Seeing a potential fight brewing on the other side of the dance floor, he said, "It's gonna be a busy night." And he left.

Jake began to apologize for leaving Katie alone. She stopped him. "Before you say anything, I want you to know that I had to do that on my own. Harold Hughes needs to understand that he can't bully me or scare me anymore. I've worried he might make a visit to my ranch to take back the sheep. Hopefully, he won't try that now. He knows that you and Sheriff Brown are watching him. That should be enough. But I do thank you for coming to my rescue." And she kissed him.

Jake twirled Katie around the dance floor, enjoying several waltzes and two steps. The local musicians appreciated the hearty applause from the crowd. "Thank you. Thank you, everyone," said Jim Bowers. "Gentlemen, find your ladies. It's time for the last dance of the night."

"Beautiful dreamer.." the band began.

"They're playing our song," Jake whispered in her ear.

Dreamily, Katie laid her head on his shoulder. "Mmmmm, indeed they are."

Afterward, Jake walked Katie back to the saloon.

Polly was wiping down the bar. "Looks like you two had a good time at the dance," she said, noticing Jake's hand around Katie's tiny waist.

"It was beautiful," Katie replied.

"I'm turning in. It was a busy day and a busier night," Polly said, giving the couple some privacy.

Still troubled by the way Dan Deacon spoke to Katie, Jake said, "About Deacon's comment..."

"Dan Deacon doesn't like sheep, and Harold Hughes doesn't like that I *have* sheep," Katie said. "That doesn't mean I'm going to stop. And I'm not going to think about them tonight.

"Jake, I had a lovely time this evening," Katie said. She softly stroked his cheek. That was all the encouragement that he needed. Jake swept Katie into an embrace. His kiss started on her lips but moved down her neck, resting on the swell of her breast. She reveled in his touch as her fingers ran through Jake's thick, dark hair.

Finally, Jake straightened up. "This is not the time or place," he said. "But perhaps..."

"Perhaps," she replied.

Capturing her lips again, Jake kissed Katie soundly one more. "Tomorrow," he said.

Katie slumped against the saloon's bar and touched her lips. "Tomorrow," she said to herself.

Even though she needed to sleep, Katie needed to confide in her journal that night.

Journal Entry – July 7, 1866

My heart! My heart! I think I am losing my heart to a tall cowboy with blue eyes and black hair. Jake Riley is everything that Patrick was not. He understands that I need to build my own life. He makes me laugh. He makes me miss him when we're apart. Yet, he is somehow there when I need him. Could this be love?

KR

Chapter 13: Under the Lone Tree

July 8, 1866 - Twin Brooks, Dakota Territory

Katie

When Katie attempted to pay Polly for two nights' room rental and use of her kitchen, the saloon owner waved her off. "You more than paid your way with your help behind the bar. Besides, friends are always welcome here."

"I'm truly blessed to have found you and Sarah when I did."

"We women need to stick together. It's a man's world on the 'wild' frontier, but when women support each other, we can make our way out here."

"My nan always said that we need women friends to be sane –and happy."

"Once again, your nan was right. I want to meet that woman someday." She patted Katie on the shoulder and said, "Now you have a safe ride back to your spread. Did you say you've named it?"

"I'm calling my claim the Shamrock Sheep Ranch for my da's pub. That reminds me, I need to pick up a pail of green paint to mark my flock. Then I'm meeting Jake at the livery. He's riding part of the way back with me." Her green eyes sparkled at the mention of his name.

Clad in sturdy boots, a split riding skirt, a white blouse, and a kelly green vest, Katie had put her old life behind her as she strode down the boardwalk toward the general store. She felt a renewed sense of purpose and an energy to push forward despite Dan Deacon's warnings.

After purchasing the paint and a brush, Katie went to the livery, saddled her horse, and packed the items in her saddle bag. Looking around, she didn't see Jake's large black stallion in the stable. She was a bit surprised but more disappointed that he'd left town without saying goodbye.

She paid the livery owner and mounted her chestnut mare. From her vantage on horseback, she could see Jake riding her way.

"I thought you'd left early," she said.

Coming alongside her, Jake said, "I gave my word, Katie Rose, that I'd accompany you part-way home. Just had a couple of stops to make before we ride out." He indicated a parcel on the back of his saddle.

The July morning was proving to be the start of a typical July day on the prairie – hot, dry, and windy.

"Thank goodness for the breeze," Katie said after the town was out of sight. She fanned herself with her gloved hand.

"About the only time the wind stops is when it's gonna change direction," Jake commented. He looked up and saw a pair of eagles weaving in and out of the fluffy clouds. "See those eagles? They're riding the wind currents up high. The Arapahoe, where I come from, tell stories about why the eagle is sacred."

Katie turned to listen. "Tell me."

"Well, the Arapahoe believe the eagle is the strongest and bravest of all birds. In their stories, the Great Spirit made all the birds of the sky when the world was young. And of all the birds, the Great Spirit chose the eagle to be master of the skies."

He looked up again at the two great birds. "The eagle flies higher than any other bird, which means it flies closer to the creator. Because of this, the Great Spirit chose the eagle to communicate with man. The eagle carries the prayers to the creator. In turn, the Great Spirit sends messages through the eagle.

"When you see an Arapahoe, a Pawnee, or any of the plains Indians wearing an eagle feather, that is a great, sacred honor. And, come to think of it, the eagle has been a symbol of greatness for many people – the Romans, the Vikings… And now it's the national bird of the United States.

"You see a lot of eagles along the river out here. They nest above the cliffs in tall trees. By now, the eaglets have left the nest. That pair up there," he nodded again to the soaring eagles, "is hunting…hunting for small animals like rabbits or other birds. I've heard that a full-grown eagle can carry off a newborn lamb, so you'd best keep an eye to the sky."

Katie tried to imagine a lamb in the claws of one of those birds. "I've seen eagles – or maybe they were hawks – flying over the flock." Then, making a slight jest, she said, "I guess I'll have to keep an 'eagle eye' out for them." Jake groaned at the pun.

They rode on for a bit until they could see the Lone Tree in the distance. "It's almost noon," Katie said. "Are you hungry? I packed some bread and cheese. We can rest under the tree."

"I'll go you one better. I asked Emma to pack another picnic for us. That's why I was late getting to the stable."

"That's a grand idea, Mr. Riley," Katie responded.

They arrived at the towering cottonwood tree, a landmark on the almost-treeless prairie. Katie noticed the tree's green leaves made a soothing sound as they rippled in the breeze. "If you take care of the horses, I'll lay out the picnic," she told Jake.

"Deal," he replied. He hobbled the two horses, allowing them to graze on the nearby prairie grasses.

Katie spread out a saddle blanket under the tree. She unpacked the basket of goodies from Emma's diner – fried chicken, pickles, sliced tomatoes, strawberry pie, and a jar of lemonade. To that, she added the loaf of bread and cheese she'd brought.

"I hope you're hungry. Emma has prepared a feast for us!" Katie called to Jake. He sank down on the blanket across from Katie. "Woo eee. Emma outdid herself," he whistled. "And I get to share it with the prettiest gal in the Territory."

Katie blushed as Jake leaned over to kiss her. She tilted her head to meet his lips, anticipating his hot kisses. He did not disappoint. Jake pulled Katie onto his lap and encircled her with his arms. She returned the embrace.

"You taste so good," Jake whispered in her ear as he trailed kisses down her neck. Her hands traced the hard muscles of his shoulders and back. Then she laughed.

"What's so funny?" he said, pulling back and looking into her deep green eyes.

"I'm ticklish. Your kisses are tickling me." She giggled again and moved off his lap.

"Well, don't that beat all," Jake said. "If kissing makes you laugh, then…" his voice trailed off.

"You'll just have to wonder about that – for now," she teased and handed him a chicken leg.

"Fair enough. You're worth waiting for, Katie Rose Kelly."

After lunch, the two enjoyed the shade of the cottonwood tree, with Jake resting his head in Katie's lap.

"That's the song of a meadowlark. See that flash of yellow?" Jake asked, pointing to a spot high in the tree.

"It's a sweet sound. I love the sounds of the prairie," she replied. "Except for the coyotes."

"Be grateful you can hear the enemy. It's when you can't hear 'em that you're in trouble," he said.

"Hmmm," she said, gently playing with a dark curl of his hair. "I'm listening if you want to talk about it."

"I don't talk much about the war. My outfit fought in the Western campaign. That's where General Grant made his reputation. The battles, they were bloody and deadly. The sounds of war are horrible, but the silence could be even worse. In the still of the night, you'd swear you could hear Johnny Reb sneaking up. Sometimes we did get ambushed. Sometimes I was the one sneaking up on the enemy." He shook his head. "I did my part. War is the stuff that nightmares are made of."

He fingered the ribbon and medal Jim Bowers had pinned on his chest the day before. "I don't like to think I earned this here medal for killing other men."

"You, and the other men on that stage, were being honored for helping to hold the country together. For defending the Union."

"Sometimes I wonder if it was worth the cost." He shook his head to clear it of thoughts of war. "Enough of that dark talk. Let's enjoy this bright summer day – and each other." He reached up and brought her head down to his for a light kiss. "We've got a ride ahead of us, and daylight's burning."

Katie packed the remainder of the picnic lunch while Jake unhobbled the horses.

They rode side by side and chatted about the dance, the picnic, and the townspeople. Finally, Jake brought up the topic of Harold Hughes. "You're pretty handy with that fan. I don't think I've ever seen one used quite like that," he laughed.

"It's not part of the 'language of the fan' that every young lady learns, but it's a pretty effective way of communicating. Harold Hughes never saw it coming."

The cowboy sized up the red-haired woman riding aside her chestnut horse. "I think you're gonna do just fine on the frontier. That city gal from Chicago has changed into a. . ."

Before he could finish the sentence, Katie said, ". . . into a lady sheepherder."

"Yep, you're tougher now – but you're gonna need to be."

"I'll take that as a compliment."

112

"And this is where I go north," Jake indicated a split in the trail. "I'd ask if you're comfortable riding the rest of the way alone, but you've got your shotgun."

"And my fan." She flipped open the lacy baton in jest.

Jake jumped down from his horse and lifted Katie off her saddle. "One more kiss before I go," he said.

"I was hoping you'd say that," and she gave herself into his arms for a long goodbye kiss.

They parted. Katie spurred her horse west, and Jake headed north.

She was happy to be "home," she realized as she unsaddled her mare. Maddie greeted her enthusiastically, jumping and yipping in welcome. Jimmy appeared a few minutes later.

"Nothin' to report, Missus," he said.

"That's a good report. How do cold fried chicken, salad, and a slice of pie sound?"

"The best thing I've heard all day. Thank you kindly," said the boy.

The next day, Jimmy showed Katie how to mark the sheep with her shamrock brand.

That evening, she reached for her journal and then remembered the packet of mail from home. She opened the letter from her father.

My darling Katie Rose,

Business at the Lucky Shamrock has picked up since the war ended. More and more soldiers and their families have moved to Chicago for jobs. The meat packers are booming thanks to the railroads. The newspapers say that soon Chicago will be second only to New York in size. Imagine that, Katie Rose!

The Shamrock Sheep Ranch, is it? I am very proud of you, and I'm honored that you have named your new home after the Shamrock Pub. The shamrock has always been a sign of luck for our family, and I'm bound that it will serve you well for your life in Dakota Territory.

Between you and me (do not tell Nan), it sounds as though Hughes was a scoundrel. I am distressed that I did not see it when I met him. Perhaps his Union blues swayed my opinion of him. I hope he got his comeuppance. You are well rid of him.

Although we miss you terribly, starting a fresh life on the frontier was a good choice. I have heard stories about other women – young and old – packing up and moving out west. And don't they deserve a bit of land, too? We Irish appreciate how important it is to have your own land.

One day, I hope to see the farm you are building in the Territory. Until then, I will think about you every day and pray for your safety and success.

Da

Chapter 14: Prairie Fire

Katie

Growing up in Chicago, Katie was used to hot summer days. But the heat of late summer on the prairie was something she hadn't experienced before. The prairie winds whipped through the tall grass, drying the grasslands to a crackling, tinder brown. When the sun went down, the nights were still and stiflingly hot.

The sheep had grazed all the viable pastures around her home. Except for the bits of green vegetables still surviving in her garden, most of the area around the dugout and the barn were barren. The garden vegetables only survived because Katie carried water from the creek daily. But the creek was also drying up.

With the help of her border collie, Katie moved the flock to the north side of her land, closer to the river, taking care to stay south of Deacon's lands. She'd learned that sheep aren't especially fond of water, and while they can swim, sheep generally choose not to go in the water. For now, the flock found decent grazing pastures on this patch of land.

After several days in this location, Katie thought about where to move the flock. Maybe closer to the creek? She'd noticed there was still grass near the water, and she could stay in the dugout rather than the sheep wagon at night. The dugout, she discovered, was much cooler and offered a respite from the heat. The sheep would be close enough that she and Maddie could patrol and protect the flock.

On what seemed to be the hottest day so far, Katie and Maddie rounded up the sheep and herded them away from the river. Maddie ran through and around the flock, keeping the animals together and moving them toward greener pastures. Rather than driving the wagon, Katie walked, leading the animal and her house-on-wheels southward.

The wind felt like a blast furnace, Katie thought. She wore only a camisole with her "work skirt" – a sturdy, reddish-brown skirt about the same color as the prairie dirt. Realizing that petticoats were unnecessary on the prairie, she nevertheless had donned the undergarment out of habit. On her head was a wide-brimmed hat tied securely with a red ribbon.

The wind shifted, and Katie looked to see clouds. "Rain clouds?" she mused. The skies were darkening, even though it was midday. In the distance, Katie could see the barn. Deciding to take shelter if these were storm clouds, she directed Maddie to move the sheep toward the barn.

Storms can build up quickly on the prairie. The skies continued to darken. A crack of thunder startled her. She looked over her shoulder to see lightning in the gray clouds. The winds whipped across the grasslands. The thunder and lightning were closer now.

Then the ground shook, and she heard a deafening crack of thunder, frightening the sheep. In the distance, she could see a red glow.

Fire.

The tinder-dry grasses provided the perfect fuel. The lightning was the "match" needed to start the fire. Thinking quickly, Katie knew she had to protect the animals – and herself.

The dugout was her only hope.

In the dugout, Katie hastily tossed the kitchen table and chair outside, along with her bed and another small piece of furniture, leaving only the cookstove on the floor. Making sure the foodstuffs were out of reach on high shelves, she left the dugout and called her dog.

"Maddie," Katie called as she ran toward the flock. She began leading one of the larger ewes toward the dugout. The sheepdog followed her mistress's direction, nipping at the stubborn sheep and pushing them toward the shelter.

The winds increased furiously. Katie could feel the first hot waves from the fire in the distance. With the last of the ewes and lambs crammed into the dugout, Maddie stood guard at the door while Katie drove the sheep wagon into the creek. Her only hope in saving the wagon was to surround it with water. Then she unhitched the horse. Slapping the mare on her rump, Katie trusted the horse could outrun the fire and save herself.

The novice homesteader then took a last look at her claim. Her mind racing, she pulled off her petticoat and soaked it in the well. Filling a pail, Katie watered down the dugout. She flung buckets of water on the dugout's grass-covered roof and slapped the soaked petticoat against the sides of the dwelling. The hours she'd spent hauling and stacking rocks against the front wall of her dugout might have been one of her best ideas, she decided.

With the fire racing toward her home, Katie grabbed a quilt she had tossed into the yard. Her final act of defiance – and self-preservation – was to soak the blanket in the well. She dashed to the dugout with the wet blanket. Inside, Katie stuffed the sodden quilt around the dugout's door to keep out the smoke.

Then they waited. Katie, Maddie, and her flock were packed tightly into the dugout.

"If I'd known that this would be an emergency barn," she said to the dog, "I would have told the Slaton boys to dig deeper." The dog licked the salty sweat off Katie's neck.

She remembered what Jake said about calming the herds by singing to them. Curled among the wooly sheep, Katie began to sing the Irish ballads that her nan had sung to her.

"My Gallant Darling," she sang, but in her grandmother's native tongue.

'Sé mo laoch mo ghile mear

Bonnie boy, ghile mear

You will be my gallant star

Oh heys to me mo ghile mear.

As the ewes settled down, so did their lambs. Soon, the flock was resting. After Katie had exhausted her repertoire of Irish tunes, she turned to another ballad she had come to love.

Beautiful dreamer, wake unto me,

Starlight and dewdrops are waiting for thee.

The song brought a tear to Katie's eye as she wondered if she would ever see Jake again.

Jake

Jake heard the thunder in the south. He saw the dark clouds on the horizon. Then he saw the red glow. The red glow of a prairie fire.

He knew where that glow was coming from – and where it was headed thanks to the strong, western winds.

"Sam, cover for me. There's a prairie fire down south. I need to check on Katie." The other cowboy nodded.

"I've got ya," Sam Goodman said as Jake wheeled his horse and galloped toward danger.

The horse and rider stopped only once to rest and get water from a small creek. And then they were off again, with the flames licking the sky in the distance.

Several hours later – nearly sundown – Katie's claim came into view. Jake could see that the barn, although charred, was still standing. The sheep wagon, at least the wagon bed and the wheels, was sitting in the nearby creek. The canvas cover had burned away.

What he didn't see were any sheep or Katie.

From atop his horse, he scanned the scorched grounds for any sign of life. Nothing. He rode closer to the dugout for a better look. Then he heard singing.

Katie's clear, soprano voice was singing an Irish ballad. He jumped from his stallion and ran to the dugout. The door was stuck; something was jamming it. He pounded on the wooden door.

"Katie! Katie Rose Kelly, open the damn door! Katie!" Before he could continue his tirade, the door opened to show a disheveled Katie holding a small lamb.

"Is it over?" she asked. "Is the fire gone?"

"Oh, my sweetheart!" Jake embraced her. "Yes, my darling Katie Rose, you've survived your first prairie fire." He stroked her back and kissed her forehead and then her lips.

The lamb struggled to escape Katie's arms, so she let the wooly bundle jump down to the dirt floor. Her arms now free, she returned Jake's embrace with a fervor, a hunger. They stood among the sheep, hugging and kissing like long-lost lovers. Then Katie started laughing.

"Why do my kisses always make you laugh?" he said.

"It's not that. Look around you. We're surrounded by my sheep – although a few have found the door – and sheep droppings. Not very romantic, is it?"

"I can remedy that," the cowboy replied.

With Maddie's help, they herded the beasts out of the dugout. Katie swept the floors and then collapsed in the middle of the barren home and started crying.

Jake sat down next to her and put his arms around her shoulders. "It's alright, sweetheart. You're safe now. The sheep are safe. The fire has passed." He pulled the scarf off her head and stroked her coppery hair.

Still crying, she turned toward him. "I know, but ..." tears ran down her cheeks.

"Shhhh…" Jake gently kissed her tears. Katie leaned into Jake's arms, and after a space of time, her crying subsided.

Katie

She looked into his clear, blue eyes as if seeing him for the first time. Then she took his face into her hands and kissed him. The kiss was long and full of desire.

"Jake, I want you," she said after breaking off the kiss. "Do you want me?"

"It's all I've thought of for months, Katie. But," he hesitated, "are you sure? You've been through a lot and…."

"Shhhh…" she responded, pulling him to the ground.

Their lovemaking was tentative at first, as each learned what the other enjoyed. Jake kissed the swells of Katie's full breasts, his mouth eventually finding the hard peaks of her nipples. Katie moaned in pleasure.

While he was teasing her breasts with his tongue, Katie's hands explored Jake's hard, muscled back. She ran her hands from his shoulder blades down to his taut buttocks. Then her hands moved to the front of his torso to find his manhood.

Jake groaned. He moved on top of Katie and once again made eye contact. "Are you sure?"

She nodded and arched her back. Jake slid into Katie's core. Together, they moved as one until they reached climax. Jake rolled off Katie but took her with him. Now Katie was lying on Jake. She laid her head on his chest, just under his shoulder. He stroked her lower back and gently kissed her head.

"Mo chroí," Katie said.

"Mmm?" he said.

"Irish. It means 'my heart.'"

"Mo chroí," he repeated.

Katie wanted to stay that way forever, but too soon the light of the moon lit the dugout.

"Oh my. It's late." She rose to reassemble her blouse and skirt.

Jake followed her lead and reached for his shirt. When he'd tugged on his boots, they both emerged from the dugout to find the sheep bedded down in the moonlight as Maddie paced around the flock, keeping guard.

Katie fished a piece of dried meat from her pocket and gave the treat to the faithful sheepdog. "Good girl," she said as she patted Maddie on the head. The dog nuzzled her.

"It'll be dawn soon," Jake said. "I can stay for a bit and round up your horse, but then I'll need to head back to the Double D."

Katie nodded, understanding that he, too, had responsibilities beyond her. "I'll get a pot of coffee going." She looked around the claim for the furniture she had tossed out and realized that all the furniture had either burned up or been carried away by the winds. "At least I still have a cookstove."

"And a wagon. That was good thinking to drive the wagon into the creek." Jake nodded to the sheep wagon. "You've lost the cover, but that's easy to replace."

"I'll need to make a trip into town for. . .for everything," she said as she realized how much she'd lost in the fire. Where would she get the money to replace her belongings? Even the small widow's pension she received wouldn't cover everything. She'd think about that when her head was clearer. She wiped away a tear.

"Hey now," Jake said. He put his arms around her again, and Katie felt as if she had always fit into his embrace. "This is just a setback. It's Mother Nature testing you. And you won."

"You're right. Now for that coffee."

Together they inspected the barn, the wagon, and the expanse of burned prairie. "The thing about prairie fires, Katie, is that the grass will come back better than before. Just wait and see. I'll scout for grazing lands while I'm looking for your horse."

Less than an hour later, Jake returned with Katie's horse. "I found her on the south side of your claim, grazing nice as could be. That's where you can move your flock."

Katie nodded at his suggestion. The sun was rising higher in the eastern sky, signaling that Jake needed to be on his way. But before he rode out, he jumped down and took Katie in his arms. She returned the embrace as they kissed.

"Thank you," she said. "Thank you for dropping everything to come here. Thank you for caring. Mo chroí." She placed her hand over his heart.

After one final kiss goodbye, Jake swung back into the saddle, tipped his hat at her, and gave her a rakish smile. Then he trotted away.

Katie watched until he disappeared over a slight rise in the horizon. And then she got to work.

First, she cleaned the soot from inside the dugout. "I cannot abide a dirty house, even if it's made of dirt," she said out loud. She began making a list of the furnishings and supplies she would need. And she decided on a way to pay for her purchases.

Sarah said 'sheep are for the cash,' she thought to herself. *I'll trade or sell a couple of sheep in town. I'll bet the new butcher shop will buy them.* She hated to part with two of her animals, but it had to be done.

With that decided, she tackled the barn. Her efforts to wet down the outside of the structure did help a bit. There were some holes in the roof, but nothing that couldn't be repaired before winter, she judged. As for the outhouse – that was a complete loss. She'd need to build a new one.

She found that Jake's assessment of the wagon was a bit more optimistic than hers. Yes, she'd need a new cover, but the wagon box was still in good shape.

"Good," she thought. "At least I'll have a place to sleep while repairs take place. The question is how to be in two places at once – here, watching the flock and in town, buying supplies and hiring a construction crew."

There was plenty to keep her busy, and Katie didn't have time to feel sorry for herself. First, she needed to get the sheep to the southern pastures that Jake had found.

"Come on, girl," she called to Maddie. "We've got sheep to feed." The dog danced at her horse's feet.

Her logistical prayers were answered one day after the fire when Jimmy Turner arrived. "Aunt Sarah sent me," said the boy. "We saw the smoke and wanted to make sure you were o.k."

"Thank the good Lord for good neighbors," Katie said to the boy. "We...Maddie, the sheep, and I...hid in the dugout during the worst of it. I could certainly use some help if you can stick around for a few days."

He nodded in acceptance. "I can watch the flock."

"And then I can ride into town for supplies," Katie responded.

After supper, Jimmy bedded down by the campfire while Katie found a scrap of paper and wrote to her family.

Dear Da, Nan and Ryan,

I guess you could call this week a "trial by fire." A lightning storm started a prairie fire out west two days ago. It spread across the dry, prairie grass like, well, wildfire. But not to worry. We are all safe. The sheep, my dog, and I took shelter in my dugout. Thank goodness dirt doesn't burn! The wagon and the barn will need repairs – and the outhouse is gone – but I thank the good Lord that was all that I lost.

Jake Riley, a cowboy from a nearby ranch, rode in while the ground was still hot from the fire. I was shaken by the fire, but he helped me realize that I was lucky to survive. Jimmy Turner, from the Wright Ranch north of Twin Brooks, is here now. He'll watch the flock while I go to town for supplies.

I'm exhausted but unharmed. I am writing this short letter to you in case you read about prairies in the newspapers.

All my love,

Katie Rose

Chapter 15: Nan's Loom

Katie

Twin Brooks was bustling when Katie drove the wagon into town. Her first stop was at Polly's Place.

"What can I get you, Katie?" Polly said by way of a greeting.

"Lemonade, please." She noticed Micah was having the same beverage at the end of the bar.

Polly poured a glass of lemonade for Katie. "Say, I heard you had some troubles out your way. Prairie fire, was it?"

Katie took a sip of the cool drink. "It was. I was moving the sheep to new grass when it started to the west. The fire came roaring through just as we – Maddie and me – got the sheep into the dugout."

"That was fast thinking," said the lawman. "The only thing the fire couldn't burn through was a dugout. You were lucky you were close enough to take cover."

"I know." She recalled Jake bursting into the soddy after the fire had passed. "The barn and the wagon need repairs, and the privy burned to the ground. I'm in town to buy supplies and hire a carpenter. Tim and Sarah sent Jimmy to check on me. He's watching the flock so I can restock. I brought two good-sized lambs with me to sell to the butcher. I'm hoping that will cover the cost of at least some of the supplies."

"You've had quite a time of it, missy," said Polly. "I bet you'd like a long bath to soak off the ash and soot tonight."

"That sounds heavenly, Polly. First, I've got some business to take care of." With her supply list, Katie departed for the butcher shop and general store.

That night, Katie relaxed in the deep bathtub filled with warm, fragrant water. She'd splurged on a bottle of lavender-scented bath oil. A small indulgence, she told herself.

The next morning, dressed in a freshly laundered blouse and her riding skirt, Katie and Polly enjoyed a quiet cup of tea before the saloon opened for business.

"With all the talk about the prairie fire yesterday, I forgot to tell you that a package from Chicago arrived for you a few days back. It's in the storeroom. Let's go take a look."

When Katie opened the large box, she couldn't believe her eyes. It was her nan's loom. "Nan said she was going to send me her nan's loom. It was in the attic all these years."

She sized up the large loom. There were rollers, about two feet long, on what she assumed to be the front and back of the loom. The loom was narrower than it was long, she noticed. "I guess it sits on a table," she speculated. "Good thing I brought the wagon. It's too big to pack in a saddle."

Running her hand along the worn, wooden frame, she said, "Imagine the women who used this loom back in Ireland. Women I didn't even know. Oh, Nan." Her voice quivered just a bit.

Polly, ever practical, eyed the contraption. "Do you even know how to use it?"

"No. But Sarah taught me how to card and spin wool, and she has a loom. I'll ask her for help. She says it helps her pass the time on winter nights."

"Sarah's woolens are beautiful," Polly agreed. "And it's good to have friends and neighbors you can rely on. So, how do you like homesteading?" Polly asked.

Katie laughed, "I really didn't know *what* to expect. Coming from Chicago, I was what the cowboys would call a 'greenhorn.' But, I did have a rough start," she shook her head, thinking of Harold Hughes' attack.

She stood up straighter and took a deep breath. "But now I've survived a prairie fire. I've shot a couple of coyotes. I'm catching on fast.

"I do have a question for you, though," she lowered her voice. "The women in Chicago used to talk about something called "Mother's Friend" to prevent pregnancies. Have you heard of it?"

"I'm familiar with Mother's Friend," Polly said. "There's a midwife outside of town who supplies ladies with medicinal powders." She gave Katie the midwife's name and where to find her.

With her business completed, Katie rode back to the claim she now thought of as Shamrock Sheep Ranch. As she neared her 160 acres of land, she saw the fluffy sheep contentedly grazing on a patch of prairie grass.

That night, Katie wrote in her journal.

Journal Entry – August 20, 1866

It's hard to believe that I'm the very same city girl who came to Dakota Territory just a few months ago. If I'd known I would be facing prairie fires, hungry coyotes, and, yes, a horrible attack by a vicious man, I might still be serving beers in da's pub. But no, I was not meant to wear widow's weeds and pine away for my dead husband. Just like Nan crossed the Atlantic to start a new life, I have crossed America to start fresh.

I've looked my attacker in the eye and let him know that he can't bully me anymore. I've defended my flock by shooting a coyote. And I've survived a prairie fire. I'll never forget those red and orange flames licking the dry grasses and the black, billowing smoke chasing across the land. When I saw the fire racing towards us, all I could think was to save the sheep. I guess that means I've truly become a sheepherder.

I'm also starting to think that marriage may again be in my future. I've given myself to Jake – something I didn't do lightly. I believe he loves me, but I'm not sure he wants to make a life as a homesteader or rancher. Also, if I married him, I would no longer own the land that I've claimed. Maybe I'm getting ahead of myself. Maybe Jake doesn't want to settle down. He's never said that.

Two years ago, I never would have dreamed that this was my life. Who knows what the future will bring?

KR

Chapter 16: Fishing and Fireflies

September 1866 - Double D Ranch, Dakota Territory

Jake

Riding herd at night gave Jake time to think. The cattle were quiet for the most part. He could hear Sam softly singing off in the distance while the cattle lowed. The night skies were clear, and the stars sparkled from the heavens.

"I wonder if Katie is watching these stars tonight," he mused. He liked to think that maybe they were both looking at the night sky and remembering their time together. Jake missed Katie. He'd never missed a woman before. Was it the coppery red hair? Or those emerald green eyes? Maybe it was the curve of her hip. Or was it the way they just seemed to *fit* together? He smiled. Whatever it was, Jake couldn't get Katie Rose Kelly out of his thoughts.

Or out of his dreams. Their love-making had changed things. He wanted – no, he needed – to see Katie again.

The ranch hands would be rounding up the herd in a couple of weeks. They'd cut out the steers bound for the market, then move the rest of the herd to winter pastures.

"That's it," he thought. "I'll visit Katie before we move the herd."

He cleared the plans with the ranch foreman, packed his saddle bags, and rode south. Unlike his wild ride after the prairie fire, he took it easier on his mount this time. Still, he was eager and made good time.

From the crest of a hill, Jake could see Katie's herd — dang it, her flock, he corrected himself. Maddie, the border collie, was minding the flock. Katie's sheep wagon was in the distance, but there was no sign of Katie.

Then he looked off to the west, toward the creek. Katie was swimming. No, she was bathing. "Timing is everything," he thought as he cantered his horse toward the water.

Climbing down, he called out hopefully, "Want some company?"

Katie's response was more a squeal than a scream. "Jake Riley! What are you doing here? Please fetch that towel on the shore and then turn your back like a gentleman."

"Never pretended to be a gentleman," he said as he handed off the thin cotton towel. "Just came to see how you were doing."

"All right, you can turn around now," Katie instructed. You almost saw more than you expected."

"Hope springs eternal," he said with a glint in his sharp, blue eyes. She was wrapped from shoulders to calves, but even so, the towel did not leave much to his vivid imagination.

"You're impossible. Turn around again so I can dress." She made a twirling motion with her free hand.

Jake could hear the rustling of clothing, and finally Katie said, "I'm decent. You can turn around again. Thank you."

She was wearing a camisole top threaded with green ribbon that matched the leaves in the flowered pattern of

131

her full skirt. Katie shook out her wet hair and combed through the loose curls with her fingers so it would dry more quickly.

The actions were more than Jake could bear. He strode over to Katie and took her in his arms.

"The truth is, I've missed you, Katie Kelly. Missed the smell of the lavender in your hair, missed how you fit into my arms, and missed the taste of your sweet lips." His deep kiss said more than his words could ever say.

Katie

Katie's body responded. Her arms encircled his shoulders, and her hands plunged into his shaggy black hair, knocking off his cowboy hat.

"The truth is," she murmured into his ear, "I've missed you, too, cowboy." She checked her flock and saw that Maddie had everything under control, and then Katie led Jake into her sheep wagon – her home on wheels.

"It's more comfortable than a blanket on the grass," she said, "and it's quite a bit more private." With that, she unbuttoned Jake's shirt and began kissing his collarbone.

Jake laid down on the mattress and pulled Katie on top of him.

He groaned. "Good God, woman. You're not wearing drawers. Do you know what this does to me?"

"I dressed in a hurry," Katie said by way of explanation. "They're rolled into the towel. Should I go put them on?" There was a teasing tone to her voice.

He gently bit her lip. "You're perfect just the way you are." Jake explored Katie's ripe body, but his hands kept coming back to her high, firm breasts.

This time, the lovemaking was more tender. They took their time, learning what pleased the other. At last, Katie curled into Jake's arms. Exhausted but sated, both lovers simply enjoyed the closeness of being together.

The sun was low on the horizon when they finally emerged from the wagon. "What a lovely way to spend an afternoon," Katie said as Jake lifted her out of the wagon, and she kissed him lightly on the lips.

Over a meal of baked prairie chicken and potatoes, Katie asked, "What brings you down this way?"

"You. Only you," Jake replied. "We'll be taking the herd to winter pastures soon, so I asked for a couple of days to go fishing before we get too busy."

"Winter's coming that soon? I had no idea. It's only September."

"We have some time, but out here on the prairie, the first winter storm can hit any time after October. Don't let today's warm weather fool you."

"The life of a cowboy seems much harder than a sheepherder's life," Katie observed.

"Maybe," said Jake. "But give me a beef cow over those cloven-hooved beasts of yours." He shivered a bit at the thought of herding a flock of sheep.

"Hmmm, then why do people say 'Cattle are for the prestige. Sheep are for the cash'?" Katie asked.

"Must be something that sheepherders made up," he countered, with a smile in his voice. "I didn't come here to pick a fight."

"That's right, you came here to fish. Let's do it. Tomorrow, let's go fishing."

Darkness fell, and they settled in near the campfire. Katie leaned into Jake, and he put his arm around her. They could see tiny lights weaving and bobbing in the tall prairie grasses just beyond the campfire.

"Lightning bugs," Katie said.

"Fireflies," Jake corrected her.

"What's the difference?"

"Nothin' except the name, I reckon. They're good luck, you know."

"Hmmm." She snuggled in closer to Jake. "When my brother was little, he'd squish lightning bugs and paint his face with the bug juice."

"See how they flash when they fly? It's a mating dance. The male fireflies are trying to attract females. If a female likes what she sees, she'll flash back. See that one over there?" He pointed to a flash coming from a clump of grass.

"You can learn a lot from bugs," Jake continued. "Did you know that crickets tell the temperature?"

"How do you know that?" she asked.

"I read it in a newspaper – the story said if you count the number of chirps in 15 seconds and then add 40, that'll be the temperature."

"Let's try it."

Jake pulled out his pocket watch and watched the second hand while Katie counted chirps from a nearby patch of wildflowers.

"That's fifteen seconds," he said.

"Thirty-three chirps, so plus 40…that means it's 73 degrees. Seems about right. I guess you *can* learn from bugs," she said.

At that moment, a flash crossed the night sky.

"Did you see that shooting star?" Jake pointed up.

"I did. And I made a wish."

"What's the wish?" Jake asked.

"I can't tell, or it won't come true." Then she kissed him. They stayed together as the night breezes gently lulled them to sleep under a blanket of stars.

In the deep of night, Katie awoke to find Jake thrashing in his sleep and calling out. "Take cover! Take cover, men. Watch that ridge! They're comin' over that ridge!" He threw his arms up to cover his face.

Katie realized that Jake was showing signs of soldier's fatigue shock. She'd heard it was the result of traumas from the war.

Taking care not to get hit, Katie held his flailing arms and tried to wake him up gradually. "Shhhh. It's all right. You're safe. Jake, sweetheart, you're safe here. Shhhhh."

Jake's eyes opened to find Katie gently holding his face. Then panic crossed his face again. "Did I hit you? Sometimes I strike out in my sleep." She shook her head and continued to gentle him.

"It's nightmares from the war…mostly from the Battle of Mine Creek. A lot of good men died that day," he explained. "I hope I didn't scare you."

"We all carry scars from the war. Some are worse than others. You didn't scare me."

They settled back on their bedrolls, but haunted by the sounds and sights of war, Jake didn't fall back asleep.

Katie woke to the aroma of coffee. She stretched and smiled as Jake handed her a steaming cup.

"Good morning, beautiful," Jake said. He looked into his coffee mug and said, "About last night...the nightmares..."

"Some men came back from the war with physical scars. Others came back with scars that are harder to see," Katie supplied. "And some didn't come back at all. I'm ready to listen if you want to talk about the war."

"Thank you, mo chroí," he said, using the Irish endearment. He touched her face, which seemed to brighten his face. "But the day is too beautiful to talk of those things now. Let's get a move on. The fish are waiting."

The autumn day was clear and warm. Katie dangled her bare feet in the creek and kept an eye on her flock. Upstream, Jake tested his luck with a fishing pole. Soon, his stringer was full of bass, walleye, and a couple of perch.

"You know what's better than catching fish," Jake asked. Katie tilted her head in askance.

He answered his own question. "Eating fish."

Back at camp, Jake surveyed the cooking pans in Katie's makeshift kitchen. "This one will do." He selected a large cast iron pan and began seasoning the fish.

"This is a side of Jake Riley I didn't expect to see," Katie observed.

Jake expertly flipped the fish, exposing a golden-brown fillet. "Life on the trail gives a man plenty of time to learn new skills – like cooking. Bring those plates over, please."

The afternoon was idyllic. Jake watched the lambs frolic in the pasture. "Are you ready for winter?"

"I'm working on it. I've ordered feed for when the snow gets too deep. I'll keep the flock close to the homestead so the sheep can shelter in the barn if need be. And then it will be time to bring in the rams. Tim Wright offered his rams if he can have a portion of the lambs when they're weaned."

He considered the plan and said, "Seems fair."

"I'll keep all the sheep until after the spring shearing. Then I'll send some to market. I'm hoping the Goyas will be back for shearing season. I owe them a debt."

"You would have done the same if you'd come upon someone in trouble. But the Goyas are good people. Even if they are sheep people."

She poked him in the arm. Jake laughed. "You know I'm joking. Some of my favorite people are sheepherders."

He sobered. "But you should also know that I've heard rumblings. The big ranchers are talking about how to 'handle' the sheep that are on open pastures. Trouble is coming. I don't mean to worry you, but you'll need to take precautions. Make sure that you're grazing well south of the river, Katie."

Dinner that night was another fish fry. Jake filleted the rest of the catch, salted it, and wrapped the meat in leaves. He put half in his saddle bag and gave half to Katie.

"I'd leave it all with you, but I'll need to show something from my fishing trip. I'll ride out tomorrow morning."

"Then we have the night."

Thinking about his nightmares from the previous night, Jake said, "I thought... Maybe I should sleep outside and let you have the wagon tonight. It's not that I...."

"Let us have the night, Jake. Please."

They made love under the stars. Katie was becoming familiar with Jake's body – his firm, muscled back and his sinewy arms. She traced the black hair from his chest past his flat stomach and ended with his hard sex.

"You are a bold colleen," Jake said. His hands had found her warm, moist center. He moved on top and gently entered her.

"Oh, Jake. I never knew it could be like this."

Afterward, Katie nestled in his arms until she heard him breathing softly. Finally, she drifted off to a dreamless sleep.

The September morning came too soon for both of them. But, once again, Jake greeted Katie with a cup of hot coffee as she woke up.

"I could get used to this," she said.

"Rise and shine, Katie Rose Kelly. We're burning daylight."

"Burning daylight – that makes absolutely no sense."

While she dressed, she watched Jake cook eggs and bacon for breakfast. "I could *definitely* get used to this," she commented.

After breakfast, Jake said, "Come walk with me."

Hand in hand, they strolled through the prairie flowers. Along the way, Jake stopped to pick a red Blanket Flower, a purple Blazing Star, and a brilliant sunflower. When he had a whole bouquet, he presented the flowers to Katie.

"Thank you," she said.

"They're just wildflowers."

"That's not what I'm thanking you for. Thank you for last night. And for yesterday. And the night before. Thank you for wanting to come and spend time with me."

He brushed a red curl off her forehead, leaned down, and kissed her. "I can't get you out of my head, Katie Rose. These days – and nights – will keep me going when the winter winds are blowing. You are an amazing woman. I love you."

She dropped the bouquet and wrapped her arms around him. "Oh, Jake. I love you, too. And I love that you think I'm amazing."

Reluctantly, they made their way back to camp.

Before leaving, Jake gave Katie a deep, lingering kiss. "That will have to keep me until I see you again."

"Something to remember me." She gave him a lock of her red curls tied with a green ribbon. "Goodbye, mo chroí. My heart."

He tucked the lock of hair in his vest pocket, mounted his horse, and rode away.

Journal Entry – September 17, 1866

The last two days were the best days I've had since coming to Dakota Territory. Jake paid a surprise visit. The days were warm. The nights were beautiful. We talked about all sorts of things. We walked through the prairie. We watched the stars at night. I learned more about Jake than I ever knew about Patrick.

The war has left scars on him that I never knew about. Maybe if enough time passes, he'll stop having the nightmares. I need to tell him that I'll be there for him.

Before he left, he told me that he loves me. And I told him I love him.

KR

Chapter 17: Colors of the Prairie

October 1866 - Shamrock Sheep Ranch, Dakota Territory

Katie

The days grew shorter, and the nights grew longer. Katie Rose enjoyed the Dakota autumn – its warm, sunny days cooled by western winds. At night, she sat by the campfire, listening to the sounds of the night. She smiled at the memory of Jake teaching her how to calculate the temperature by counting the chirps of crickets. Less comfortingly, she could also hear the coyotes and the wolves howling at night.

In mid-October, the sheep camp was on the northern edge of her claim, far from her dugout. The sheep wagon, however, was outfitted with enough food and ammunition for a week at a time. As she watched the flock, she meandered through the prairie, collecting flowers, berries, and wild vegetables that she would use to dye the wool.

It had been more than a month since Jake had ridden off. And, thankfully, her monthly visitor arrived on time. "Thank you, Mother's Friend," Katie whispered in the wind.

Her life had slipped into a comfortable routine of watching the flock, hunting for prairie chicken or deer, cooking, and sleeping. From a pamphlet she found at the mercantile, Katie had learned how to dry meat for the winter. She fashioned drying racks on the side of her wagon and used the heat of the October sun to dry the venison. The drying meat was also a special treat for Maddie, but the dog knew better than to steal from the racks.

When Katie was closer to the dugout – and her garden – she planned to harvest the remaining potatoes, beets, turnips, and carrots. On the back side of the dugout, the Slaton brothers had carved out a small cellar to keep the vegetables cool, protecting the food from extreme temperatures.

Katie's To-Do list for winter was nearly complete. She had scouted some winter bedding grounds for the sheep. She made a mental note to visit with Sarah Wright about other winter preparations she would need to make before the snow flew.

As if Katie's thoughts about Sarah had sent a silent invitation, Katie was delighted to see Sarah ride into camp late one October morning.

"Jimmy said your flock was nearby, so I thought I'd ride down to see you. I was so worried for you when I heard about the prairie fire," she said as she dismounted her horse.

"Jimmy was a great help." Katie hugged her friend.

"That's what neighbors do. And," Sarah said in a conspiratorial tone, "Jimmy is keen to get out from under his uncle Tim's rule once in a while. I think he likes the opportunity to be 'the boss,' even if it's on someone else's ranch."

"I really do appreciate his help," Katie replied. "He knows sheep – and he's taught me a lot about sheepherding. He's a good boy. Almost a man, actually."

"Yes, I'm afraid he'll want to strike out on his own when winter's over. We took him in when his pa died. My sister had her hands full with the two little ones, and Tim was happy to gain an extra hand on the ranch. Although," she laughed, "a teenage boy eats his weight in provisions every day!"

Sarah was happy to share her knowledge of sheepherding. She assured Katie that sheep were fairly self-sufficient in the winter. "Unlike cattle, sheep will paw at the ground like horses to find edible grass in the winter. But we still stock up on some feed just in case the weather turns. They need to be healthy for lambing in the spring.

"That reminds me, Tim said he'd bring the rams over after the first of the year. After about five months you'll be seeing little lambs dancing around here."

The women moved on to talk about more domestic topics, including spinning and weaving.

"My nan sent me *her nan's* loom," Katie said excitedly. "It had been tucked away in the attic, and when I wrote her that you were teaching me how to spin. The next thing I knew, Nan was shipping me her family's loom. You should see it, Sarah! It's straight from Ireland! There's even a tiny shamrock carved into the frame."

"It was meant to be yours, my friend." She patted Katie on the hand. "And I see you have used the shamrock brand on your flock. It's so…it's so Katie Rose Kelly. I'm very happy for you. I'm looking forward to seeing a huge flock of shamrock-branded sheep grazing on this land. It will be a beautiful sight!"

Both women smiled at the thought.

Changing subjects again, Sarah said, "And your young man? The cowboy we met at the Independence Day Picnic. Jimmy mentioned that you said Jake arrived even before the ground was cool from the prairie fire."

Katie blushed. "Yes. He found me and the sheep huddled in the dugout. I'm afraid I was in quite a state."

"Well, who wouldn't be 'in a state'? Surviving a prairie fire is no small feat. You certainly had your wits about you."

"Truly, I was acting on instinct. Chicago has had fires now and again. Waiting out the fire in a safe place was part of our lives in the city. I was lucky to have the creek close by. That saved the wagon."

Sarah shook her head. "You've a cool head about you, girl."

Katie grimaced. "You could call it 'trial by fire.'"

Persisting, Sarah said, "But what about your young man? Have you seen him since the fire?"

"Yes," Katie admitted. "He stopped by to do some fishing about a month ago. Jake said they'd be moving the herd to winter pastures, and he wanted to check on me before the snow flew."

"'Check on you,' is it? Hmmm." The older, married woman crinkled her eyes and smiled at Katie.

"Well, we did go fishing. We even caught some fish."

"Fishing…"

Katie blushed again. "It was a nice visit. Even though he's a cattleman."

"Cattlemen and sheepherders have been known to get together, my girl. Just look at Tim and me."

"We'll see." With that, Katie changed the subject, asking her friend about dying the wool and setting up the loom.

"I'd love to help you set up the loom, Katie. I tell you what, I'll make a trip to your place in a couple of weeks – weather permitting. We'll set up the loom, and I'll give you some weaving lessons. But for now, I should be heading back home. I don't much like riding at night."

Sarah saddled her horse and gave Katie a final hug. She turned and waved to Katie as she trotted northward toward the Wright ranch.

As Katie watched her friend and neighbor ride off, she felt lighter and happier. She was making a new life for herself on these vast prairies. She had friends. She had land. And she had to laugh at herself. "Look at me getting all philosophical! Now, back to work, Katie Rose Kelly."

The next day dawned cooler and reminded Katie that winter would soon be upon her and her flock. Checking the pastures and deciding it was time to move the sheep, Katie called Maddie. "Let's move them south, girl." Together, they herded the flock toward Katie's dugout. When Katie saw the outline of her dugout's hill, she realized she was happy to be home again. She'd grown fond of that little hillside home in just six months.

With the sheep in nearby pastures, Katie spent her days watching the flock and preparing for winter. She dug up the last of the garden's harvest. She carefully stored it in the cellar, along with chokecherry jam, applesauce, and pickles she'd put up earlier.

Then it was time to try her hand at dying the wool. First, she carefully washed the raw wool, taking care to remove dirt and lanolin. Next, Katie set up a campfire outside the dugout and hung a large boiling pot over the fire. She had gathered ingredients for three dyes – onion skins, which would turn the yarn a golden hue; sagebrush for a soft, green tint; and blueberries. She was especially excited to see how the sage would "boil up."

Katie kept an eye on the flock but trusted that Maddie was doing her job.

Placing the onion skins in the boiling water, Katie allowed the skins to simmer for a time, turning the water a deep yellow. Katie fished out the onions and put several bundles of clean wool into the solution. Now she just had to be patient. After the wool had simmered for about an hour, she allowed the fire to go out and let the fibers soak the rest of the day. Before nightfall, she pulled the wool from the cooking pot and hung it to dry on the racks she'd used to dry meat. Satisfied with her work, she spent the night with Maddie and the flock.

In the distance, Katie could hear coyotes calling to each other. She re-checked her shotgun before bedding down for the night.

The next day, she was up with the sun. Autumn on the prairie was a beautiful season. The last of the prairie flowers cover the meadows with yellow sunflowers, purple blazing star, and orange-red blanket flowers. Eyeing the gorgeous hues of these blooming flowers, Katie promised herself she would experiment with more plants next year, but for now, she had sage to boil.

She repeated the washing, boiling, and simmering process with fresh sage leaves and then with a basket of blueberries. When the wool had reached the colors that

Katie had hoped for, she removed it and spread it on the drying racks.

"I'll have to write to Nan about my new skills," Katie told Maddie that evening as they watched over the flock. To Katie's ears, the coyotes sounded closer tonight.

The moon was high overhead when Katie heard Maddie's low growls. She grabbed the shotgun and ran toward the flock.

Maddie was facing off with four coyotes. The sheep were bleating as two more coyotes circled the flock from the far side. The largest of the coyotes had a lamb in its jaws, but Maddie was on the move. She attacked the coyote, causing it to drop the lamb and retreat.

Katie thanked the heavens for the moonlight, which helped her get a bead on one of the predators. Her first shot was wide, but the second shotgun blast found its mark. Katie reloaded while Maddie continued to hold several of the coyotes at bay. Two beasts advanced on Maddie, attacking the sheepdog from both sides.

"Keep calm, Katie Rose. Find your next target," she said to herself. Katie saw a third coyote about to join the fray with Maddie. She aimed, and this time, her first shot was true. That left four coyotes standing.

The sound of the coyotes and the dog fighting was truly terrifying. The snarling, barking, and howling were ear-shattering, especially given the odds in favor of the coyotes. Maddie battled furiously. She had one of the coyotes on its back and went for the kill, ripping out the coyote's throat.

Three attackers left.

Maddie went after the other coyote, tearing into the side of the predator. But the coyote fought back, ripping Maddie's ear and biting the dog's neck. Maddie fought on. Finally, the coyote yipped and retreated with the remaining two attackers. They disappeared into the darkness to lick their wounds.

Maddie collapsed from exhaustion and from pain. Katie ran to the dog, still carrying the shotgun in case the predators returned. A quick assessment told Katie that Maddie was severely injured. Her ear was half torn off, and there was a large bite on her right shoulder, but her neck wound did not appear to be too deep. The dog lay still, her chest heaving.

Katie poured water from her canteen on Maddie's wounds, all the while murmuring to the dog and stroking her uninjured back. She tore a length of material from her slip and fashioned a bandage for the dog's shoulder. Katie wasn't sure how to mend Maddie's torn ear. In the end, she decided to let nature take its course. But she'd keep an eye on the injury.

Even though the night seemed eternal to Katie, the sun finally peeked over the horizon. That allowed Katie to get a better look at the dog's injuries. Maddie lay still while Katie checked the dog's battle wounds. "The bleeding has stopped," she told the dog. Maddie licked some of the smaller bites.

"What a brave dog you are. You deserve an extra treat today," Katie said. The rest of the day, Maddie rested while Katie kept watch over the flock.

Journal Entry – October 20, 1866

I love autumn on the prairie – but after autumn comes winter. The sheep will be pastured closer to the dugout because living in a wagon during the winter just sounds awful. The dugout will be much cozier.

I've tried my hand at dying and have two beautiful piles of gold and green wool to show for my efforts. I'm carding the wool now, and then I'll spin it into yarn. Sarah has promised to help me set up my loom and teach me how to weave. Maybe someday I'll be as good at weaving as Sarah is.

The nights are getting longer, and it's lonely on the prairie. Working the wool keeps my hands occupied. And I enjoy seeing how the wool becomes yarn. While I'm carding and spinning, I think about what I could make with the yarn. Scarves? Mittens?

Maddie showed her mettle last night when a pack of coyotes attacked the flock. She fought off two of the beasts, killing one of them. My shooting is getting better, and I was able to shoot two more of the attackers. My darling Maddie was badly injured, but I think she'll heal – not sure of her ear, however. I am so thankful for that sheepdog. She fought bravely and protected our flock. More than that, she's my companion and a really good listener.

KR

Chapter 18: Weaving a Dream

November 1866 - Shamrock Sheep Ranch, Dakota Territory

Katie

Katie took a more active role in herding the flock while Maddie healed. But soon, the black and white border collie was again moving the sheep from pasture to pasture, making sure that the frisky lambs didn't stray too far.

"You are a wonder," she said to her dog. "And your ear seems to be healing just fine. It will never stand up like the other one, but I think it gives you character, Maddie girl." The border collie's other ear perked up at the mention of her name. Her bushy black tail wagged, and her pink tongue hung crookedly from her mouth. Katie laughed and rubbed the white patch of fur on Maddie's chest.

On the horizon, Katie could see a rider headed toward the dugout. When the rider and the horse were closer, Katie recognized Sarah Wright returning to set up the loom.

"Hello, my friend!" Sarah called out as she rode in.

"And hello to you," Katie responded. "It's so good to see you, Sarah. I hope you can stay longer this visit."

"At least for a night or two."

Sarah dismounted and noticed that the sheepdog was limping. "What happened to Maddie?"

"Maddie's a hero, Sarah. She fought off a pack of coyotes a few nights back. She's actually getting around pretty well now."

"Good dog," Sarah said when Maddie approached her. "They are amazing, aren't they? Sheepdogs work hard. They don't ask for much. And they're fierce as lions. She comes from good stock. Her mama is a fighter, too."

Katie gave her dog another pat. "I've got the kettle on. Let's have some tea."

The women sat on a bench outside the dugout and enjoyed their tea.

"This seems warm for November," Katie observed.

"That's fall on the prairie for you. Just when you think it will be a mild winter, Mother Nature hits you with a three-day blizzard. But yes, this is an unusually nice day for November."

Together, they chatted about Sarah's family. Katie was surprised to learn that Sarah and Tim were originally from Indiana. "After the war, Tim and I packed up the kids and headed west. We were one of the first homesteaders near Twin Brooks. Tim's folks were farmers, but he always wanted to have a big herd of cattle."

"And the sheep?" Katie asked.

"Oh, my family always had sheep," she replied. "I convinced Tim to start with sheep and then add cattle to our ranch. The sheep were a good investment. You know what they say…"

Together, the women chanted, "Cattle are for the prestige. Sheep are for the cash." They both laughed.

Sarah confirmed that Jimmy had decided to strike out for the gold fields next spring. "I'm not surprised," said Sarah. "He's got the wanderlust in him. But, he's a hard worker and will do well whatever he chooses."

"I'll miss his help," Katie replied.

"You might want to think about hiring someone to help with the flock and to work around the ranch."

"I could never afford that." Katie motioned to her flock. "Shamrock Sheep Ranch isn't a money-making venture – yet. Thank goodness for Patrick's war pension. That's helping to pay the bills for now, although I did have to sell two sheep after the fire."

The other woman nodded. "You'll double the flock size after the next lambing. And when you get the hang of the loom, you can sell rugs, blankets, and fabric to help make ends meet. Still, an extra hand around the ranch would take some of the pressure off you," Sarah sipped her tea. "You never know who's going to ride over the horizon. That brings us to Jake Riley. Has that cowboy been back 'fishing' lately?"

She said the word "fishing" with a tone that suggested something else.

"Haven't seen hide nor hair of Jake since his visit in September. And we really did fish!"

"Hmmm," was Sarah's response. "I heard that some of the Double D cowboys had trailed part of the herd to market. After that, they'll move the rest of the cattle to winter pastures. That, and making sure there's feed ready, has probably kept him busy."

Changing subjects, Sarah asked, "Are you ready to learn how to weave, Katie?"

"Oh, yes!" Katie put her teacup down and hurried into the dugout. She returned with several skeins of gold, green, and blue yarn.

"These are beautiful, Katie! What did you use for the dyes?"

"I used your recipes. Onion skins for the gold yarn, sage leaves for the green, and blueberries for this one." She held up a ball of light blue yarn. "I think they turned out pretty good for my first attempt."

"You did, indeed. We'll set up the loom tonight and have our first lesson."

After a dinner of prairie chicken, potatoes, and beans, the women unpacked the Irish loom.

With her fingers, Katie rubbed the shamrock carved into the frame. "It's almost as if this was meant for me."

Sarah smiled. "This is a beautiful family heirloom. Now, let's put it to work." She pointed out the parts of the loom – the heddle, the warp roller, the rachet, the crosspiece, the shuttle, the beater.

Then she explained the basics of weaving – warp and weft. "Warp and weft are how yarn becomes fabric. The warp yarns," she indicated the lengthwise strands as she strung the green yarn through the grooves of the loom, "must be kept taut. This is the shuttle that holds the thread we'll weave with. Then yarn – the 'weft' – goes crosswise on the loom."

Sarah showed Katie how to load yarn onto the shuttle. "When all the warp threads are on the same level, it's called the 'neutral position.'" She pointed to where the heddle was positioned on the frame. "We move the heddle 'up' and pass the shuttle through the 'shed' – the space made

153

when we move the heddle. Then we put the heddle in 'neutral' and 'beat' the yarn that we've just passed through." She demonstrated how to press the lengthwise strands together tightly.

Katie nodded. "I think I'm getting this. When we beat the yarn, it tightens the weft and strengthens the fabric."

"That's right. Then we move the heddle to the 'down' position and pass the shuttle through again."

"And we beat the weft down to tighten the fabric," Katie was excited to learn this new skill.

"Now, it's your turn to sit at the loom," Sarah rose and let Katie take her seat.

Katie worked at the loom until she had woven several inches of fabric.

"This would make a fine scarf, Katie."

"That's what I was thinking, too. The green isn't a 'kelly green,' but I have an idea for that, too." Her eyes sparkled as she imagined the final product. "And I think my nan will love it. She has green eyes, like mine."

"Let's turn in for now. We can work on the scarf again tomorrow," Sarah suggested.

Unlike the previous day, the November morning was cool and overcast. Before starting the weaving lessons, though, Sarah and Katie pulled their shawls off the hook on the wall and took a walk.

"Winter's coming, I'd judge," said the older woman as she wrapped the shawl tighter. "Those clouds look like they could be bringing snow. We'll do a little more work on the loom today, then I'll head back if you don't mind. The weather can be unpredictable out here."

"Of course, Sarah. Just let me check on Maddie and the flock."

"From one shepherdess to another, I think that's an outstanding idea. I never tire of watching my sheep. Which reminds me, I spoke with Tim about bringing over a ram for breeding."

"...and?" Katie asked.

"We generally put our rams in with the ewes in January. That means the lambs arrive in June – about five months later. Tim thinks that lambing in late spring is better than in the heat of the summer. Besides, that's when the shearing crews arrive."

Katie nodded, remembering Ben and Lara Goya at Hughes' ranch. "How do I contact the Goyas about shearing my sheep?"

"Oh, they'll know about it. But when they come to our ranch, I'll make sure they plan to stop at your..." she corrected herself, "at the Shamrock Sheep Ranch. My goodness, I like the sound of that!" She squeezed Katie's arm, "I'm so happy that everything is working out for you. And it's good to have another woman to visit with. It's just icing on the cake that she's a sheepherder!"

"My nan always told me that beaus are nice, but we really need girlfriends."

"There are just some things you can't talk to men folk about." Both women nodded in agreement.

Back in the dugout, Sarah continued her lessons. "When you're ready, you can add different colors of yarn into patterns. But let's finish this scarf first. Then I want to see you load the warp and the shuttle."

Katie worked at the loom until lunchtime. After the midday meal, Sarah taught Katie how to remove the finished scarf from the loom.

"First, pull the loops of the warp out from the notches on the top. After you've removed the warp from the top of the loom, do the same on the bottom. Now your weaving is entirely removed from the loom." Then, she showed Katie how to tie off the loose threads of the warp.

"Ta-dah! Your first project is complete, Katie Rose. And it's a lovely color."

Katie ran her hand over the finished scarf. "Thank you so much for the weaving lessons. I'll never be the weaver you are, Sarah." Sarah started protesting. Katie continued, "The first time we met, you were trying to sell a beautiful piece of blue fabric to Jim at the mercantile."

"I remember that. You stepped in to help close the sale," Sarah nodded. "I've been weaving a long time, Katie. Don't underestimate yourself. You quickly caught on to the entire process – the carding, the spinning, and the weaving."

With very little assistance from her teacher, Katie could re-thread the warp on the loom and load the shuttle. "This time, I think I'll use the golden yarn."

"You're a natural weaver, Katie, ready to solo." Sarah praised her student. "But now, I need to pack up and head back home. The clouds still say snow to me."

Before mounting her mare, Sarah gave Katie a final hug. "Stay safe, my friend. …and think about hiring someone to help this spring. You'll have your hands full with a growing flock. And," she smiled, "you'll never get back to town if you're out here alone."

"It's good advice. I'll see what the spring brings." Katie waved as Sarah turned her mare northward.

The next morning, Katie was not surprised to see a light covering of snow dusting the prairie.

Getting dressed, she prepared to ride the flock. Once again, she congratulated herself for switching from long skirts to more practical men's trousers. "Fashion – and tradition – be damned," she said as she attached the suspenders. She made a mental note to purchase another pair of trousers the next time she was in Twin Brooks.

The sheep seemed more restless than usual, Katie observed. She wondered if it was the weather or just "sheep being sheep." She smiled to herself. "I sound like I've been herding sheep all my life instead of just a few months."

"Maddie," she called out to the sheepdog, "let's move them to the east pasture." Katie started herding the flock, and Maddie immediately took up the work, ensuring all the ewes and lambs were headed in the right direction.

By the time the sun was low on the western ridge, Katie was satisfied the sheep had settled down in the nearby pasture.

Before entering her home, Katie gathered an armful of "meadow muffins" – the droppings left by buffalo. In a world with few trees, the buffalo chips were indispensable.

During her time as a barkeeper at Polly's Place, Katie had learned that the buffalo herds used to be enormous. The railroad companies had hired buffalo hunters to kill the animals by the thousands to "clear out the prairies" for the iron horse. Still, some smaller herds roamed Dakota Territory, and Katie took advantage of their leavings. She was just glad the massive beasts kept their distance.

Inside, she shrugged off the heavy coat and replaced it with her favorite shawl, the one from her nan.

Soon, the cookstove had taken the chill off the one-room dugout. Katie warmed up a meal and considered sitting at the loom for a bit. Instead, she pulled out her journal.

Journal Entry – November 11, 1866

The first snow arrived this morning. Winter is setting in on the plains. I've moved the flock to a nearby pasture that offers some good shelter from the winds. Sarah and Tim have assured me that sheep are hardy animals and are accustomed to winter weather.

Speaking of Sarah – she arrived yesterday to teach me how to use nan's loom. It seems that sheepherders who weave call it "sheep to shawl." Sarah says I have a talent for weaving!

I didn't make a shawl, but I finished a nice scarf for Nan. It's a lovely shade of green and will be my Christmas gift to her. Now I just need to weave two more – one for Da and one for Ryan. Won't they be surprised when handmade scarves arrive from Dakota Territory! I'm sure it will be the talk of the pub – as if Da doesn't already tell all his mates about his daughter, the girl homesteader!

KR

Katie's eyes grew heavy. She surrendered to sleep in the warmth of her dugout.

Chapter 19: Blizzard

November/December 1866 - Shamrock Sheep Ranch, Dakota Territory

Katie

Snow continued to fall throughout November. It actually helped to insulate the dugout, making the home cozier and easier to heat. Now, weaving occupied much of Katie's time – when she wasn't checking on the sheep. Since Sarah departed, Katie had finished the gold scarf she planned to send to da, and she'd begun working on a blue scarf for her brother.

When she did her daily rounds to check on her flock, she was surprised at how adaptable and self-sufficient the animals were. Noticing that many of the sheep had snow piled on their backs, she realized that the wool insulated their bodies, just like snow insulated her dugout. Their thick fleece and the lanolin in the wool prevented moisture from getting to their skin.

And, unlike cattle, the sheep would paw at the snow and dig to find grass under the snow. They also relied on snow as a water source, so Katie didn't have to haul water or pasture them near the creek – which was frozen now anyway.

Her daily rounds allowed Katie to stretch her legs and ensure the flock found sufficient grass for grazing. When she wasn't with the flock, she trusted Maddie to protect them. Still, Tim Wright had suggested she move them to the barn for shelter if a blizzard looked likely.

"A Dakota blizzard ain't something to fool with, Katie," Tim had said last summer when he gave her tips on sheepherding. "The winds alone can knock a ewe off her feet, much less a lamb. Best to keep the flock grazing nearby in the winter." Katie had taken his advice and used pasture closer to the dugout.

The Dakota weather was capricious, Katie had been warned. Coming from Chicago, she was, of course, familiar with winter storms. But being alone on the prairie brought a blizzard to an entirely new level. "The morning will start out nice as can be, but by noon the clouds are gathering. And by nightfall, you'll find yourself in a raging blizzard," Sarah had said during her recent visit. "If you're in doubt, bring the woolies back to the barn for peace of mind."

Katie recalled those words of warning one morning when the skies seemed darker and heavier than usual. There was already a thin layer of snow on the ground. Maddie gloried in the cold, white stuff. She rolled in the snow, scooting around on her back as if she'd never seen snow before. Her antics always made Katie laugh.

But assessing the skies, Katie said to the dog, "I don't like the look of those clouds. Let's bring the sheep in."

Together, they started herding the flock toward the barn. The sheep, however, were moving more slowly than usual, stopping to nibble on any shoots of grass they found along the way. Even the increasing winter winds didn't spur on the sheep.

On foot and wearing her now-favorite pair of men's trousers and a heavy winter coat, Katie was unrecognizable from the pretty Irish girl who had lived in Chicago. With her nan's shawl covering her head and used as a muffler, only her green eyes were peering out from the pile of winter clothing. Still, the layers of clothing allowed her to brave the winter winds and keep the sheep moving toward the barn.

By mid-afternoon, the snow started falling, and Katie could see the barn in the distance. Then, through the waves of falling snow, she could make out two riders coming toward her.

"Katie! Katie Rose Kelly, is that you under that pile of clothes?" she heard from the first rider.

Jake Riley, also dressed for the weather in a long duster, leather chaps, and his signature black cowboy hat, came into focus.

"Jake!" Katie called. "I'd kiss you but my face would freeze if I took off the scarf."

The cowboy laughed. "You can owe me the kiss. For now, let's get these sheep to the barn before the blizzard hits."

He motioned to the other rider. "Sam, circle around the back of the herd – er, flock." Sam was already turning his horse in that direction.

Working as a team, the two cowboys, the woman sheepherder, and the border collie continued to drive the confused and now skittish sheep toward shelter. The howling winds increased, and the snow fell harder. It was after sundown when the last sheep was finally penned in the barn.

Relieved to be out of the storm and in the shelter of the barn, Katie put out feed for the sheep while Jake and

Sam unsaddled their horses in the stall next to Katie's horse.

Jake shook the snow from his hat, and Sam brushed the snow from his coat. "That blew up fast," Katie said. "Thanks for your help in moving the flock."

"Oh, you and Maddie would've gotten them here, but sooner's better than later," Jake said.

"It reminds me of herdin' sheep on the plantation," Sam laughed, "except for the snow, the wind, and the cold temperatures."

They all saw the humor in his remark.

"Well, I was glad to have some help. And sooner is better than later," Katie agreed. "So…what brings you to Shamrock Sheep Ranch, fellas? Shouldn't you be tending your cattle?"

"This here is open-range country," Jake explained. "The cattle can go pretty much wherever they like. We moved most of them to winter pastures where there's some canyons and hills to block the storms. What we didn't move went to market. That means there's not much for cowboys to do in the winter. So, the foreman told Sam and me to take a few weeks off. We've got a couple months of greenbacks burnin' holes in our pockets, and we're lookin' to spend it."

Katie looked skeptical. "Last time I checked, this," her hand swept around the barn, "isn't on the way to Twin Brooks."

Sam cleared his throat and grinned at his partner.

"Well, um, no, it's not," Jake responded. "But I was thinkin' maybe you'd like to come to town with me for a few days. That's why Sam came along. He could babysit the sheep while you take a break. What do you say, Katie? But first…don't you owe me something?"

Katie threw her arms around Jake's neck and pulled him in for a long, tantalizing kiss.

"That will do – for now," he said.

Before they left the barn, Jake found a long piece of rope and tied it to a pole by the door. As they trudged through the snow drifts to the dugout, Jake fed out the rope. When they reached the dugout, he tied the other end of the rope to a stake by the dugout's door.

"What's that for," Katie asked.

"In case the blizzard gets worse, you can find your way to the barn by holding on to the rope."

"He's right," Sam said. "I've seen blizzards that near blind a man. If you can't see where you're going, you might get lost in the storm. The rope is good insurance."

"I have a lot to learn about this country." Katie shook her head.

Inside, Katie peeled off the layers of clothing, hanging the coat, hat, and shawl on a peg. The cowboys followed suit. The small dugout provided cramped quarters for the three, but it was warm, dry, and out of the weather. They ate venison stew and soda bread by candlelight.

"What did you call this bread," Sam asked. "It's pretty darn tasty."

"It's Irish soda bread – a specialty in my family. And it's easy to bake out here because there are just a few ingredients – flour, salt, buttermilk, and, of course, baking soda."

163

"Where did you find buttermilk out here?" Jake inquired.

"Sarah Wright visited a few weeks back and brought provisions. She came to give me weaving lessons, so I could use that loom." Katie motioned to the contraption in the corner. "I baked up several loaves with the buttermilk she brought. I think I'll get a milk cow next spring and some chickens, too."

"Well, ain't you turning into a farm girl," Jake laughed.

"Mmmm, more like a girl homesteader," she corrected.

"You sure ain't the green horn city girl I met at the boarding house," he said, recalling their first encounter.

"That seems like a lifetime ago," she answered, somewhat wistfully. They were both silent for a beat. Sam cleared his throat before things got uncomfortable.

Jake changed the subject. "Now, about that trip to town."

"Did you forget about the blizzard?" Katie asked.

"That'll pass in a day or so. It'll give Sam a chance to get to know your animals."

"I can't expect Sam to watch my flock while I go traipsing off to town."

"Sure, you can, Miss Katie," Sam interrupted. He looked around the dugout. "This is a good place for me to hunker down durin' our winter break."

"Are you sure, Sam?"

"Yes'm. Besides, not havin' to share a bunkhouse with a bunch of snoring cowboys will be a pleasure."

"It's settled," Jake said. "Once the weather clears up, we're goin' to town, Katie Rose!"

Katie had been worried that sleeping quarters would be awkward, but the men had brought their bed rolls with them. After moving her few pieces of furniture, there was enough room on the dugout floor for both Jake and Sam to stretch out.

Katie heard Jake moan once during the night. She and Sam watched their friend with concern. Sam shook his head in understanding. She lay awake for some time after that, thinking about Jake's time in the army and listening to the blizzard winds howling outside.

The snowstorm lasted another full day. By noon, the snow was knee-deep in some places, with drifts as high as her dugout. Katie was grateful for the rope that connected the dugout to the barn, as well as the rope that Jake had strung to the outhouse.

The following day, the December sun glistened on fresh snow. Katie consulted with Sam, and they decided it was time to move the sheep out of the barn and back to winter grazing.

"I'll take it from here," Sam assured Katie. "These critters will be happy to stretch their legs. Now, you and Jake saddle up for town."

Katie admitted that she was eager to leave the homestead. "I know how they feel, Sam. It's been ages since I've been to Twin Brooks. And I have a shopping list a mile long," she laughed.

The snow drifts slowed the riders, but Katie and Jake entered Twin Brooks just as the sun slid under the horizon. After leaving the horses at the livery stable, the couple headed for Polly's Place.

As if frozen in time, Polly was behind the bar serving beers. Micah leaned against the polished bar in deep conversation with Polly.

"Howdy, Sheriff and Miss Polly, " Jake said, making his presence known.

"Welcome back, strangers," Polly greeted Jake and Katie. "I'm guessing you'd like a cold draught, Jake," the saloon-keeper smiled as she poured a tall draught for Jake. "Katie, what can I get you?"

"Polly, it's so good to see you. I'd like a cup of hot tea if it's not a bother," Katie said warmly.

The saloon keeper assessed Katie's attire. "Katie Rose Kelly, when did you give up your fancy Eastern skirts for Western britches?"

Katie laughed. "I'm taking a page from your book. It's so much easier to ride and to herd sheep in long pants."

"Britches are more practical. The ladies back East call them 'bloomers.' I haven't seen them in Godey's Lady's Book yet, but there's talk of them in the newspapers."

"Enough about fashion, ladies," Jake interrupted. "What's the news around town?"

Like every barkeeper, Polly knew the business of most of the townspeople and a good portion of the nearby homesteaders.

"The last time I was here," Katie said, "the town was bustling with soldiers and Army wagons."

"Has it been that long?" Polly said. "Well, there's a Sioux leader, Red Cloud, out in Montana. He's stirring up the Arapaho and Cheyenne; they're gathering by the Bozeman Trail. Seems the soldiers and settlers are violating the Fort Laramie Treaty, and the Indians are trying to hold the Army to the agreement."

"The ink's hardly dry on the treaty, and Army is already encroaching on the Indian's hunting grounds." The sheriff shook his head and continued the tale. "There's gonna be hell to pay. Indians and soldiers alike. I hope it doesn't spill over into our area."

"This country's seen too much fighting. An Indian war is the last thing we need." Micah nodded, and the two men found a nearby table to continue the conversation.

"How's life on your sheep ranch? And who's watching the woolies while you're 'vacationing' in town?" Polly inquired.

Katie answered the last question first. "Sam Goodman is in charge at Shamrock Sheep Ranch. He and Jake rode over a couple of days ago. Seems there's not much for cowboys to do on a cattle ranch in the winter. So, the foreman gave them a couple of weeks' leave to spend their earnings.

"Jake suggested a trip to town. And having Sam watch the flock while I restock for the winter seemed like a good idea. Besides, I've got to admit that it does get lonely out there with just Maddie to talk to."

Polly looked puzzled. "Maddie? Have I met her?"

"Maddie is my sheepdog. She's from Tim and Sarah's litter last spring. Maddie's a good herder – and good company. Sometimes when I talk to her, she tilts her as if she understands every word!" Katie laughed at herself.

Jake strolled up to the bar for a refill. "She's a damn good fighter, too. That dog took on a pack of coyotes a few months back."

"Her right ear will never be the same…." Katie said.

"It's the scars and the experiences that make us stronger," commented Polly.

Shaking off the memories, Polly said, "So, what are your plans while you're in town?"

Jake spoke up. "We're gonna do this trip up right. Two of your finest rooms, please."

"Since I have only three rooms – and they're all empty right now – I can certainly accommodate your request," Polly replied.

"And a hot bath," Katie said, even now dreaming of the warm, sudsy water.

Polly pulled out two room keys and slid them across the bar. "I'll have Josie bring up the hot water directly."

Jake interrupted, "I'm mighty hungry and was hoping to visit Emma's for a hot meal first. Katie, what do you say? Can the bath wait?"

"I'll never turn down Emma's cooking. Lead the way."

Jake crooked his arm like a perfect gentleman, and Katie took his elbow. Together, they headed to the town's only restaurant.

As they left, Katie heard Polly tell Micah, "They fit together."

Jake ordered a steak that was so immense Emma had to bring a separate plate for the hot, buttered potato. Katie requested a smaller version of Jake's meal and could barely finish it.

"I'm not leaving a crumb," Katie told the proprietor. "Mrs. Jackson, you are a fabulous cook. The meal was delicious!"

"Call me Emma – everyone else does. It's a treat when I can cook for someone who appreciates a good meal."

"Who wouldn't like your cooking?" asked Jake.

"Oh, you'd be surprised," the black woman's eyes clouded at the thought.

"My father would call them 'eejits.' That's Irish for 'idiots,'" Katie translated.

"He'd be right," Jake added.

"Have you left room for apple pie?" Emma asked.

"Bring it on. There's always room for your pie, Emma!" said Jake.

Fully sated, the couple made their way back to the saloon. Katie shivered from a gust of cold, December night air. Jake noticed and put his arm around her, bringing her closer to him.

"What a lovely evening," Katie said as she tilted her head toward him. "Thank you for dinner. Actually, thank you for insisting I come to town with you. It's very thoughtful of you, Jake."

Jake

Jake stopped walking and took Katie's face in his hands. He leaned down and kissed her gently. "I've missed you, Katie Rose. You're stuck in my head and in my dreams."

"And I've missed you, mo chroí." She returned the kiss with a passion that Jake had hoped for.

The saloon bar room, when they entered, held a handful of customers all standing at the bar. Polly smiled at the couple and waved them through to their rooms. "Good night," she called after them.

Key in hand, Katie opened the door to her room and gasped in delight. That got Jake's attention as he opened his own door. He glanced over to see steam rising from the bathtub in the corner of Katie's room.

"Just as you requested," he said.

"Yes," she said, reaching for his and leading him into her room. "Just as requested."

She slipped out of her coat, pulled off her boots, and removed her trousers. Standing in the middle of the room in only her white blouse, Katie said, "You'd better close the door."

Just watching her shimmy out of her long pants made Jake hot with desire. "Wait for me," he said, throwing his winter coat on the bed. He quickly undressed and then just looked at Katie.

"Is there something wrong with me," she queried.

"No, mo chroí. There's something so right."

He closed the space between them and wove his fingers through her tumbling locks of coppery hair. Firmly now, Jake held her head and kissed Katie deeply. Standing on her tiptoes, she wrapped her arms around his neck and returned the kiss with a heat of her own.

Breaking free, Katie unbuttoned her blouse, slipped out of her chemise, and stepped into the steaming bath water. "Join me."

Quickly, Jake finished undressing and did as she commanded. He moved her to the center of the large bathtub and settled in behind Katie, his long legs stretching the tub's length. She leaned back, and he cradled her in his strong arms.

"I've longed for this," he murmured in her ear.

"Mmmm," was her only response.

Jake found the soap and slowly washed Katie's arms, her shoulders, her neck. Eventually, his soapy hands found their way to Katie's full, ripe breasts. Katie moaned at the exquisite feeling of Jake's hands intimately moving across her body.

"I don't know how long I can do this," she said.

"You want me to stop?"

"No, I want to continue over there," she pointed to the bed.

Jake stood up, soapy water streaming down his chest and finding its way to the dark hair around his manhood. He picked up Katie and carried her to the bed. Throwing the quilt back, he joined Katie in the four-poster bed.

They made tender love, taking time to please each other. Afterward, Jake turned toward Katie and rested his head in his propped-up hand. "What's your plan, Katie Rose?"

She looked confused. "My plan?"

"Everyone has a plan – whether they know it or not. For instance, some of the boys back at the bunkhouse don't think they have a plan. They just drift from job to job. But that's their plan. What's your plan?"

"After Patrick died, I didn't have a plan either," she shrugged. "Then Harold Hughes offered me a plan. It wasn't *his* plan, but he didn't know that. I needed to new start. That was my plan a year ago before I came West to work on a sheep ranch. I didn't *plan* to start my own ranch the way I did. I did plan to stake a claim, but the sheep, well, I have Micah Brown to thank for that."

"No thanks to Hughes," Jake growled.

"I wouldn't have planned it that way, true, but it's working out. And, as Polly said, we all have our own scars to deal with. Harold Hughes is one of my scars. Patrick Kelly is another scar. Someday I'll tell you about Pat, but not tonight."

"Instead, I want to hear what your plan is, Jake Riley."

He nodded his head, thinking how to put his plan into words. "After I got out of the Army, I drifted for while, like the boys in the bunkhouse. I like cattle – but I didn't like the cattle drives. We were always on the move. I need something more. I need roots. And I like it here. Dakota Territory reminds me of Kansas, where I grew up."

Katie snuggled into Jake's arms. She stroked the black fur that was Jake's chest hair. "Hmmm," she murmured.

172

"I haven't actually told anyone yet – but my plan is to have my own ranch. Like I said, I like it here. I want to make a life here. You know, settle down."

He waited for Katie to respond, but she had drifted off to sleep.

"Sweet dreams, mo chroí."

Katie

The following morning, Katie slipped out of bed, leaving Jake to sleep. Wrapped in Nan's shawl, she followed the aroma of fresh coffee to Polly's kitchen.

"Good morning, Katie!" Polly said brightly. She poured a cup of coffee for her guest.

"It smells heavenly." She took a sip.

"How was your evening? I hope the bath was to your liking."

"Oh, it was indeed." Katie's eyes sparkled. Polly just gave her a knowing nod.

"Before I forget, I picked up a packet of letters for you from the post office." She handed Katie the stack of mail.

"Thank you!" Katie untied the packet and opened da's letter. He wrote –

My darling Katie Rose,

It was so good to hear from you. I am more pleased and proud of you than you'll ever know. I hope that your new life is everything you were hoping for. I've heard from the men who went west – and came back east – that life on the frontier is tough. But you and I know that Sullivans (I

still think of you as a Sullivan) are made of sterner stuff.
You'll succeed and prosper.

Family news – Nan is doing well. That woman is the
heart and soul of our family! Your brother is learning the
family business. Believe it or not, he has a head for
numbers! He's doing the books for the pub. (You recall how
I hated that part of the business.)

I've said it before, but I want you to know that I plan
to visit you and walk the green grass of the prairie. I think
about you every day and pray for you.

Da

Feeling a wave of homesickness, Katie folded the
letter back into the envelope. How different her life would
have been if she'd stayed in Chicago. Would it have been
better? No, she was certain that her future – her plan – was
meant to play out on the Dakota prairies.

Chapter 20: Making Plans

December 1866 - Twin Brooks, Dakota Territory

Katie

When Jake ambled into the kitchen, Katie was finishing up the last letter from home. "Good morning, ladies. Do you mind if I join you?"

Polly set a cup of hot, steaming coffee at an empty chair, and Jake sat down.

"Did you sleep well, Jake?" Polly inquired.

"It's a sight better than my bedroll on the hard ground."

"That's a pretty low bar," Polly replied.

"A cowboy's life," he growled.

"So, how long are you two planning to stay in Twin Brooks?" asked Polly.

Katie looked at Jake. "Maybe one more night? My list of supplies is a yard long. We can leave for the ranch tomorrow morning if I finish my shopping today."

"I've got a few things to tend to, too," said Jake. "And one more night of Emma's cooking won't be a hardship, either."

Katie excused herself to get dressed. She had packed a change of clothes, including her favorite green dress. Emerging from her room a while later, Katie Kelly looked every inch a lady. She'd gathered her hair into a fashionable snood at the back of her head, although several wisps of red curls escaped to frame her face. She was rewarded with an appreciative look from Jake when she rejoined the group in the kitchen.

"Thank you kindly for the eggs and bacon, Polly." He looked at Katie. "I'll be back in time for supper tonight." He tipped his black cowboy hat, grabbed his duster, and was gone.

"Join me for another cup of coffee, Katie," Polly suggested. "I just pulled a pan of muffins out of the stove, and I can't eat them all myself."

Over coffee and delicious cinnamon muffins, the two women caught up on each other's lives.

"I heard that Harold Hughes is having a hard go of it since he...since the incident with you," Polly said. "No one wants to do business with him. He'd showed his true colors when he attacked you."

The other woman shrugged. "He's an evil, awful man. I did like his wife, though. She was kind to me. Together we learned how to live on the frontier. Then, she'd had enough and went back East."

"That happens a lot around here," said Polly. "Life's tough on the frontier. It takes grit and determination to make a go of it. Enough about Hughes. How are *you* doing? I must admit I was a bit surprised to see you and Jake walk into my place together yesterday."

"Not as surprised as I was to see Jake and Sam ride into my ranch a couple of days ago. But their timing was good. They arrived just before that snowstorm hit and helped me get all the sheep into the barn. Then we waited out the storm in my dugout. It was close quarters with both of them sleeping on the floor, but we were all warm and dry."

Katie pursed her lips and continued. "Last night Jake asked me what my plan was. I didn't have an answer for him, but I realized that I can't make a living with a flock my size. Don't get me wrong, I appreciate Micah's help. And the size of my flock has been a good way to learn the ropes. But if I'm going to herd sheep, I need a 'real flock.' Tim and Sarah have offered a ram for breeding, but I need a lot more sheep."

"Are you asking for advice?"

"Yes. You're a businesswoman. What would you do in my situation?"

"While you're in town today, ask around. Put out some feelers to see who might have sheep to sell."

"But that takes money I don't have right now."

Polly nodded. "That's why we'll visit Jeremiah Albers at the bank first. You might not need a loan today, but this is a good time to start the process. Besides, Jeremiah hears things, too. He knows who's pulling up stakes and who's expanding their claims."

"But will he make a loan to a single woman?"

"He's a banker and a businessman. He'll weigh the risks and decide. And he's been known to loan money to women before." She winked at Katie.

The bell on the door tinkled when Polly and Katie entered the Dakota Frontier Bank. A large, rolltop desk anchored the far wall of the front office. At the desk sat a slightly stout, gray-haired man reviewing a ledger.

"Good morning, Polly. How's business?"

She laughed. "Business is good, Jeremiah. I've brought you a new customer. This is Mrs. Katie Rose Kelly. Previously from Chicago, Illinois. Currently, she has a claim southwest of town and is running sheep."

"It's a pleasure to meet you, Mrs. Kelly." He extended his hand in greeting. "Uh…is there a Mr. Kelly?"

"I'm a widow, Mr. Albers. As the Homestead Act allows, I've staked a claim as head of household."

"My condolences and congratulations, ma'am."

"Thank you. Polly suggested that I might need a banker in the future if I decide to enlarge my flock. My family owns an establishment in South Side Chicago, so I have experience in managing a business. I'm not here to apply for a loan today, Mr. Albers, but Polly thought you were someone I should meet."

"Jeremiah, you do know the comings and goings of most people in this part of the Territory…."

He nodded. Albers understood the direction Polly was going. "…and if I hear of someone who's quitting their claim, I can certainly let you know."

"And that's when I might need that loan. In the meantime," Katie opened her reticule and drew out a small handful of cash. "I'd like to open an account. As a war widow, I receive a monthly pension from the government."

"I can certainly assist you with that, Mrs. Kelly."

The transactions were completed, and all parties were satisfied with the new relationship.

"Opening an account was a smart move," Polly told her friend as they left the bank.

Katie shrugged. "It's part of doing business. And it lets Mr. Albers know that I have some income already. Now, I'll part with more of that money at the mercantile. Would you care to join me?"

"I'm not much of a shopper. Besides, I have work to do. I'll see you and Jake later." And the two women went their separate ways.

Katie's first stop was the post office. She had packed the three scarves: a green one for Nan, a golden one for Da, and a blue one for her brother. Each scarf was adorned with a bright green shamrock that Katie had embroidered into a corner. Now, along with a Christmas greeting, she addressed the package to her family and sent it to Chicago.

Her next stop was the mercantile. Katie's eyes adjusted to the dim light of the general store. Not seeing anyone else in the store – including the proprietor – she pulled out her list. She began noting the locations of some of the items she needed.

"Thought I heard someone come in," said a man's deep voice. "It's Mrs. Kelly, isn't it?" The store owner recognized Katie from previous visits.

"It is, indeed, Mr. Bowers. I've got a supply list to fill." Together, they gathered flour, sugar, cornmeal, molasses, cured ham, and other foodstuffs. Katie looked over the bounty. "Do you have any eggs?" The shopkeeper added a dozen eggs to the bag of corn meal. "This'll keep them from cracking," he explained.

She scanned the shelves of fabric and noticed that Sarah's bolt of blue wool was gone. Katie nodded in approval. "I see Sarah's blue wool sold. It was a beautiful length of fabric."

"Yep. Quality goods," the storekeeper responded. "Will that be all?"

"Ummm. Do you have any fishing line?"

Jim Bowers gave Katie a quizzical look, then turned to scan his shelves. "Yep, here's some."

"Please add two spools to the purchases. Thank you, Mr. Bowers. I'll stop by tomorrow to collect everything."

After a stop at the butcher shop, Sarah went to the livery to fetch her horse and noted that Jake's horse was missing. A short time later, having completed a visit to the midwife for more Mother's Friend, Katie returned her mare to the stable and saw that Jake's stallion was also back. *This could be an interesting conversation*, she thought to herself. *I wonder if he'll ask where I went.*

Jake was leaning against the polished bar in Polly's Place in deep conversation with Micah. They both stopped talking when Katie entered the saloon.

"Did you spend all your money, Katie?" Jake asked.

"Almost all of it. I saved enough to treat you to dinner tonight." Jake started to protest, but Katie said, "Jake Riley, consider this a thank you for helping round up the flock. Besides, you always buy. Let me buy dinner tonight."

Knowing that arguing wouldn't get him anywhere, Jake gave in to Katie's request. "My mama taught me not to argue with a lady. You win."

Over a delicious meal of pork chops, apple sauce, and green beans, Katie and Jake compared their days.

"So Polly introduced me to the town banker, Mr. Albers," Katie said. "I opened an account, and Polly told him I might be looking to expand the flock."

Jake looked puzzled, and Katie continued. "Our conversation last night got me thinking about plans. I can't make a living on a dozen sheep, so ..." she lifted her hands in a gesture that indicated possibilities. "Both Harold Hughes and Sarah have flocks of two hundred or more sheep. I think that's where I need to be.

"And what were you up to today?" She didn't mention that she'd seen his horse was absent from the livery.

"I went to see a man about a parcel of land. Our conversation last night got me to thinking, too. It might be time for me to put down roots. You know, to make plans."

Katie was surprised at the news. Surprised and pleased. "Where's the claim?"

"Just west of here."

Before Katie could interrogate him further, Emma brought out two pieces of peach pie.

"This pie is gonna go to waste if somebody doesn't eat it. The peaches were canned fresh last fall," she said as she set it down.

Walking back to Polly's Place, Katie said, "I'm stuffed. It's a good thing I don't live in town, or Emma's food would make me as big as a house!"

Jake had a hard time visualizing that, instead commenting, "Nothing beats Emma's cooking, that I'll agree with."

There were several customers at the saloon, so Jake and Katie took a table near the bar. Over beers, Katie and Jake continued the conversation about the future.

"Are you going to tell me about your new claim," Katie inquired.

"It's not mine, yet. I still need to do the paperwork. When it's warmer, we can pack a lunch and I'll show it to you."

"Oh, it must be close," Katie said. "We'll be neighbors?"

Jake nodded. "Wouldn't have it any other way."

Satisfied for now, Katie moved on to another topic. "Sarah said I should hire someone to help with the sheep. What do you think, Jake?"

"I don't much like you living so far out there all by yourself."

"I've survived a prairie fire and a blizzard. What else can Mother Nature throw at me?"

"Shhhh, don't say that out loud," Jake cautioned. "She'll hear you, and then the game's on. But it's not just Mother Nature, Katie. The world is full of bad people. Micah told me about a gang that came through town a few weeks back. He swore he'd seen one of them on a Wanted Poster. But, they were out of town, headed south before he could make sure." He shrugged. "Just be careful. Sarah might be right about a hired man. Think about it."

They made small talk for a while, but the warmth of the saloon caught up with Katie, and she realized she was sleepy. "It's been a long day. I'm going to turn in for the night." She kissed Jake on the cheek and left the bar room.

Jake

Jake waited a respectable amount of time. After one more beer and a conversation with Polly, Jake went to his room. Tossing his duster on the bed, he silently closed his door and tried the doorknob to Katie's room. It was unlocked. He found Katie at the desk writing a letter. She looked up and smiled.

Almost like magnets, the two were drawn to each other. Jake carried Katie to the big feather bed. Soon, they were under the heavy quilts, but Jake didn't think he'd need a quilt to keep him warm.

It was another night of pleasure for both of them. Afterward, Katie moved into Jake's embrace and gently slipped off to sleep.

Katie

This time when Katie awoke, she was alone in the feather bed. She dressed quickly, pulling on what she had come to think of as "working clothes" – trousers, a warm shirt, and boots. Catching a look at herself in the mirror, she added a green velvet hair ribbon to her loose curls.

Katie entered Polly's kitchen to find the saloon keeper and Jake talking over cups of steaming hot coffee. Again they stopped talking when Katie entered the room.

"Good morning," Katie greeted them. "If I didn't know better, I'd say you two were talking about me."

Before Jake could protest, Polly said, "'Tis the season of secrets. Christmas is just around the corner."

Katie thought about the reels of fishing line and the package from the butcher and put a finger to her lips.

"Thank you kindly for the breakfast, Polly," said the cowboy. Addressing Katie, Jake said, "I'll saddle the horses and stop by the mercantile to pick up your purchases. You stay here and enjoy Polly's cooking and company until we're ready to hit the trail."

Katie watched him leave and said to Polly, "He's not much for small talk in the morning, is he?"

"He talks when he's got something to say."

Katie wondered at the comment but didn't pursue it. It was, after all, the season of secrets. The two women talked about the upcoming holidays. Katie filled in Polly on her growing skills as a weaver, and Polly mentioned that there was talk of a newspaper coming to town.

"It's becoming a real city," Katie declared.

Polly laughed. "Don't get ahead of yourself. Still, a newspaper is a sign of civilization, and I welcome it."

Katie nodded. "The town *is* growing. I noticed several new shops in town. And, thanks again for the tip about the butcher, Polly. I never would have guessed that he was a tanner, too!"

Soon, it was time for Katie to take her leave. She pulled on her winter coat, wrapped Nan's shawl over her head, and hefted her carpet bag. Before going, she hugged Polly. "You know, you and Sarah were my first friends here. Thank you."

Polly hugged her back and said, "We women need to stick together and support each other."

The ride back to the ranch was long, cold, and windy. The winter winds kept conversation to a minimum, but when they reached the halfway point, Jake said, "Let's give the horses a rest. We can take cover under Lone Tree."

After hobbling the horses, Jake returned to the shelter of the now-leafless tree with a wicker lunch box.

"Don't tell me you stopped at Emma's. You think of everything," Katie said.

"She had a couple of pork chops left over from last night. Not sure what else she tucked in there. Take a look."

Katie started unpacking the lunch box. At the bottom of the box was something wrapped in tissue.

"Go ahead," Jake urged. "It's for you."

Katie unwrapped the parcel and shook out a full-length duster coat lined with sheepskin. Jake grinned. "Put it on. I wasn't sure if the sheepskin lining would be a deal breaker for you, but it'll keep you warm and toasty when you're ridin' herd – er, watchin' the flock, I mean."

Katie was astounded. "Jake, this is too much. But…thank you. And, no, the sheepskin lining isn't a deal breaker. Someday I hope my sheep will be keeping someone warm, too." Quickly, she pulled the duster over her thin, woolen jacket. "It feels wonderful."

He shrugged. "I told you those greenbacks were burnin' a hole in my pocket. When I saw this in the store window, well, I knew that was the perfect Christmas gift for you."

She hugged him and then broke away to retrieve her gift for Jake. Holding it behind her, she said, "I planned to wrap it, but this seems like a good time to give it to you, so…"

He unwrapped the parcel to find a sheepskin vest. Jake started laughing.

"What's so funny?" Katie asked.

"We'll both be wearing sheepskins."

"I just said that I hoped my sheep would keep someone warm. Well, this vest is made from the sheep I sold at the butcher shop last fall. Polly said he was a tanner, too."

Jake ran his hand over the sheepskin lining. "Is it too corny to say that now I can have part of you close to me?"

"No, it's the perfect thing to say. So you like it?"

Jake kissed her deeply and whispered in her ear, "Thank you, mo chroí."

"I love it when you talk Irish to me," she laughed as she kissed him.

They finished their lunch and completed the ride to Katie's ranch. As they neared the dugout, Jake said, "You know, you need a ranch sign for Shamrock Sheep Ranch. I know just the man to carve it for you."

Together, they unpacked the parcels and unsaddled their horses in the barn. Katie saw that the sheep had been put out to pasture again. The dugout was empty when she entered. Katie was lighting a fire in the cookstove when Jake entered.

"Sam must be out with the sheep," he said. "I'll ride out and let him know we're back."

"Thanks. I'll put away the supplies and start supper. Oh, and bring this for Maddie." She handed Jake a container of food for the dog.

It was past sunset when the two cowboys – today, they were sheepherders – entered the warm dugout. The aroma of stew and hot biscuits greeted them.

"Smells delicious!" Sam said as he removed his winter gear. He stood by the stove and warmed his hands. "After the storm passed, I moved the flock out to the west pasture. The hills give some shelter from the winds, and there's grass poking through the snow."

"Sam, I can't thank you enough for giving me a break. The trip to town was a tonic." She continued, "I've been thinking about how busy it gets during lambing time. If you ever decide to leave the glamorous life of cowboying, I could use a hand around here. I'd pay you, of course."

"That's a mighty nice offer, Miss Katie," he said. "I'll think on it."

For proprieties' sake, the two men bedded down on the dugout floor again, with Katie tucked away in her small bed.

They went on this way for several days, with Jake and Sam watching the flock while Katie worked in the dugout. When she wasn't cooking or baking, Katie spent time weaving. She had woven the first three scarves for her family. Now, she was working on a gold scarf for Sam and a blue version for Jake.

Over dinner that night, Jake spoke up. "It's almost time for us to head back to the Double D, Katie."

"I thought you had the winter off," she replied.

"It's not quite like that. We work in shifts in the winter, and it's our turn to spell one of the other teams."

"When are you leaving?"

Sam joined the conversation. "We should move the flock to new grounds before we leave. If we push 'em near the dugout, they'll have new grazing, and they'll be closer to you. We could get that done in a day or two."

Katie nodded. "I'll help. It's time I get back to sheepherding. Besides, I want to wear that new duster."

The following two days were busy. The three took their time moving the flock, allowing them to graze along the way. Maddie, of course, kept the lambs from straying too far.

That night, Katie cooked a special dinner for the trio. "We're celebrating Christmas tonight," she announced.

For the holiday dinner, she had stuffed and baked prairie chickens, along with potatoes and turnips. "It's not a stuffed goose, but it will have to do."

After dinner, she brought out packages for the men. "These are both thank-you gifts and Christmas gifts."

Sam opened his package first – a reel of fishing line. But along with the fishing line was a beautifully woven, soft gold scarf. He wrapped the scarf around his neck and said, "It fits! Thank you, Miss Katie."

Jake opened his package. Along with a reel of fishing line, Jake found a deep blue colored scarf. He followed Sam's lead and wrapped on his scarf. Katie was pleased that the blue scarf was the same shade as Jake's eyes.

"Thank you, Katie. You noticed that I needed more fishing line. I'll use it to catch us some big ones this spring."

Katie nodded in delight. "You both look very handsome. Merry Christmas, gentlemen!"

While Jake retrieved a bottle of whiskey from his pack to toast the holiday, Sam pulled a large, flat package out from under his bedroll. "This is for you, Miss Katie. I do some carving now and then."

Katie unwrapped the heavy package. "It's a board?"

"Flip it over, Katie Rose," Jake said with a laugh.

On the reverse side, Katie found a beautiful wooden sign with "Shamrock Sheep Ranch" meticulously carved into the pine board. Shamrocks anchored each corner of the sign.

Katie gasped. "Oh, Sam! It's beautiful. Jake just said I needed a sign. I love it!"

"Yeah. He kind of mentioned that to me. I've been working on it for a few days. Sheep herding gives a body time to carve."

Katie hugged Sam. "This is so special." She started to tear up.

"Hey! I didn't get that response from the duster," Jake complained.

"You would have if you'd made the coat yourself, Jake," Katie teased back.

"This spring we'll post it on the road to your house," Sam suggested.

"Here's to Shamrock Sheep Ranch," Jake said as he lifted his glass.

"Here's to good friends," Katie said.

"And Merry Christmas to all," Sam joined in.

Over coffee the following day, Katie asked Sam, "Have you given any thought to my offer?"

"I have, and I guess I'm wonderin' why you didn't ask Jake to work here."

"But you're the sheepherder, Sam. You understand those woolies. Besides, Jake will always be a cowboy." She looked at Jake. "You're not offended that I didn't ask you, are you?"

"You got it just right, Katie. Don't fret." He kissed her on the forehead in reassurance.

Katie looked back at Sam.

He paused before replying. "Miss Katie, when I was a slave on the plantation, my job was to tend the sheep. When I became a cowboy, I felt like I'd 'moved on' to bigger things. Does that make sense?"

"It does. And it wasn't my intention to bring up bad memories, Sam…"

"Oh, no, it's not that, Miss. I just need to think on this a while longer."

"We've got time, Sam. The offer stands and just know that I'd consider myself very lucky to have you here."

Jake lingered in the dugout after Sam left to saddle his horse.

"I'm gonna miss you, Katie Rose Kelly." He swept Katie into an embrace and kissed her soundly. "Did you think I'd leave you with that brotherly kiss on the forehead?"

"Not for a minute, Mr. Riley." She pulled him in for another kiss. "I'll miss you, too. This has been a wonderful holiday – and I don't mean just Christmas. Our trip to town, the time on the range, everything was so wonderful. You make living out here bearable."

"I was hoping for more than 'bearable.'"

"You have my heart, mo chroí," she said, using their special endearment.

"And you have mine." He kissed her one more time. "If I don't leave now, I don't think that I'll be leaving today at all."

"Out with you," Katie said to lighten the mood.

She waved goodbye to the two cowboys. She smiled at seeing them each wearing their new scarves as they rode out.

That night, she opened the journal and counted the days to date her entry.

Journal Entry – December 23, 1866

Christmas came early this year when Jake and Sam arrived unexpectedly a few days back. Sam watched the flock while Jake and I made a trip to town. I'd forgotten how wonderful a hot bubble bath could be! It was delightful, and Jake is fun to travel with. We dined at Emma's, I opened a bank account, and I restocked my dwindling supplies.

Most importantly, I made some big decisions, thanks to Jake's nudging. He asked me what my plans are. To be honest, I hadn't given the future much thought. I've been working to survive day to day. But our conversations made me think. In order to survive out here and have a

191

successful ranch, I'll need to grow the flock. I'm still working out the details of how to make that happen, but I will.

More than that, Jake is also making plans. He wants to stake a claim on land near here. He wouldn't say where it is, just that we'd be neighbors. When I listen to my heart, I want to be more than neighbors. He spoke of putting down roots. I want to be part of that plan.

He is mo chroí. And I am his.

KR

Chapter 21: Drifters

Katie

Katie had been dreading spending Christmas alone, so Jake and Sam's surprise visit made the holiday one to remember – and to cherish. Now it was 1867. A shiny new year lay before her, and, thanks to Jake's prodding, she was thinking about and planning for the future.

She was starting the year with twelve "proven ewes" – adults that had lambed at least once, along with six first-year ewes and six rams. Katie began doing some calculations. After breeding all 18 females, she could grow her flock by 18 to 20 new lambs, assuming a couple of twins were in the next lambing. That would put her flock size at about 40 animals this summer since she planned to sell or trade half of the male sheep.

Sarah Wright had said Tim would bring the rams in January or February, depending on the weather. That meant the lambs would start arriving in June or so. "Don't count your chickens – your lambs – before they're born, Katie," she laughed at herself.

The winter continued to be brutally cold, with wicked winds whipping across the prairies. Given how unpredictable the winter weather could be, Katie kept a close eye on the flock. She was actually thankful there were so few animals to tend, allowing her and Maddie to move the flock fairly quickly. She followed the flock with the sheep wagon, setting up winter housekeeping in her house on wheels.

She passed the time knitting on those nights when she wasn't in the dugout and couldn't weave. From mittens to shawls, Katie became proficient in the fabric arts. And, given the season, her new mittens were very practical. She intended to bring a stack of them to town to sell at the mercantile. She surveyed the pairs of mittens in the wagon and felt like she was accomplishing something.

Mid-January brought a respite from the severe winter weather. And with the January thaw came a visit from Tim Wright. He arrived with two rams in the back of his wagon. "Howdy, Katie Rose!" he called out as he neared the flock.

"I wanted to get these fellas over here during the break in the weather," he motioned to the two rams in the back of the wagon. "This seems like as good a place as any to introduce the boys," he said. "Normally, a flock this size needs only one ram, but we – Sarah and me – wanted to give the young guy here some experience. You know, to 'see how it's done.'"

Katie blushed, and then she laughed at the absurdity of the situation.

Tim cleared his throat. "Um, sorry if I was being indelicate."

"Not at all, Tim. I'm a sheepherder. This is part of the business." She paused and then continued, "I was just about to have lunch. It's venison stew with garden carrots and potatoes."

"And it smells mighty good. Let me get these boys settled in with the flock, and I'll be back. Um, do you want to..."

Katie considered the question and decided she would have plenty of opportunities to "see how it's done," as Tim had called it.

"Thanks, but I'll check on them later."

"Okay. I'll be back in a bit. Let's go, Buddy." The Wright's border collie jumped off the buckboard and sniffed the ground. Then he followed Tim and the wagon to the grazing flock.

Tim returned from his duties to find Katie had set out a fine lunch with stew, fresh bread, and canned peaches. "The peaches are a treat. Thank you, kindly."

They chatted about Jimmy's plans to leave for the gold fields in a few months. "He's still intent on going to California," Tim said. "He heard about a gold strike at a place called Dutch Flats. What I've learned about mining is that the saloons and shopkeepers get rich on the gold fields."

He shook his head. "You can't convince a boy like Jimmy. He'll learn. 'Course, maybe he'll be one of the lucky few who does strike it rich. He's gotta get that out of his system. But he knows there's always a place for him back at the ranch."

"He was heaven-sent after the fire," Katie offered. "He's a hard worker, and from what I heard about mining, it's a combination of hard work and luck. Luck – I have just the thing for him." She hurried into the sheep wagon and emerged with a bundle. "These are for Jimmy," she said.

"It's a fitting 'thank you,' and hopefully, the shamrocks will bring him luck."

Katie handed Tim a pair of green mittens. Tim saw that Katie had embroidered a bright green shamrock on the wrist of each mitten.

"I know he'll cherish them, Katie." Tim tucked them into his vest. "I'll be back to fetch the rams in a month or so. Now, I'd better skedaddle. It gets dark pretty early these days." He looked around for his sheepdog. "Now, where's that dog?" He whistled. The brown and white border collie sprinted into camp and jumped on the wagon bed. His goofy pink tongue lolled out of his mouth, almost like a grin.

Katie laughed at the dog's antics and handed him a treat. "Good dog," she said. Then she thanked Tim and Sarah again for the loan of the rams.

"We'll get some fine lambs," He assured her. He climbed onto the buckboard wagon, and Katie waved goodbye to her neighbor.

About two weeks later, another blizzard blew up on the prairie. This time Katie and Maddie didn't have time to herd the animals to the barn. She barely had time to make it to the dugout before the snow began falling, coming in fierce waves, small and icy. In the dugout, Katie could hear the winds howling. She worried about the sheep and Maddie but feared for her own safety, too.

It was two days before Katie could venture outside. She bundled herself for the cold, thankful for the extra warmth the sheepskin lining of the duster gave her. A green scarf covered every inch of her face except her eyes.

It was an alien terrain that greeted her. Everything was white, with snow drifts higher than her dugout. The north side of the barn had disappeared under a drift that reached the roof's edge. She made her way to the barn to check on her horse. The animal had eaten all the hay in its stall, and Katie saw that the mare needed water. The water in the trough had frozen solid.

Instead of using water from the well, she found the cooking pot she'd used to make dye. Filling it with snow, she hung the pot over a fire, using an iron pole between two posts. She warmed her hands on the fire while the snow melted. When her horse had sufficient feed and water, she saddled the mare and set out to find her flock.

After searching for nearly an hour, she followed the sounds of bleating and discovered the flock had taken shelter on the lee side of a small hill. She counted heads and realized, to her dismay, that one of the lambs was missing. Still, Maddie had done an admirable job protecting the flock during the storm.

Still, a shepherd's job is to watch over their flock, Katie told herself. She began crisscrossing the snow-packed land in search of her lost lamb. Finally, on the far side of the pasture, she found the lamb, frozen and lifeless. It must have wandered away from the flock, she decided. Not knowing exactly what to do, she hoisted the frozen, dead animal in front of her saddle. She didn't want predators to get "a taste" of her sheep.

Back with the flock, she realized the snow drifts prevented the sheep from finding any passable grasses, so Katie decided to bring the sheep back to the barn where she'd stocked hay for the winter. Along with Maddie, Katie herded the flock toward the barn. And by dusk, the sheep were safely tucked into the barn.

That night, Katie collapsed into bed, exhausted from the day's work. Maddie curled up next to Katie's bed as if the border collie was now protecting her mistress instead of her mistress's sheep.

Katie donned her duster and scarf in the morning and went through the deep drifts to the barn. Maddie scampered alongside Katie, mainly staying on top of the drifts. She re-lit the fire under the cooking pot and melted more snow for the animals. Addressing her companion, Katie said, "Let's give them one more day inside, Maddie. Then we'll move them out."

On her way back to the dugout, she saw a pair of riders headed her way. She didn't recognize the horses or the riders, so she hurried to the dugout to retrieve her shotgun. When the riders trotted into the clearing, Katie and Maddie were ready to meet them.

"Hello," she greeted them. "Are you fellas lost?" Both men were wearing long coats and slouch hats. She noticed they both carried long guns and pistols.

"I think we got turned around in the storm," said the first rider. "We was headed to Twin Brooks when the blizzard hit."

"The town's northeast of here." She pointed in the direction of Twin Brooks.

"Could we rest a spell an' water the horses before ridin' on?" asked the second rider. "Ummm, Jed and me, we ain't eaten in a couple of days…" he continued.

"Is yer man nearby?" questioned the first rider as he scanned the clearing.

"My hired man is out hunting but should be in directly," she replied, wary of appearing to be alone on the claim.

The other man nodded and said, "About that grub.."

"You can water the horses and fill your canteens at the well. I'll fix you lunch for the ride."

Katie went into the dugout while the riders were occupied at the well. She quickly grabbed a half loaf of bread and some cold venison and wrapped it in parchment paper. Returning outside, she and Maddie watched as the two men filled their canteens.

"This should keep you until you reach town." She handed them the package of food while still holding the shotgun under her other arm.

"Thank you, ma'am. Appreciate it," said the second man. They mounted their horses and rode off. Katie noted that they rode to the southeast instead of toward town. She was going to call out but thought better of it. They made her feel uneasy, and she was glad to be done with them.

The days began to get longer as winter wore on. Katie spent her time watching the flock, weaving, planning, and writing letters.

Dear Da, Nan and Ryan,

The life of a sheepherder is certainly solitary. Thank goodness I have Maddie to talk to. Sometimes I think that dog even understands me. She'll tilt her head as if considering something I've said, then yip in answer.

I hope the scarves found their way to you. Nan, you'll be pleased to know that my weaving is improving. Thank you again for the gift of the loom! And, when I'm not weaving, I've taken up knitting. I have so many pairs of mittens that they're starting to take over the house!

My neighbors lent me two rams for breeding. If my calculations are correct, I'll have new lambs in May. After that, it will be time to shear the sheep.

I'm looking forward to shearing time. Ben and Lara Goya helped me last year; seeing them again will be good.

We've had several blizzards this winter. It's a blessing that my flock is small enough to shelter in the barn – when I have ample warning that a storm is coming. I've learned that blizzards blow up very quickly out here. They can be fast and deadly. During the last blizzard, I couldn't see the barn even though it was just a few yards from the house. Mother Nature is a grand thing to behold.

How is everyone? I recall that winter is always a busy time for the pub. I miss the noise and the bustle of the Shamrock and its customers. Will I even recognize Chicago the next time I'm back? It sounds as though the city is growing by leaps and bounds!

Please know that I'm doing fine out here on the frontier. It's a new adventure every day.

Love and prayers to all of you,

Katie Rose

Chapter 22: Sheep for Sale

March 1867 - Shamrock Sheep Ranch, Dakota Territory

Katie

By March, Katie had a stack of letters to send home the next time she went to town. She wondered when that would be.

As luck would have it, the Wright's wagon appeared on the horizon one warm spring morning. Katie hurried back to the dugout to put coffee on for her visitors. She could make out two figures in the wagon, with a rider trailing.

Tim Wright called out, "Good morning, Katie Rose. We came to collect our rams and thought a neighborly visit would be in order."

Sarah continued, "Cabin fever was getting the best of us. Thank goodness spring is in the air!"

The couple climbed down from the wagon. "Jimmy, I'll take care of your horse while you drive the wagon out yonder and load up the two rams," Tim instructed his nephew.

While Jimmy was working, Tim and Sarah enjoyed coffee and warm biscuits with Katie. "How's the weaving coming?" Sarah inquired.

"I've made a couple more scarves," Katie answered. "And when I'm in the sheep wagon, I occupy my hands with knitting. I have quite a collection of mittens. But I've run out of yarn, so my weaving and knitting are done for now. I'm also running low on supplies. Do you think Jimmy could watch the flock for a couple of days while I make a trip to town?"

"That's why we brought him along," Tim said. "He needs a change of scenery and likes being 'in charge' at the Shamrock Ranch."

"Oh, thank you. I'll pay him, of course." She paused, then continued, "But I should tell you about the drifters who came through a few weeks back."

That got Tim's attention. "Drifters? What did they look like?"

Katie told of her encounter with the two riders. "They said they were headed to Twin Brooks but got turned around in the snowstorm. They asked where my 'man' was, and I told them he was hunting but would be back soon. I kept my shotgun with me the whole time they were here. They said they were hungry, so I packed a cold lunch and gave them directions to town." She paused, thinking about the incident. "The funny thing was, they headed southeast." She shook her head, recalling the conversation.

"That is odd," Sarah commented.

"Headed toward Hughes' place, you think?" Tim asked.

"I have no idea. But I understand if you'd rather Jimmy didn't stay here alone."

"Oh, he'll be fine," Tim responded. "The gold fields aren't for cowards. If the drifters show up again, this will be a good experience – but I doubt they will."

At that point, Jimmy poked his head in the dugout. "The rams are loaded up, Uncle Tim." Looking at Katie, he said, "I see that Maddie is in a motherly way."

That took Katie by surprise. "I noticed she was putting on weight, but I just thought it was because she doesn't get as much running in the winter."

"Uh oh," Tim said. "I'm guessing that Buddy is going to be a father again," he said, referring to the male border collie that had accompanied him when he delivered the rams in January.

"Puppies!" Katie clapped her hands.

"Yep, probably in another month or so," said Tim. "That's good. It'll give her enough time to wean the pups before lambing season."

After lunch, the Wrights hooked the horses to the wagon and drove toward their ranch. Jimmy took up residence in the sheep wagon, and Katie planned her trip to town.

The promise of spring was everywhere as Katie rode toward Twin Brooks. Bird songs filled the air, patches of green grass replaced piles of snow, and pasque flowers, the first blooms of spring, appeared. Katie was so taken with the lavender prairie flowers that she gathered a bouquet for Polly.

In town, she noticed Army soldiers were again present. Her first stop, as usual, was to Polly's Place. She was pleased to see her friend and proprietor behind the long oak bar.

"Well, look who made it through her first Dakota winter. Congratulations!" said Polly. "I mean that sincerely, Katie Rose. It's the winters that are a trial for homesteaders."

"What brings you to town?" said Micah from the end of the bar.

"Jimmy Turner offered to spell me for a few days so I could restock and just take a break." Looking at Polly, Katie said, "Is that nice room with the bathtub available?"

"It's all yours, Katie."

"Perfect. I'll be back after I finish my business." With that, Katie made the rounds – the mercantile, the post office, and the bank.

At the bank, Katie learned some surprising news. While she was depositing Pat's pension money, Jeremiah Albers said, "Say, did you hear that one of your neighbors is pulling up stakes and going back east?"

"I don't hear much out on the claim, Mr. Albers."

"Seems the winter was too hard for him. And, he's got some sheep to sell. Are you interested?"

"Hmmm, I might be. Tell me more."

"It's Harold Hughes. He was in the bank a couple of days ago. You're acquainted with him?"

"Yes, I'm afraid I am, Mr. Albers. What's his plan for the sheep?"

"He was going to herd them to the river with the other sheepherders this spring, but seems they – Tim and Sarah Wright and some others – want nothing to do with him. So he's stuck. Needs to sell the flock before he leaves." The banker hesitated, "He asked me to broker the deal. If you're interested, we could work out a sale that's good for all parties."

"I am interested, but I certainly don't have enough money to buy the Hughes' flock."

Albers used his fingers to count the ways Katie could buy the sheep. "You have a reliable income from the pension. This spring, you'll have the wool and mutton money. That, and a bank loan could finance the purchase."

"It sounds like what I'm looking for, Mr. Albers. I do want to grow my flock. But my da taught me to look at all the options. Let me sleep on it. I'll come back in the morning with my answer. How does that sound?"

"Sounds right as rain, Mrs. Kelly."

After a delicious dinner at Emma's that night, Katie treated herself to the first hot bath since her last trip to town. This time, she bathed alone. The memory of sharing the tub with Jake made Katie miss the cowboy even more. Still, the singular luxury of soaking in the warm, soapy water was a tonic. While she soaked, she considered her business opportunity.

In the morning, rested and refreshed, Katie was having coffee with Polly when Micah stopped by.

"Morning, ladies," he greeted them. "Katie, I've heard reports of gangs. Have you seen anything suspicious out your way?"

"Now that you mention it, two drifters came by a couple of weeks ago. Said they 'got turned around' in the snowstorm on their way to town." She recounted the story to the sheriff and Polly. "I pointed them toward town, but they didn't ride in that direction. What have you heard?"

"That tracks with what I've been hearing," he said. "Did they ask if you were alone?"

"Yes, but I told them my hired man was hunting and would be back shortly. That seemed to put them off. And I kept my shotgun visible the whole time. They didn't stay long. Enough time to water their horses and fill their canteens."

"Mentioning the hired man was smart," he said. "Stay on the lookout."

Katie nodded and hoped Jimmy hadn't encountered the pair when she was gone.

"I had an interesting conversation with Mr. Albers at the bank yesterday," Katie said. "He said there's a homesteader who wants to sell his flock."

Polly nodded. "That would be Harold Hughes. There was talk of it a few days ago."

Micah said, "I'd heard the same. Folks need to rely on their neighbors out here, and he didn't make any friends. It wasn't just his attack on you. He has a way about him that puts off people."

"Gosh, I should have said something, Katie. We had so much else to talk about that I didn't even think about Hughes' flock. Are you interested in buying it?" Polly asked.

"Mr. Albers thinks that, given my savings and profits from the sheep, along with a bank loan, I could do it. What do you think, Polly and Micah?"

"As one businesswoman to another, I say 'yes,'" said the saloon keeper.

206

"Polly's right," said Micah. "But don't give Hughes a penny more than he deserves."

"I'll need to see the flock before I can make an offer. That means I'll have to go to Hughes' ranch." Katie made a sour face. "I'm guessing I'm the last person Harold Hughes wants to sell out to. After my last trip to his place, Hughes won't be happy about seeing me."

"I can accompany you if you'd feel safer, Katie," said the sheriff.

"Or," said Polly, "the offer and inspection could be made by a third party. Another sheepherder, maybe? Hughes doesn't need to know who's the final buyer."

"I'll ask Mr. Albers about that," Katie answered. "It would make sense for Tim and Sarah to make an offer, wouldn't it?" Polly nodded.

"Well, I guess I'm going to the bank before I head home."

Eager to earn his broker fee, Jeremiah Albers agreed to the blind-purchase arrangement. "As long as the Wrights approve of the deal, this should work out for everyone. I know Hughes wants to get back to Illinois before spring planting begins. I'll ride out to his place tomorrow and let him know there's a potential buyer."

"While you're there, I'd like an inventory of the flock – the ewes, rams, wethers, and lambs I'll be buying. That way, we can determine a price."

"Of course, Mrs. Kelly," said the banker.

Even though Katie did a lot of thinking about her new acquisition on her ride back, she still marveled at the beauty of the prairie. Yes, there was snow here and there, but the colors of spring were winning the battle. The lavender pasque flowers and yellow dandelions were reaching toward the spring sun. High overhead, she saw hawks sailing on spring winds.

Jimmy and Maddie were with the flock when Katie climbed a low hill by Lone Tree. She was pleased to see how well the first-year lambs were doing. She realized it would soon be time to separate the bucks from the flock.

That night, she talked with Jimmy about buying Hughes' flock. "Why don't you ride up and ask Aunt Sarah and Uncle Tim tomorrow? It's not a hardship for me to stay with the flock for another day."

When she put the plan to Sarah and Tim the next day, they were more than willing to act as potential buyers. "Thank you so much," Katie said. "I'll ride through Twin Brooks on my way home and let Mr. Albers know."

Albers was pleased that Katie had acted upon her plan so quickly.

On her way home, Katie spied a familiar rider in the distance. It was Jake, and he was headed toward her ranch, too. Jake reined in his horse next to Katie's mare when the two riders met up.

"Howdy! Looks like we're headed in the same direction. Mind if I ride along?"

"Jake, it's so good to see you. I have news, and it's partly thanks to your advice."

The cowboy looked puzzled. "How's that? I haven't seen you in two months. But I reckon I'll take the compliment. It *is* a compliment, isn't it?

She beamed.

"Did you know your eyes get bright green when you're excited, Katie Rose?" He leaned from his saddle and kissed Katie lightly on the cheek.

She cocked her head, then turned and kissed Jake on the mouth. "Let's not get too carried away on horseback. There's time for that later," she promised.

"Go on with your story. Your plan."

Katie filled in Jake on the plan to purchase Hughes' flock, with the Wrights acting as buyers.

Then, all I need to do is herd the new flock – my new flock – to their new home." Katie concluded.

"So, when does this rodeo happen?"

"The Wrights and Mr. Albers will meet with Harold a week from tomorrow."

"Sam and I can be waiting in the distance."

"And I'll be there, too," said Katie. "I won't show myself until the deal is signed, sealed, and delivered. No sense in tempting fate."

"No sense at all," he agreed.

"So, tell me why you were coming to visit."

"To celebrate St. Patrick's Day, of course. I figured there would be a big party at Shamrock Ranch." Then he looked deeply into Katie's eyes, "And I've missed you something fierce, mo chroí." With that declaration, he jumped off his horse and pulled Katie from her mount.

After a good and thorough kiss that took Katie's breath away, both the riders re-mounted and trotted happily toward Shamrock Sheep Ranch. They stopped at the sheep wagon and filled in Jimmy on the arrangements.

"I'll head back to Uncle Tim's tomorrow morning," Jimmy said. "If it's all the same to you, I'll stay here in the sheep wagon tonight."

"Thank you, Jimmy. I'll pay you tomorrow morning before you leave."

"No need, ma'am."

"Think of it as a stake for your gold mine," she said with a smile. Jimmy nodded.

Katie had been riding from dawn until late afternoon. When Jake offered to unsaddle both horses, she eagerly accepted the offer.

A hearty Irish stew was simmering on the cookstove when Jake entered the dugout. Ignoring the stew, Jake twirled Katie around and embraced her. "You promised more kissing when we were off the horses," he said when they broke apart.

Katie laughed. "You're right. So right." And she wove her fingers through his black hair and pulled him toward her for another kiss.

"My Irish beauty. A woman with a plan," Jake murmured in her ear. "I have plans for you. But first, let's eat. If the stew tastes as good as it smells, I'm in for a treat."

"It's a grand meal for St. Paddy's Day," Katie said with a pronounced Irish lilt.

After dinner, Katie winced when she got up from the table. Massaging her lower back, she said, "I'm not used to that much riding in one day. It's a good thing I can herd sheep on foot."

"A back rub is what you need. Lie down, and I'll work out the knots in your back."

Katie did as he suggested, and soon she was sound asleep.

"Well, that didn't go as expected," he said ruefully, laying his bedroll on the floor next to the bed.

In the morning, Katie awoke to Jake's snoring on the floor by her bed. Careful not to wake him, she warmed yesterday's coffee on the stove and picked up her packet of letters from home. Opening Nan's letter, she read:

Mo Stór (My Treasure),

We received your hand-woven scarves. I am so pleased that my nan's loom is making beautiful pieces again. Many's the times I recall her weaving shawls, rugs, and other finery when I was a young girl in Ireland. My green scarf with the shamrock is the best of the lot. Of course, I wouldn't say that to your da or brother. They are very thoughtful gifts.

Your da is seeing Seamus Murphy's widow. She is a cheerful woman, and I think she is a good companion for your father. I would welcome her into our family, but it is too soon to make the wedding cake.

As for your brother, he is embracing his new responsibilities at the pub. Your da relies on him more and more as time goes by.

I hope this letter finds you healthy and happy. That has always been my wish for you. It was troubling to see you in widow's weeds. Perhaps, as you start your new life on the frontier, you'll find love again.

My love to you, Katie Rose,

Nan

Katie thought about the news that her da was courting Mrs. Murphy. Like her nan, Katie thought it was time for Brian Sullivan to find love and companionship. She smiled wryly at Nan's advice for her to do the same. She would have to write to Nan about Jake Riley.

Chapter 23: The New Flock

March 1867 - Shamrock Sheep Ranch – Dakota Territory

Jake

Jake stayed at Katie's claim for two more days and another night. Then he returned to the Double D to recruit Sam to help move Hughes' flock.

"Heck yeah," said Sam when Jake put the question to him. "You know, I'm thinking I'll take Katie up on her offer and become a sheepherder again."

Jake winced at the announcement. "Now, don't go making rash decisions, partner."

"She's gonna need help, what with lambing season coming on, and the size of Hughes' flock. That's not a one-man, err, one-person job anymore. She'll need a hired man, and I'm going to step up – unless you're thinking that's the job for you."

"I don't see myself counting sheep, Sam. But you're right, Katie will need another hand, and I'd rather have you watching her sheep than any man in the Territory."

Sam decided he'd talk it over with Katie just to be sure she still wanted him to work at the Shamrock – they'd already shortened the name of the ranch.

Katie

Before Katie knew it, the sale day arrived. They all agreed to meet at Lone Tree, at the edge of Katie's ranch. Jimmy had arrived the previous afternoon. He'd watch

Katie's small flock while she went to collect Harold Hughes' larger flock.

When Katie rode up, Jeremiah Albers and Micah Brown were waiting at the meeting spot. "Sheriff Brown, I didn't expect to see you today. Has something happened that requires your presence?"

"Nope," said the lawman. "But if something goes sideways and Hughes gets his dander up, I think having me along might help."

Albers spoke up, "I suggested to Micah that I'd appreciate it if he'd ride along since there's money being exchanged."

The sheriff nodded. "When the Wrights get here, we'll head over to Hughes' place."

"Jake and Sam said they'd help move the flock once we're away from Hughes' claim," said Katie.

"Good plan," the lawman agreed.

It wasn't long before Tim and Sarah arrived. Both were on horseback, with a couple of sheepdogs trailing alongside. Shortly after that, Katie spied Jake and Sam in the distance.

"Thank you again for helping make this happen," she said to the Wrights, Jeremiah, and Micah. "I can't tell you what this means to me. We'll hold back," she indicated to the two cowboys riding up, "until you're clear of Hughes' place, then we'll join up."

The Wrights, Albers, and Sheriff Brown were disappearing past a small hill when Jake and Sam got to Lone Tree.

"Howdy, Katie," said Jake.

"Morning, Miss Katie," Sam greeted her.

"Good morning, fellas," she replied. "It's a beautiful morning for sheepherding, isn't it?"

"How long do you reckon they'll be at Hughes' place," asked Jake.

"Sarah said she wanted to inspect the sheep to see their condition. Then they'll count the sheep…."

"That'll put 'em to sleep," joked Jake.

Katie smiled and shook her head.

"I'm thinking that's enough time to get in a little fishing." Jake motioned to the nearby creek. "We brought our poles and the line you gave us at Christmas. I even brought a pole for you, Katie Rose."

"Fresh fish for dinner, it is!" she said.

"Don't go jinxing it for us," Sam said.

They had good luck at the creek, having pulled in several bass and a couple of perch. Sam added his latest catch to the stringer, then set his pole down. "Miss Katie, I've been thinking about your offer."

Katie turned to listen to him.

"You're gonna need that extra help with the new sheep. If the offer still stands, I'd like to come to work at the Shamrock Ranch."

"You're the answer to my prayer, Sam. When can you start?"

He shrugged. "Now, I reckon. You're gonna need the help once we get the sheep to the ranch."

"I like how you said 'we,' Sam. You're hired!" She extended her hand, and two shook hands on the arrangement.

"So that's what you were talking with the foreman about, Sam?" asked Jake.

"Yep. I told him that I had another job offer. I cleaned out my bunk and packed up my gear." He indicated the stuffed saddle bags.

"Well, shoot," said Jake. "I'm gonna miss you, partner."

"Oh, I'm thinking you'll be seeing plenty of me," said Sam with a smile.

"Maybe so. Maybe so," Jake agreed.

He looked at the midday sun and said, "But we're burning daylight right now. Hopefully, Tim and Sarah have those woolies on the move. Let's join them."

Jake was correct in assuming that the Wrights, Albers, and Brown had concluded their business with Hughes and were indeed herding the flock westward. When Katie, Jake, and Sam hooked up with the group, the sheep were well out of sight of Hughes' place.

"How did it go?" Katie asked Sarah when they were close enough to talk.

"When we got to Hughes' homestead, I was surprised at the poor condition of his house," Sarah said. "The door was hanging by one hinge, and one of the windows was gone. It looked to me as though Harold Hughes had given up months ago."

A frown passed Katie's face, and she started to speak.

"Don't worry. I took extra care in inspecting the sheep. Hughes was surprised to see Micah with us, though. He wasn't happy to see Sheriff Brown since Micah's last visit resulted in Hughes losing a dozen ewes with lambs to you. Jeremiah assured him that there was a fair amount of money changing hands. He thought it better to be safe than sorry.

"That calmed him down a little – until I asked to inspect the sheep. I told him I wanted to see what I was buying."

Tim started chuckling as Sarah recounted the conversation. "Yeah, that got his goat," Tim chuckled at his own joke.

Sarah smiled. "I explained how life is on the Rocking W Ranch: Tim runs the cattle, and I run the sheep.

"Hughes said something about 'uppity women-folk'," Tim supplied.

"But I didn't let his crankiness bother me," Sarah continued. "I went through the flock, checking for diseases, like foot rot. They're clean as far as I could tell. But, they're a little on the lean side. With your pastures, you'll be able to plump them up in no time."

"He made excuses about the winter being tough," Tim said. "I told him that winters on the plains are usually tough. But he also said that raiders came through this winter."

That got Micah's attention. "Raiders? What happened?"

Tim said, "Hughes said it was in January. He was out separating the ewes for breeding. He came back to the house, and a bunch of the yearlings had been clubbed to

217

death. Whoever did it also had some 'fun' with the house. That's why it looked so bad."

"In January?" Katie exclaimed. "Do you think it was those drifters that stopped by my place? They looked suspicious, and they were headed southeast toward Harold's claim."

"Sounds like the gangs I've been hearing about," Micah said. "I'll be putting out the word when I'm back in town."

"Well, now that he's sold his animals, he'll be on his way back to Illinois," Katie said. "And someone else can file for his claim. So what was the final head count, Sarah?"

"By my count, you're taking possession of 311 animals."

"And here's your bill of sale," Jeremiah Albers said, handing a document to Katie. "I'm just happy that Hughes didn't study it too closely since it didn't specify Tim and Sarah as the buyers. Your signature goes right here," he indicated the buyer's line and handed it to Katie to sign," Albers said.

"Thank you, Mr. Albers," Katie said.

"My pleasure, Mrs. Kelly," said the banker. "And with that paperwork completed, I am returning to Twin Brooks." He turned his horse toward Micah Brown. "Sheriff, are you riding back with me?"

"I think Katie and her crew have everything in hand," said Micah. "Congratulations, Katie."

"Thank you, Micah. Please give my best to Polly." He tipped his hat to Katie and rode north with Jeremiah Albers.

Jake reined his horse in by Katie and said, "Tim and Sam think we can continue on for a couple of hours, then bed down for the night. How does that sound, boss lady?"

Her eyes sparkled. "Boss lady. I like the sound of that." Putting on a thoughtful, serious look, Katie said, "Yes, that will be acceptable." They all laughed.

Sam found a good patch of grass for the sheep, and the group made camp for the night. Tim and Sarah planned to accompany the flock to Katie's ranch the next day and then ride back to the Rocking W with Jimmy.

After a dinner of perch and bass, Sam took the first watch along with the Wrights' two sheepdogs.

Sitting around the campfire, Tim and Sarah discussed their partnership on the Rocking W. "I think we thoroughly confused Harold Hughes when Tim told me to take the lead on inspecting the animals," Sarah said. "My family ran sheep back east," Sarah explained. "It's all I knew."

"And my family raised cattle in Indiana," said Tim. "When we decided to get hitched, Sarah said she wanted sheep. Her pa even gave us a small flock to get started."

"With sheep, you get paid for the wool, and later you get paid for the mutton. It just makes sense to me," Sarah commented.

Tim nodded. "I'm still a cattleman at heart."

"So am I," Jake said. Looking out toward the flock where Sam patrolled, he said, "But...not all cowboys are *always* cowboys. I'm happy Sam's gonna be at the Shamrock now."

"So am I," said Katie. She curled into the crook of Jake's arm, looking very contented.

The conversation died down as the group stared into the campfire, each thinking their own thoughts.

Finally, Sarah said, "Well, I'm calling it a night," and she crawled into her bedroll.

Tim followed her lead. Only Jake and Katie remained by the fire.

"This was a big day for you, mo chroí," Jake said.

"Mmmm," Katie murmured in agreement. Jake drew her closer and just enjoyed her nearness.

Katie was sound asleep in Jake's arms when Sam tapped Jake on the shoulder. "I can take the second watch if you want," Sam said.

"Nope, a deal's a deal," Jake whispered as he disentangled himself from Katie. He gently lowered her to the waiting bedroll.

Sam shrugged and found his bed by the campfire.

Katie was the first to wake up the following day. She fed the smoldering campfire and put the coffee pot on. While she waited for the coffee to heat, she added a short entry in her journal.

Journal Entry – March 26, 1867

My flock grew by more than three hundred sheep yesterday. Now I am well and truly a sheepherder thanks to Jake, Sam, the Wrights, Jeremiah Albers, and Micah Brown.

Jake pushed me to think bigger and to make plans. Sam agreed to work for me. I couldn't handle a flock this big alone. Jeremiah Albers told me about Harold Hughes wanting to sell his flock and loaned me part of the payment. The Wrights inspected the sheep and agreed to be my stand-ins for the purchase. And it all started when Micah Brown insisted that Harold Hughes pay for his attack on me. Should I add Harold Hughes to the list? I'll think about that.

I hope Jake was listening when Tim and Sarah told their story about sheep and cattle. If they could make it work, maybe we could, too.

It will be a busy spring with lambing coming up – and now I have a lot more ewes to watch over. Thank goodness for Sam!

KR

Chapter 24: Spring Flooding

April 1867 - Shamrock Sheep Ranch

Katie

Katie and Sam settled into an easy working relationship. As the hired man, Sam made his home in the sheep wagon. He told Katie it was "a sight bigger" than his bed in the Double D bunkhouse, and he was "mighty comfortable" in his new house on wheels. Katie, for her part, appreciated Sam's experience and understanding of sheep.

The flock, which numbered some 334 ewes, first-year lambs, wethers, and rams, flourished on Katie's verdant pastures. The tender green shoots of spring grass were a treat for the sheep used to dry winter rations.

"We'll put 'em in the spring pastures gradually," Sam cautioned. "Spring grass is a might rich for their bellies after a winter on dried feed."

To manage the flock, Sam, Katie, and Maddie moved the sheep from green pastures to areas that required they supplement the animals' diets with winter forage. As they worked together, Sam talked about his early life as a slave in Missouri, where he tended sheep.

"I was one of the lucky ones," he said.

Katie frowned. "Lucky? As a slave?"

"I didn't have a wife or young'uns when the war started," he explained. "The Western Campaign came through Missouri in the first years of the War. For me and a lot of other slaves, that was our chance for freedom. Me and some others escaped to Kansas and joined up with the Union Army. I served in the Kansas 2nd Colored Infantry," Sam said proudly. "In the Army, I learned to shoot a rifle, learned to read and write. Now, I'm not saying war was a good thing – a lot of good men died in the war – both negro and white. But the war ended slavery, and that was a terrible evil. After that, I drifted down to Texas and signed up for a cattle drive. That's where I met Jake."

Katie listened with rapt attention. "Where's your family now?"

"Don't know where my ma and pa are. I was sold away from them when I was just a boy – only about ten or eleven. That's how slavery worked. We were property to buy and sell."

He shook his head, remembering the horrors of the "peculiar institution," as John Calhoun had labeled slavery many years before. Then his face changed, and he said, "Can't dwell on the past. It'll eat you up. Now I'm my own man. Some day, if the good Lord sees fit, I'll have a family and a farm.

"I've heard that freed slaves can claim land through the Homestead Act, just like you did, Miss Katie. Don't you worry though, I'm not gonna up and leave you. I'm still getting comfortable in this new life."

"Thank you for trusting me with your story, Sam. That means a lot to me. And I'd welcome having you as a neighbor, but let's get through lambing season first. I can't do this without you," Katie said as she surveyed the sea of wooly critters in her pasture.

"I reckon we've got another month or so before the first lambs come. Mamas don't usually 'show' until about six weeks before lambing, and they just started showing a week or so ago."

Then he turned and looked at Maddie. "But Maddie there, she's gonna have pups any day now."

"Puppies and lambs! Green grass and birds singing! Spring is a wonderful time of year, Sam!" Katie exclaimed. Sam just laughed.

Sam's prediction that Maddie would soon have her litter was accurate. In fact, that evening, when Katie brought out a pan of scraps for the dog, the border collie was nowhere to be found. Katie didn't think anything of it at first. Then, before she turned in for the night, Katie noticed the pan of food was untouched. Since the sheep wagon was visible in the east pasture, Katie walked over and asked Sam if he'd seen the sheepdog.

"No, ma'am," he said. "But I'll keep an eye peeled for her."

The food dish was still uneaten the next day, sending off alarm bells in Katie's head. She dressed in her now-usual trousers, blouse, and vest and grabbed her hat and shotgun. Katie thought about saddling her horse but decided to start the search on foot.

The morning dew had disappeared from the grass and spring flowers by the time Katie rounded a slight hill to find Maddie curled around four still-damp puppies.

"Oh, Maddie, you're a mama," Katie whispered to her four-footed companion. The dog raised her head at the sound of Katie's voice. "They're beautiful." There were two puppies with Maddie's coloring, black and white, and two in shades of brown and white, just like Buddy, the Wright's dog.

Katie hurried back to retrieve the food dish and a bowl of fresh water. "You're going to need this, mama," Katie said as she placed the food and water beside Maddie.

Then she found Sam to give him the good news. "…and mama and babies are doing well," she concluded.

"She'll be back in the barn in a day or so, and she'll bring the pups with her," Sam predicted. "Dogs like to go off alone to have their pups. Maddie will be herding sheep again in a few weeks. And she'll teach the young'uns how to herd."

Katie clapped her hands in excitement. "Oh, Sam, isn't it wonderful!"

But she changed her mind when the April rains began a few days later. Thanks to the lanolin in their wool, the sheep were not affected by the constant showers. Katie noticed they were becoming accustomed to the richer spring grass and gaining weight. Then she realized that most of the ewes were pregnant, which also added pounds.

Still, the rains created muddy fields, which made it difficult for Sam to move the sheep wagon across the soggy pastures. Some nights, rather than fighting the water and the mud, Sam would leave the wagon on higher ground and camp out with the flock as he'd done as a soldier in the Union Army.

In the barn, Maddie's puppies were starting to explore their surroundings. They didn't stray too far from the warm nest of straw that Maddie had made for them. Katie laughed at their clumsy first attempts at walking.

And that's where Jake found Katie late one afternoon. She was seated in a shaft of sunlight, watching the black-and-white and the brown-and-white puppies play tug of war with a scrap of leather.

"Donnie, let your brother and sisters have a turn!" Katie laughed as she admonished the large, brown puppy who was dragging around the short leather strap.

"I've missed your laugh, mo chroí," Jake said as he entered the barn. "So you've already named the pups?"

"Jake! What a grand surprise! Of course, I've named Maddie's babies! Let me introduce you."

She pointed to the brown puppy. "That's Donnie, short for Donnacha, which means brown-haired warrior in Irish. The other male is Conan, which means 'wolf.' And the girls are Colm, Irish for 'dove,' and Lorcan, which means 'silent.' Lorcan rarely barks," she explained.

Jake took it all in and correctly identified the four puppies. "Let's see. Donnie, Conan, Colm and Lorcan. Got it. Maddie has a fine litter here."

He picked up Colm and nuzzled her. "I like the sweet smell of puppies," he said. Then he turned to Katie and buried his face in Katie's red curls, still holding the light brown puppy. "But I prefer red-haired Irish women."

Katie kissed Jake full on the mouth. "If you put down the puppy, I can hug you without squeezin' the life out of little Colm."

He did as instructed. Even though they stood in the shaft of sunlight, not a bit of light could be seen between them.

"How long can you stay?" Katie asked when they finally pulled apart.

"Only a day or two. It will be calving season soon," he explained. "I lit out before the river got too high."

"How high is 'too high'? she asked worriedly. "We've been so busy here that I haven't ridden out since the rains started."

"A horse can still make it across, but I wouldn't chance it with a wagon."

Katie pondered this for a moment. "Let's ride out tomorrow. I'd like to see it for myself." She dusted herself off from sitting on the dirt floor. They walked out of the barn to Jake's horse. "I'm a fright. Why don't you ride out and invite Sam in for dinner while I start supper."

"Yes, ma'am. And I didn't come empty-handed." He handed Katie three grouse. Then Jake mounted his horse, leaned down to kiss Katie, and rode off to find his friend.

Jake

It didn't take Jake long to find the sheep and the sheepherder.

"Howdy, Sam!" Jake called out.

Sam waved him in. "Howdy, yourself. How's life on the Double D?"

As Jake got off his horse, he said, "That's what I wanted to talk with you about."

"Sounds serious."

"It might be," Jake admitted. "Now that Katie has a 'real flock,' she's got the attention of Deacon. And that ain't good."

"Nope, it ain't."

"Deacon says sheep are ruining land that's meant for cattle. He's not alone. The other big ranchers are making noises about sheep on open range. I heard things are really heating up to the south and west. Hired gangs are stampeding sheep off cliffs, clubbing them, shooting them…it's getting serious. People are gonna get hurt or killed."

Sam thought about the news, then commented, "Cattlemen have never understood that sheep can graze on pastures that won't support beef cows."

"Maybe, but I can't tell Dan Deacon that," Jake replied. Then he shook his head. "I wanted to warn you. But let's keep it from Katie a might longer. No need to worry her yet."

"You're gonna need to take sides on this, Jake."

"Yeah," was all he said in response. Then, changing the subject, Jake said, "Katie sent me to invite you to supper. We're not too far from the dugout. Can you leave these critters and eat with us?"

Sam looked at the skies and to the horizons. "I can take a dinner break. I'll be happy when Maddie is back on the job, though. Have you seen her pups yet?"

"Oh yeah. Learned their names already, too." Both men laughed as they walked back to the dugout together.

That night, dinner was a celebration of old friends getting together, Katie's triumph over Hughes, and a promising future on the Dakota frontier.

Sam left shortly after dinner, leaving the lovers to themselves.

"I thought he'd never leave," joked Jake.

"You weren't very subtle."

"Subtlety was never one of my strengths," Jake replied as he untied the scarf from Katie's upswept hair. Her curls tumbled down to her shoulders. Jake pulled Katie into an embrace and began kissing her. He started at her mouth, then his lips roamed to her left ear. He loosened the bow at the top of Katie's blouse and continued the kisses down her neck to her collarbone.

Katie laughed. "That tickles."

"Then I'm doing it right."

"Hmmm. Let me try." Standing on her tiptoes, she started placing angel-soft kisses at the top of his neck. She trailed the kisses down the open neck of his shirt to the dark mass of chest hair.

"Woman, before I'm too weak in the knees to carry you…." his words fell off as he picked her up and carried her to the small bed at the far end of the dugout. Neither complained about the bed size, which allowed them to remain in each other's arms after they made love.

Katie

They slept soundly until thunder cracked just before sunrise. Jake screamed and shot up in the cramped bed. "They're coming! They're coming!" he yelled, with his eyes still shut.

Katie recognized what was happening. The war still haunted Jake. Slowly and gently, she stroked his back and shoulders. "Shhhh, my love. Shhhh. It's a nightmare. It's only a bad dream. You're here with me. You're safe."

Jake woke in a sweat. "I did it again, didn't I?"

229

"I think the thunder set you off. It was loud enough to wake the…." She didn't finish the sentence.

The reference didn't seem to bother Jake. Instead, he sat on the side of the bed, stretched, and reached for his long johns. Going to the door, he peered out. "It's really pouring out there. I'm surprised we didn't hear the rain before now."

"It's the dugout's sod roof. It dampens the sounds outside." She joined him at the door. "Oh my! There's water everywhere."

"I'll get dressed and see how Sam and the sheep are doing," he said.

"I'm coming, too."

The sun was peeking from the eastern horizon as they rode out toward the flock. "A thunderstorm like this can spook a herd of cattle, Katie. Let's hope Sam has 'em under control."

Maddie had joined Sam. They were circling the flock, attempting to calm the skittish animals. Sam was relieved to see reinforcements arrive.

"What's Maddie doing out here?" Katie asked.

"She showed up a couple of hours ago. I guess she figured it was time to get back to work," Sam replied.

"What can we do?" Jake asked.

"Let's get 'em to higher ground," answered the seasoned sheepherder, pointing to a distant hill. "Go slow. Otherwise, we'll lose 'em."

Together, they began moving the sheep in the direction Sam indicated. Another crack of thunder and a bright flash of lightning split the dawn. This was too much for the already-skittish sheep. About a third of the animals broke off from the main body of the flock and began running in the opposite direction.

Maddie was the first to respond. She circled back and tried to stop the stampeding sheep, but she was no match for more than one hundred frightened sheep.

"Katie, try to turn 'em back," Sam yelled over the din. He was unaware he hadn't used the genteel "Miss Katie" when addressing her.

Katie wheeled her mare around, intent on overtaking the leaders of the runaway sheep. The driving rain and the sticky mud made it nearly impossible for her horse to maneuver in the storm.

"They're getting away," she called.

"You stay with the flock," Jake shouted to Sam. He raced off after Katie, spurring his powerful stallion into a flat-out run.

But the sheep had the advantage over the riders and the border collie. The moving mass of bodies gave them momentum, and the continuing storm fueled their frantic adrenaline. Katie could see they were headed toward the creek.

But this wasn't the placid trickle of water she remembered from last fall. The creek was a raging torrent that had broken out of its banks. Katie saw that it had tripled in size, fed by tonight's storm as well as days of constant rainfall this spring.

"I can't turn them," she called back to Jake, who was rapidly catching up with her.

He assessed the situation and considered racing to the other side of the stampede. *That might confuse the dumb animals more,* he thought. *Better for two people – and a dog – to try and push them away from the creek.*

Maddie, despite her recent pregnancy, was keeping pace with the flock. The border collie instinctively tried to herd the sheep away from the water. Along with Katie and Jake, the three were able to head off part of the flock before they reached the surging waters.

But about half the frightened sheep continued to run recklessly into the creek. Sheep are not good swimmers and generally fear large bodies of water. In another situation, they would have avoided the moving waters. Still, the thunderstorm seemed to blind them to the dangers.

Helplessly, Katie watched as half of the runaway sheep entered the angry creek, eventually disappearing under the raging waters.

"Don't stop to think about it now, Katie," Jake yelled over the tumult. "We've got to get the rest of the critters away from the water's edge. We've got to get them back to the rest of the flock."

Katie nodded in understanding. She steered her horse to what seemed to be the front of the runaways. Jake joined her, and together they redirected the remaining sheep away from the creek and back toward the rest of the flock.

The sun had risen, and Katie could see a rainbow in the west. Together Katie, Jake, and Maddie had accomplished the seemingly impossible task of saving most of the frightened sheep.

Katie looked up. "The storm stopped. Thank goodness."

"I've been in a few cattle stampedes, but this," Jake motioned to the now-peaceful flock, "was nearly as crazy. The only difference is a thousand-pound steer instead of a hundred-pound sheep. Either way, a stampeding critter is tough to stop."

"Thanks, partner," Sam said as he joined Jake and Katie. "Having an extra 'hand' here made the difference. I've seen herders trampled by sheep, too. It ain't pretty."

The danger and the realization that she'd lost fifty or sixty animals hit Katie. Her face crumpled, and she began to cry.

"I can't do this," she sobbed. "I thought I could make it out here, but I'm just like Hughes. I…I can't beat the frontier."

The men looked at each other. Sam said, "Miss Katie, this is part of sheepherding. Sheep aren't the smartest of God's creatures. And when they're scared…" his voice trailed off.

Jake took up where Sam had left off. "Thunderstorms are part of nature, Katie. You know that. But they're nothing to cry about."

"You don't get it," Katie responded. "I had to borrow money to buy Hughes' flock. Now part of that investment is floating in the creek over there. And, and…one of us could have been hurt or killed today." Her sobs began again.

For Katie, it wasn't just about losing the sheep. Emotions run high during a stampede, making her understand that running a ranch can be dangerous – even life-threatening. Was she up to it? She wasn't sure.

"But no one was hurt, Katie," Jake said unhelpfully.

Sam tried another tactic. "Miss Katie, we've got this under control. The storms have stopped. The sheep have forgotten why they were running. Now they're just hungry. Let Maddie and me do our job." He looked at the other cowboy, "Jake, why don't you take Miss Katie back to her house."

Jake nodded and motioned to Katie to follow him.

Back at the barn, Katie dismounted and started to unsaddle her mare. "I'll take care of it. You go inside."

Katie complied. When Jake entered the dimly lit dugout, he found her quietly weeping in her bed.

Jake

This time, Jake knew that words were not going to soothe her. He sat on the edge of the bed and stroked her gently on her back. Eventually, Katie's shoulders stopped heaving. Her breathing became more regular, and Jake could see she was sleeping.

He filled his time by raking out the stable, grooming the horses, and playing with the puppies. When Maddie returned to tend her litter, Jake checked on Katie. She was just sitting in the dugout. She didn't move.

"Katie?" Jake said

"I can't do this, Jake. What was I thinking? I can't run a sheep ranch – even with Sam's help. We were lucky that you were here today. This is too much for me. If a man like Harold Hughes can't prove a claim out here, how can I do it?"

"You're right. This is too much for a little Irish gal like you. You should pack up, turn tail and go work for your pa at the pub."

"Damn you, Jake Riley," Katie shot back at him.

The cowboy just shrugged.

"Damn you, Jake! You're making fun of me. I'm serious." Her green eyes sparked.

"So am I. 'Course, I'll miss your sweet smile and the swing of your hips, but you'll be safe in Chicago. The Dakota Territory ain't for everyone."

He considered his next words. "Tell you what. Before you cash it in – if you even can – before you abandon the claim and the sheep, give it a couple of days. I'm guessing your decision to come West wasn't a spur-of-the-moment decision, was it?"

"No, I considered my options before I threw my lot in with Harold Hughes."

"See there. You should consider your options now, too." And before she could argue with him, Jake kissed her soundly.

"I reckon it's time for me to get back to the Double D." He started to leave, then turned back. "If you decide to go, will you tell me goodbye first, mo chroí?" Then he was gone.

Katie

Katie sat down in the middle of her dugout and started crying again. This time, she didn't know if she was crying because she had lost the sheep or because she had lost her way.

In her confusion, she turned to her journal to sort out her thoughts.

Journal Entry – April 10, 1867

I was so full of hope when I came west. I thought starting over in a new place, in a new life, was what I needed to get over Patrick's death. Maybe I was wrong. Maybe I'm the same girl I was before I came to Dakota Territory. A little worse for the wear, in fact. If I'd stayed in Chicago, I wouldn't have been attacked and raped by Harold Hughes. I wouldn't have nearly died in a prairie fire. And I wouldn't be in debt to the banker for sheep that are now floating down the creek. What a mess I've made of my life. Is it time to pack it in, as Jake said? I'm so tired of fighting to survive every day. I'm just so tired.

KR

Chapter 25: First Anniversary

May 15, 1867 – Shamrock Sheep Ranch, Dakota Territory

Katie

In the days after Jake left, Katie kept hearing his words in her mind. *"I'm guessing your decision to come West wasn't a spur-of-the-moment decision, was it? You should consider your options now, too."*

But it was his final request that tugged at her heart, *"If you do decide to go, will you tell me goodbye first, mo chroí?"*

She didn't want to leave Jake, but could she survive the challenges the frontier presented? She'd heard that about half of the homesteaders out here gave up and went back home or to "greener pastures." Maybe she should go back to Chicago. She longed for the comfort of her da's home and her nan's calming presence.

Then her thoughts returned to why she had begun this grand adventure. What was her purpose in life? What kind of a future did she want? Would Jake consider spending his future with her?

All those questions were pushed aside in early May when Sam hammered on Katie's dugout door in the middle of the night. "Miss Katie, it's begun!"

She grabbed her shawl and answered the door. "What's begun, Sam?

"Lambing season."

Katie had arrived at Hughes' place after most of the lambing was done. As for the few ewes that did lamb while she was there, she was so busy with her chores as a house girl that she didn't see any actual lambing.

"Don't the ewes…. Uh, do the ewes need help with this, Sam? This is my first lambing season. I didn't see any of that at Hughes' place."

"For the most part, the mamas let nature take its course. But it's a good idea to keep an eye on them – especially the young ones. Sometimes they need help."

Katie nodded. She wondered what kind of help might be required.

"Give me a minute to get dressed."

Actually, it took Katie less than a minute. She tucked her nightgown into the waistband of her trousers and pulled on her boots. On her way out the door, she grabbed her coat despite the mild night air.

"What can I do to help, Sam?"

"I've been watching 'em, Miss Katie, and moving the pregnant ewes in from the far fields. They're in the west pasture, near the barn. We can bring 'em into the barn if they need extra care. Especially the downed ewes."

"I should have asked more questions about lambing. What's a downed ewe?"

"Sometimes ewes go off by themselves, or they don't graze enough to stay healthy. Lambing is harder on them."

Katie heard the familiar bleating of her sheep as she got closer.

"It's important to keep the newborn lambs near their mamas," Sam continued. "The mamas recognize their lambs by smell. Those first hours are when they get to know each other.

"Here we are. Here's the first lamb of the season," Sam said as he knelt beside a ewe and her still-wet lamb.

Katie was captivated by the sight. The ewe was on her feet now, cleaning the new baby. Unsteadily, the lamb got up and wobbled a bit, finally finding mama's milk.

Katie sighed. "This is so beautiful, Sam."

Sam chuckled. "That is is, Miss. 'Course, after you see a few hundred of 'em it becomes a little less precious."

"I don't believe you," Katie whispered.

She gazed at the sunrise's pink glow, touched the new grass's dew, and heard the meadowlarks singing. *This is home. This is MY home,* she realized.

She turned back to Sam. "This is why I was meant to be here. I found my purpose. Happy birthday, little lamb," she said to the newborn lamb.

During that first night and day of lambing, Katie and Sam watched seven ewes birth nine lambs, including two sets of twins. "We'll keep an eye on those twins, Miss Katie, to make sure the lambs are getting enough milk. Sometimes one of the twins takes more than their fair share. Can't *always* let nature take its course," he chuckled.

Later that day, Katie leaned against a large boulder and looked out over the flock. "This has been quite a day, Sam. I'm exhausted."

"Best get some shut-eye, Miss Katie. We're not nearly done. I'm figuring you have couple hundred pregnant ewes if Mr. Hughes' rams did their work. These mamas are just warming up."

"It starts again tonight?"

"It's gonna go non-stop for the next few weeks, Miss. Most of the time, the lambin' happens in daylight – which is good for us. It's easier to see what's going on."

He eyed the exhausted woman and said, "You should get some sleep while I keep watch. Then you can spell me later this evening. We'll work in shifts until most of the lambing is done."

Katie dragged herself back to the dugout. She washed her hands, splashed some cool water on her face, and, fully clothed, collapsed onto her bed.

As she drifted off to sleep, Katie thought about her momentous year on her claim. She sat straight up and looked at the calendar on the wall. The date was May 15. She started laughing. She'd been so busy feeling sorry for herself that she'd completely forgotten about the first anniversary on her claim! She promised herself that there would be a celebration – once she could take a breath. She had so much to celebrate!

Sam's prediction that lambing would consume them for the coming weeks was correct.

Most of the ewes let nature take its course, as Sam described it, but sometimes, especially with the smaller sheep, the birthing process was more difficult.

A couple of weeks into lambing season, Katie was watching over the ewes when she heard a sheep that was obviously in distress. The ewe was smaller than most of the other sheep. Katie knew from experience that could result in a difficult labor, especially since this was probably the ewe's first time lambing.

The ewe was restless. She was constantly bleating. As the contractions began, the ewe stood still, eyes closed, and breathed deeply. Finally, the ewe squatted, and Katie saw two hooves emerge from the ewe's backside.

And then nothing. Katie waited. The ewe waited. After what Katie estimated to be half an hour, she knew she had to take action, or both the mama and the lamb surely would die. She gently massaged the birth canal, hoping to encourage the lamb to keep moving through. When Katie could feel the lamb's head in the birth canal, she carefully and slowly pulled the lamb out by both legs.

Katie was so absorbed in the birthing process that she didn't hear Sam approaching. "You're doing good, Miss Katie," Sam coached. "Keep pulling. Be patient. And keep talking to the mama. She needs encouragement."

With one more pull, the slimy little lamb entered the world. "Welcome to Shamrock Sheep Ranch, little one," Katie said.

"Best check to make sure that's the only one," Sam suggested.

Sure enough, there was a second lamb in the birth canal. But the birthing was much faster this time – probably because the first lamb had eased the passage.

"This one's a boy," Katie said as she examined the second newborn.

"You are becoming a mighty good midwife, Miss Katie," said Sam.

"I learned from the best," she returned the compliment.

They continued in this rhythm for several weeks until almost all of the ewes were tending to new families. By Katie's count, about 220 ewes had finished lambing, and the flock size had nearly doubled in size.

Sam

"How many more are still pregnant, Sam?" Katie asked her foreman one day in mid-May.

"My last count was around forty. They're all pretty close to lambing, so we should be done in a week or so.

"Forty more lambs!" Katie exclaimed. "That will put my flock at over five hundred head! And that's after losing nearly a hundred in the flood. I'm going to need more pasture land if this keeps up."

Sam frowned. He recalled what Jake had said about Dan Deacon. And he knew that competition for grassland could end up in a range war.

Cautiously, he said, "You've got 160 acres of prime grazing land now. And, after we – after you – sort out the sheep for market, you'll have a more manageable flock."

"You're right, of course. But before that, we'll have shearing season. I'm looking forward to seeing the Goyas again."

She looked out over the flock. The ewes kept watch as their lambs frolicked and played in the prairie grass. "You know, Sam, before lambing began, I was in despair. I was ready to give up, especially after the flood took away so many animals. But now, I'm seeing new life on the prairie. Every new lamb is a miracle, and I am blessed."

"Yes'm. I see it same as you do."

They sat together on a slight incline and watched in silence.

"You know, Miss Katie, I never sat and watched the cattle like I do the sheep. I wonder why that is."

"It means you were meant to be here, Sam."

The foreman just smiled.

The remaining ewes delivered their lambs as Sam had predicted, and lambing season was completed before June.

June weather was erratic on the Dakota frontier. One day warm, gentle breezes would carry the smell of grass and flowers. The next day, the skies erupted in a downpour.

After the thunderstorm that caused the creek to flood, Katie was a bit skittish in stormy weather. She mentioned this to Sam one day, and he alleviated her fears as best he could. "The creek flooded because we'd had a lot of rain comin' into that storm. The ground and the creeks couldn't take any more water. Now, though, the rains are soaking in as fast as the water hits the dirt. I don't think we're in for another flood any time soon, Miss Katie."

"That's good. I don't think I could take more bad weather this year," Katie responded as she watched the gathering clouds on the western horizon.

"We could use some rain to cool us off, though, couldn't we? It's a scorcher today."

"Yes'm," Sam agreed. "I'm moving the flock down into low country by the creek."

"Sounds good. We still have a couple of ewes with lambs in the barn…the ones that needed a little extra help. You and Maddie take the flock to water, and I'll keep an eye on the ones in the barn. I wish I could switch places with you, Sam. I'd love to cool off in the creek. Enjoy it!"

Sam and Maddie went to work, herding the sheep toward the cooler pastures. The flock moved easily, grazing along the way, but the smell of the sweet water drew them to the creek.

Katie

Back at the dugout, Katie worked on her garden. She'd planted beans, squash, corn, and, of course, potatoes. Now, it was time to weed and water the new shoots.

When that chore was done, she checked on the animals in the barn. One of the ewes had not bonded with one of her two lambs. Katie and Sam had decided to move that newborn to one of the other ewes whose lamb was stillborn. Sam had shown Katie how to create that bond.

"Sometimes it works. Sometimes it doesn't. But it's worth a try," Sam said as he rubbed the orphan with the stillborn's scent. When the adoptive ewe allowed the orphan to nurse, Sam said, "I think it's gonna work. But let's keep 'em in the same pen for a couple of days so they get used to each other."

Katie was in the barn, checking on the adoption progress, when she heard the winds come up.

Putting down the feed bucket, she went to the barn door and saw a black funnel cloud coming straight at the dugout and the barn. She was familiar with tornadoes but had never experienced one in Chicago.

She knew she'd never reach the safety of the dugout – a home built into the side of a hill. That meant she needed to find the safest area of the wooden barn. Looking around, she decided the horse stalls had the most reinforced walls. Briefly, she wondered if she should close the barn doors, and then she laughed at how ridiculous that was.

Before taking cover, Katie opened the gate to her mare's stall and swatted the horse on the butt. She hoped letting the animal run free might allow it to escape harm's way. One of the new lambs wobbled toward her. She picked up the new baby while she looked for a safe place to ride out the storm.

Katie crouched low in the stall, still cradling the lamb. She covered her ears to block out the roar of the tornado. People were right, she thought. The tornado did sound like a locomotive coming down the track. The sound was deafening. She pulled her apron over her eyes to protect them from the straw, and hay picked up as the winds whipped through the open barn.

The roaring got louder and louder. The tornado seemed to be right on top of the barn. Katie could hear the barn creaking and finally tearing apart. She kept her head covered and curled into a tighter ball in the corner of the stall, still protecting the lamb. The wood began crashing down. The sheep were bleating. The winds continued to roar. She felt the barn walls and roof crash down. Then the world went silent and dark.

Sam

Sam noticed the skies darken to a sickly shade of green. The air became still – too still, in his judgment. Then he saw it – a massive twister coming over the hill. It touched down near the homestead, picking up dirt and debris in its path. He prayed that Katie had hunkered down in the dugout, which probably offered the best shelter from a tornado.

Out on the flat prairies, there were few places to hide. The roaring winds were deafening, so loud that Sam's calls to Maddie couldn't be heard over the din. Instead, he grabbed an armful of puppies and laid flat in a low spot. Maddie found them and curled up next to Sam and her pups.

The sheep, for the most part, lay down in the high grass. As the tornado raced toward the flock, Sam watched as several sheep were swept up in the twirling winds. He'd heard-tell of twisters picking up livestock, but he'd never seen it until now. Sam watched as the tornado rose into the clouds and disappeared. The winds subsided. The sheep got up and started grazing.

"I think we're in the clear, girl," he said to Maddie as he released the four squirming pups. For her part, Maddie nosed her offspring to reassure herself they were unharmed.

Katie

When she finally came to, Katie didn't know how long she'd been unconscious. There was a lump on her head, and she had a throbbing headache. She thought one arm might be broken. But she couldn't move even to check her aching arm. So much debris had rained down on her that she was trapped. She couldn't hear the sheep, so she assumed they had taken cover elsewhere or were dead.

"No time to mourn," Katie thought to herself. She began to yell. She shouted and screamed until her voice was gone. The exertion had tired her, and she dosed off to sleep.

She awoke to hear Maddie barking furiously. "Maddie girl, I'm here. Maddie, go get help." Briefly, she wondered where Maddie's puppies were. She hadn't seen them in the barn before the tornado hit.

Maddie continued to bark. Then Katie heard Sam calling her name. "Miss Katie! Miss Katie, are you in here?"

"Sam! Sam! We're here… in one of the horse stalls." Her voice was not loud, and it wasn't strong, but it was enough for Maddie to hear. Katie could hear the dog's barking closer, and then she heard scratching and pawing at the wood and wreckage on top of her.

Sam moved the boards and cleared away the broken boards and rubble that covered Katie. Finally, she could see a shaft of light.

"Sam! How long have I been here? Are you all right? Where are Maddie's puppies."

"One thing at a time, Miss Katie. I've just about got you free." He continued clearing debris away, pulling scraps of timber and pieces of the barn roof. With the last bit of wood removed, Katie tried to stand, but she didn't have the strength.

"Help me up. I need to get circulation back in my legs. I think my left arm is broken. Here, take this lamb." She handed the now-orphaned lamb to Sam.

He placed the lamb on a pile of straw. And, putting her uninjured arm over his shoulder, Sam lifted Katie out of the pile of broken wood.

She again started peppering him with questions. "How did you stay safe during the storm? How did you find me? What about the flock?"

"Me and Maddie and her pups hunkered down in a low spot near the creek," Sam explained. "The twister passed over us, taking three or four sheep with it. It was the darndest thing to see!" He shook his head, still in disbelief.

"I could see it came from the direction of the dugout and the barn, so Maddie and I skedaddled back here." Before Katie could ask, he said, "Maddie brought her pups to the creek today. I put 'em in a sack and brought 'em back with us. They're safe. So is the flock – most of 'em, anyway.

"It looks like the twister up and took away the sheep in the barn, too. I've heard tell of tornadoes picking up animals and putting 'em down miles away. Don't you worry. We'll look for 'em directly. But Maddie here is the hero of the day. She came directly to the barn and started sniffing around. That's how I knew to start digging for you."

Away from what used to be her barn, Sam put Katie down on a stump. "Let's take a look at you," he said as he lifted a piece of blood-soaked hair from Katie's forehead. "The cut don't look deep, but head wounds always bleed like the devil, excuse my language, Miss."

He went to the well and pulled up the bucket. After dipping his neckerchief in the cool water, he returned to Katie and began dabbing her head wound.

"That cold water feels so good," she said. "Can you take a look at my arm?"

He did as Katie asked and recognized the seriousness of the injury. "I'm gonna have to set that bone, Miss Katie."

"I figured as much. Have you ever done that before?"

"Yes'm. In the war…and before that on the farm in Missouri. It's gonna hurt something awful, though," he warned her.

He handed her a stick to clench between her teeth while he moved the bones in place. Katie nearly passed out again from the pain.

"The worst is over, Miss." Sam commenced wrapping the broken arm with splits to keep the bones in place while they mended.

"Did the sheep wagon make it through the storm?" Katie asked.

"Yes'm. It wasn't in the twister's path, and it's just fine."

Katie laughed. "That wagon survived a prairie fire, and now it's survived a tornado. It's the luck of the Irish!"

She thought about her words. "I've survived a prairie fire, a flood – and a tornado! It IS the luck of the Irish, faith and begorrah, as my nan would say!"

Exhausted and badly in need of sleep, Katie asked Sam to help her into her dugout.

"I can make you some tea before I go back to the flock, Miss," Sam offered.

"Sam, you read my mind. Ummm, could you leave Maddie and her puppies here for the night? I know that's a silly request, but…"

"Say no more, Miss Katie. I'm sure Maddie could use a rest, too."

With her cup of tea on the table, Katie reached for her journal to record the day's events.

Journal Entry – June 5, 1867

Mother Nature is trying her best to send me back home. But she's not going to win. Today a tornado ripped through my barn, covering me in what's left of my barn. I've heard stories that tornadoes can whip up in minutes. The stories are true. One minute, it was a hot June day. Then I heard a terrible roar and saw the tornado headed my way. I didn't even have time to shelter in the dugout – which I am sure would have been safer.

I am a bit 'worse for wear' – a broken arm and a lump on my head. But I'm still alive and kicking! Maddie found me in the rubble – bless that creature! And Sam dug me out – double blessings on him!

Sam assures me that most of the flock was spared. After the tornado whipped through the barn, it headed away from the lowlands where the flock was grazing.

Not to be taunting Mother Nature, but I think I'm winning so far.

KR

Chapter 26: Full Circle

June 1867 – Shamrock Sheep Ranch, Dakota Territory

Jake

It was a long night riding herd for Jake. When he entered the bunkhouse, he heard a couple of the other hands talking about a twister that had touched down to the south. He was so tired that, at first, it didn't register that the tornado might have gone through Katie's claim.

"Where did you hear this, Rory?" Jake asked one of the cowboys.

"I was having a few beers at the Gulch Saloon in Twin Brooks the other night," the ranch hand replied. "Somebody, I don't remember who, said they'd heard about the twister from another cowboy. Word was the tornado went through a sheep ranch and wrecked the barn. Why? It was only a bunch of sheep, Riley. Who cares?"

"Sam's working at a sheep ranch down that way," Jake replied. He didn't want the world to know his business about Katie Rose. "I've got a couple of days off this week. I was gonna go into town. Maybe I'll ride down that way and check it out."

"Kinda out of the way if you're headed to Twin Brooks," the other man snickered.

Jake might have decked the man if he hadn't been so tired, but he could only think about getting some shut-eye. He was asleep before his head hit the pillow.

Since Jake didn't intend to go to town, he pointed his horse directly south toward Katie's ranch and made good time. He could see the swath of destruction the tornado left. Trees, what few there were, had been ripped out of the ground. There were bare strips of land where the twister had cleanly removed any grass that had been growing. Now, he could see new shoots emerging. Soon, he thought, some of the traces of the storm would be gone, thanks to the fast-growing prairie grasses.

As he got closer to Shamrock Sheep Ranch, he noticed more damage. "My god," he thought, "this twister must have been a quarter-mile wide when it hit." The nearer he got to Katie's claim, the more apprehensive he became. Jake was stunned when he came to the rise overlooking Katie's homestead. There was no barn to be seen, just a pile of wood where Katie's barn used to stand.

From his vantage point, he could see the flock of sheep and the sheep wagon that Sam called home. But he didn't see Katie anywhere. Jake hoped she was in the dugout. He spurred his horse in that direction.

He called out to her when he entered the clearing. "Katie! Katie Rose!" He leaped from his horse and raced to the dugout, still calling her name as Katie came to the door.

Before she could say a word, Jake pulled her into an embrace and rained kisses on her face, ending with a deep, passionate kiss on her mouth. Then he pulled back to take stock of the woman he had come to love and long for.

"Your arm. It's in a sling. The tornado?"

Katie

"Yes, it happened when the tornado hit. I was lucky, actually. The twister came over the hill so fast that I couldn't make it to the dugout, so I took cover in the barn. The dugout would have been safer." She chuckled a bit. "The barn probably wasn't the safest place to be, considering how the barn looks."

"You were in the barn when it collapsed?"

"Uh-huh," she replied. "Everything landed on top of me. I was still holding a new lamb when Maddie found me."

"That dog deserves an extra treat."

"Oh, she got a reward," Katie assured him. "Sam dug me out of the rubble that used to be my barn. Did you know he could set broken bones? Thank goodness for Sam!"

"It's a skill that a lot of us had to learn during the war. You're right, though. Thank goodness Sam was here. So, you have new lambs now?"

"Yes. You missed all the fun. Lambing season is mostly done. There are a few stragglers, but we have a new crop of lambs to tend. That's keeping Sam, Maddie, and her pups pretty busy these days."

She gingerly waved her broken arm. "I've been staying close to home, bringing meals out to Sam and the dogs."

Taking care not to hurt her injured arm, Jake again took Katie into his arms and held her for several moments. "I've missed you, mo chroí," he whispered into her ear.

Katie's eyes teared up as she stroked his thick, black hair. "I almost gave up. After the flood, I almost packed up and went back to Chicago. But the new lambs made me realize I've made a new life here. I have a life and a purpose on the frontier. And I'm strong enough to meet whatever Mother Nature throws at me. Even a tornado."

She looked into Jake's deep blue eyes, "And I couldn't leave you."

Their reunion was sweet and passionate.

Jake carefully unbuttoned Katie's blouse. Next, he untied the ribbons of her camisole and slipped off her garments. Before she could cover her breasts, he said, "I never tire of admiring you, Katie Rose Kelly. You're in my thoughts every day and in my dreams every night."

She stepped out of her skirt as Jake hurried to catch up. Soon they were reacquainting themselves with the other's body. After making love, Katie nestled in Jake's arms. She twirled his wavy black hair in her fingers.

"I still have the lock of hair you gave me," he murmured. "I carry it in my pocket watch. Whenever I check the time, I see you."

"I didn't see you as the romantic type when I first met you at the boarding house in Ft. Randall," Katie said. "I was wrong. So wrong."

He made a sound deep in his throat. "You've been right about a lot of things. And I think you've gotten it right about your purpose out here. You belong on the prairie, Katie Rose."

"We both belong on the prairie, Jake. I've come to love my life here. And we're coming up on shearing season."

"I see we're back to talking business."

"I am a businesswoman," Katie replied as she slid out of Jake's arms. "My absence will be noted if I don't start dinner for my crew."

"What's for dinner?"

"Mutton steaks. One of the sheep stepped in a prairie dog hole and broke a leg. Now he's dinner."

"I'd better steer clear of prairie dog holes if that's what happens," Jake said with a laugh.

She rubbed the meat with salt, pepper, and spices and put it in the sizzling pan. While the steaks were frying, she tossed together spring greens for a salad. "I wish the potatoes were ready, but we'll make do with bread."

When the meal was ready, Katie packed it into a basket. Katie and Jake rode out together to where Sam was watching the flock.

"Well, look what the cat dragged in," Sam said when he saw his friend. Eying the picnic basket, he continued. "You don't need to keep cookin' for me, Miss Katie. But I'm mighty glad you do."

"I'm not much use herding right now," she countered.

Maddie bounded up to Jake, followed by two of her four puppies. "Hmm, let's see if I remember their names." Jake correctly called out Colm and Lorcan, the two females in the litter.

"The boys are out yonder," Sam indicated with a nod. "But they'll be coming in as soon as they get a whiff of the food Miss Katie's brought us."

He was right. Conan and Donnie arrived shortly to join their siblings for a hearty meal of meat scraps.

While they ate, Jake and Sam caught up on each other's lives. "I'd ask what brought you out for a visit," Sam said, "but I already know the answer."

"It's a little more than that," Jake replied. "Rory Olsen, remember that hand from Minnesota? Well, he heard about a twister. It sounded like it might have come through here, so I wanted to make sure everyone at the Shamrock was okay."

"We lost a few sheep. And, of course, there's Katie's arm. It could have been worse if it hadn't been for Maddie."

Jake nodded in agreement. He patted the border collie. "She's a keeper, this one."

"Yep, that she is. How's the Double D?" Sam asked.

"Same as always. Deacon bought out a rancher to the north. He's running more than three thousand head now."

"He's gonna need more land," Sam surmised.

"He is. That's the other reason I'm here. He's looking at sheepherders, like Katie and the Wrights, as competition for the range lands. I'm hearing talk about range wars. Things are heating up between cattlemen and sheepherders in Texas and Colorado. I've been thinking that those raiders at Hughes' place could have been scouting for Deacon and the other cattlemen."

"Deacon made it pretty clear that he doesn't like sheep or sheepherders that day at Polly's during the Independence Day celebration," Katie said. "There will never be enough land to suit men like Dan Deacon.

"I've been keeping my flock on my land to the south and the east, just like you suggested, Jake. Deacon can't complain that I'm grazing sheep on his land."

"You said it yourself. There will never be enough land for guys like Deacon. I'm just saying, be smart." He looked at Sam. The other man nodded in agreement.

They changed subjects and discussed the next momentous "season" in sheep herding – shearing season.

"The Goyas should be here soon," Katie said. "After shearing's done, we'll cut out the animals going to market."

"Jake, we need to build some pens for the shearing," Sam said. "I've sorted through the lumber from the barn, and there's enough to build a couple of pens. Do you think you could give us a hand?"

"Put me to work, buddy," Jake said.

By using walls and boards from the barn stalls, it didn't take long for Jake to assemble several good-sized pens.

Katie surveyed his work and said, "You'd make a passable carpenter. Maybe your talents are wasted as a cowboy." Jake just laughed.

The next day, Jake and Katie had a "fishing holiday," as she called it. The cowboy-fisherman collected a stringer of perch and bass while Katie dosed in the summer sun. That night they camped by the river.

"Not much of a moon tonight," Jake observed. "Just a sliver. But that makes it easier to count the stars. See that bright star?" Katie followed his outstretched hand. "That's the Dog Star. But that really bright one over there, by the moon? See that one?" Katie nodded. "That's not a star. It's Venus. It's a planet."

"How can you tell the difference?" Katie asked.

"It's not twinkling. See? Compared to the Dog Star, it shines but it doesn't twinkle."

"Hmmm." She enjoyed star gazing, but she enjoyed it even more in Jake's arms.

"I could get used to this," she murmured.

"I've been thinking about that, too, Katie Rose."

She looked into his eyes.

"Katie Rose Kelly, I love you and I want to spend my life with you."

"If you're asking me to marry you, the answer is yes."

He gathered her in his embrace. Their lovemaking was both a promise and a commitment. After they made love, they drifted off to sleep with the stars as their canopy.

In the morning, they packed up and headed back to the dugout by way of the flock.

"It was good to see you, my friend," said Jake. He shook Sam's hand and continued, "Watch over these critters – and watch over my girl."

"You've got my word, Jake."

At the dugout, Katie watched Jake unsaddling and currying her mare. "I'm not much good at taking care of her, but at least my arm has stopped aching. That's a good sign. I'll start taking it out of the sling for a while each day. It's weak as a kitten right now."

"Take it easy, Katie. Leave all the heavy lifting – literally – to Sam."

She nodded and reached up to stroke his cheek. "You take care, too, mo chroí," she said.

After thoroughly kissing her, Jake mounted his horse and cantered out of the clearing.

When he was out of sight, she returned to the dugout with Colm and Lorcan following her. "It's fish for supper, girls." And she started her chores for the day.

The Goyas arrived the following day. A baby basket was strapped behind Lara as she rode up to Katie's dugout.

Katie ran out to welcome the family. "A baby! Congratulations, Lara and Ben. I am so happy to see both – all three – of you. And my sheep will be relieved," she laughed.

Ben introduced Katie to their son, whom they named Antton. "It means 'priceless one' in Basque. It was also my father's name."

The dark-haired, dark-eyed baby boy enchanted Katie. "It's a beautiful name for a beautiful baby."

"Thank you," Lara said. "He was born last December. And," she said ruefully, "he's already got his first teeth."

"Ouch," Katie said. Lara laughed and nodded. The two women chatted while Ben left to check out the flock.

"You have a good-sized flock. The sheep look healthy. Good grazing lands," Ben observed.

"And you're partly to thank you for that," Katie said.

Ben cocked his head, not quite understanding Katie's comment.

"You rescued me after Harold Hughes attacked me. I can't thank you enough for that."

"I still think about that horrible night," Lara said. "We could have done nothing less. That Mr. Hughes, he was a bad man."

"He was a horrible man," Katie agreed. "And this spring, when he decided to quit his claim I bought him out. Sometimes things just work out."

"We are happy for you, Mrs. Kelly," Ben said. To his wife, he said, "Best make camp. Who is watching your flock, Mrs. Kelly?"

"I hired Sam Goodman from the Double D Ranch. He worked on a sheep ranch before the War," Katie explained. "And please, call me Katie."

Ben nodded and walked toward the sheep wagon. "I will speak with him about shearing."

Lara began unloading their tent and cooking supplies. She looked around at the grounds and spotted the pile of ruined lumber. Before she could ask, Katie said, "That's what is left of my barn after the tornado." She held up her wrapped arm and said, "Just a broken arm. We were lucky."

She watched as Lara set up camp. "What can I do to help?" Katie asked.

"When Ben gets back, he'll sharpen the shears and begin. He will need a bucket of warm, soapy water to wash the lanolin from the shears. And we'll need another pot of warm water to wash the fleece and separate the lanolin from the wool. Do you have a large pot?"

"I do. I used it last fall to dye wool. It's already set up by the well. I'll fill the pot and light a fire under it. You've got enough to do, Lara. Especially with little Antton."

"He's a good baby as long as his tummy is full," Lara agreed.

Ben returned from assessing the flock. "Sam will start moving the sheep into the pens over yonder," he indicated the newly built pens where the barn used to stand. "We'll get going after the noon meal."

He prepared his tools by honing the shears on a stone. Ben was ready when he was satisfied that all the blades were sharp enough.

Sam had moved ten or twelve sheep into each of the three pens, then asked Katie, "Miss Katie, when Ben's done with the first pen, you can herd 'em back to the flock. We'll keep it up until all the sheep have been clipped."

Katie agreed with Sam's suggestion.

When the Goyas were at Hughes' ranch last spring, Katie had spent most of her time planning meals and cooking. Now, she watched as Ben and Lara began working.

Ben grabbed the nearest sheep by the neck and turned the animal on its side. Then he began clipping. The sheep shearer started in the center of the animal's belly and systematically clipped the wool from the skin until he reached the sheep's backbone. All the while, he took care not to cut the animal. When he was done, a large woolen fleece was at his feet.

Lara picked up the fleece and carried it to the warm water simmering in the large caldron using a wooden paddle to submerge the wool. Katie noticed that Lara had also set up a series of racks near the well. She surmised these would be used for drying the fleece.

Ben worked steadily, taking time to clean his shears after every two or three sheep.

When he finished the first dozen sheep, Katie herded them back to the flock. She returned with the next group to find that Ben was already half done with the second pen, so she joined Lara at the drying racks.

"Mrs. Kelly – uh, Katie – careful of your arm," Lara cautioned.

"I'll be careful. But let me help," Katie replied. Together, the two women transferred the heavy, wet fleece to the drying racks. The fleeces weighed only a few pounds when they were dry, but the wet fleeces were a bit ungainly, Katie learned.

By supper time, Ben had completed shearing two pens of sheep. Katie herded the second group back to the flock.

"Ben's making good time, Sam," Katie told her foreman. Sam nodded. "I reckon we've got more than three hundred sheep to shear. That'll take him a week or so. If it's all right with you, Miss, I'd like to trade places with you tomorrow so's I can watch for a bit. Sheep shearin' is something I always looked forward to when I worked the flocks before."

"As long as I have Maddie and her pups out here to help, I'd be happy to spend time with the flock. It's a deal.

I'll come out after breakfast tomorrow and spell you," Katie agreed.

That night, she commemorated another milestone in her life on the frontier.

Journal Entry – June 17, 1867

The Goyas arrived today to begin shearing my flock. Nan always said that people are put in our path for a purpose. I am thankful that the Goyas' path and my path joined together.

They brought their baby son, Antton, with them. He is a happy baby as long as he can see his mama. Lara props him up in his basket so he can watch her work. The warm spring breezes are like a lullaby, and soon he drifts into dreamland. Do babies dream? I expect they do.

I hope that one day I'll have babies of my own to watch over and to love. Jake and I have spoken about marriage. I know I want to spend my life with Jake. But I also know that I will lose my claim to this land the moment I am married, since only single women can own a claim.

For now, I'll enjoy my time with the Goyas and their beautiful baby. While they're here, my days are filled with bleating sheep and wool fuzz tickling my nose. In one sense, it feels as if I've come full circle, from shearing season to shearing season. Yet, this is a new chapter in my life.

KR

Chapter 27: New Neighbor

June 27, 1867 – Shamrock Sheep Ranch

Katie

Katie's journal entry was correct. While the Goyas were at work, her days *were* filled with bleating sheep and wool fuzz floating on the summer winds. But she found shearing season to be glorious. After losing their heavy winter coats, the sheep leaped to their feet and danced away. They were so relieved to be rid of the weight and warmth of the thick wool.

On the final day of the Goya's stay at Shamrock Sheep Ranch, Katie cooked a feast to celebrate their work. Her arm was nearly healed, and she rarely wore the sling, giving the excuse that she needed to work her arm muscles again.

She found a large sheet of lumber from the "pile of barn," as it was now called, and dragged it near the front of the dugout. That sheet of lumber and smaller posts became a table and benches for an outdoor picnic. While the Goyas and Sam finished up the last of the shearing, Katie cooked.

The main course was a wild turkey that had the bad luck of foraging near the sheep wagon a few days earlier. She stuffed the bird with chopped-up bread crumbs and sage. Along with the turkey, Katie prepared wild turnips and asparagus. Dessert was bread pudding topped with raisins.

Earlier in the day, Katie had convinced Sam to join the group for supper even though he was reluctant to leave the flock.

"Maddie and the pups can watch the sheep for a bit," Katie said coaxingly. "We *all* deserve this meal of thanksgiving. It's also a belated anniversary meal. Last month was my first anniversary on the claim. We have a lot to celebrate. I'll pull rank on you if I need to, Sam Goodman."

"If you say so, Miss Katie. If you say so."

Before she called the workers to the supper, she surveyed her table. The table brimmed with love and fellowship, even with mismatched plates and silverware.

Nan would be proud of this spread, Katie said to herself.

As if on cue, Katie saw Jake riding toward the ranch. He neared the clearing, and she went out to welcome him.

"This is a surprise," she said. "I thought this was branding season at the Double D." He dismounted, and together they walked toward the dugout.

"We're done branding, and I've got some news for you and Sam," Jake said. He saw the table laden with food. "The news can wait. What's going on here?"

"We've finished Shamrock Sheep Ranch's first shearing season. I wanted to celebrate. You're just in time!"

She called the Goyas and Sam to the table.

"Hi, buddy," Jake said to Sam.

He introduced himself to the Goyas, "I'm Jake Riley. Katie told me how you helped her after the…" his voice trailed off.

"Hello, Mr. Riley," Ben replied. "We are honored to be among Mrs. Kelly's – Katie's – friends. This is my wife, Lara. And this is our son, Antton Goya."

They found places at the table, and all held hands. Katie searched for words to express her gratitude and friendship. She chose a well-loved Irish blessing.

"May the road rise up to meet you. May the wind always be at your back. May the sun shine warm upon your face. May the rains fall soft upon your fields and, until we meet again, may God hold you in the palm of His hand."

"Amen," intoned Sam.

"Amen," the others joined in.

"This is quite the feast, Miss Katie," Sam said as he cut the first slices of turkey.

"This has been quite a year, Sam," Katie responded.

Laughter and happy conversations punctuated the meal. After the last portion of bread pudding was gone, Katie rose to clear the table. "Nope, I'll do that, Katie. You've earned a break." Jake gestured for Katie to sit down.

As he gathered the empty plates, he asked, "Who's the next ranch on your schedule, Ben?"

"We will go north to the Wright ranch," he replied. "But it's good to spend time with friends. We will wait until tomorrow."

Katie recalled that Ben and Lara had left the Hughes ranch immediately after finishing their work. She smiled to herself to think that they counted her among their friends.

They sat around a campfire until the moon was high overhead. Before long, Sam said his goodbyes to the Goyas and returned to the flock.

Finally, Ben and Lara drifted back to their tent.

"It's just you and me, mo chroí," Jake told Katie. He put his arm around her shoulders.

"So it would seem. There's something on your mind, Jake. Do you want to tell me about it now?"

"I quit the Double D."

"Can I just say it's about time, Jake Riley! You talked about a claim months ago. What prompted this?"

"There's trouble coming," Jake explained. "Trouble over grazing rights. Dan Deacon and some other ranchers are making noises about 'getting rid of the hooved locusts.'"

"Yes, I recall that particular insult," Katie said, remembering Deacon's "big talk" at Polly's.

"Well, I'm not gonna ride on your claim, Katie. It's been brewing for a while. And you're right, it is time that I make some changes. There's some land just south of yours that's been surveyed for homesteading. I went into town yesterday and filed a claim right next to yours. What do you say to that, Katie Rose?"

Katie squealed in delight and threw her arms around him. She gave him a good and proper kiss and said, "I say, welcome neighbor!"

Jake kissed her back. "I was hoping you'd say that." He kissed her back. "We should…we should celebrate," he said with a wink.

"Yes, we should!" Katie led Jake into the dugout to continue the celebration.

The following day, Katie and Jake waved goodbye to the Goyas.

"Thank you again, Ben and Lara…and Antton," Katie said. "See you next year!"

As the Goyas rode out, Jake said to Katie, "We might see them sooner than that. Let's make a trip to Wright's ranch to let them know about Deacon's plans."

"Good idea," Katie agreed. "I also need to talk with Sarah about shipping sheep and wool to market. We'll need to tell Sam about your news and our trip to see the Wrights."

The prairie was ablaze with wildflowers. Katie gazed out on fields of golden sunflowers, yellow black-eyed Susans, red blanket flowers, pink coneflowers, and the white clover that sheep found so delectable.

"The flowers smell grand," Katie said to Jake. "I love the sweet smell of summer."

"All I smell are the sheep," he replied.

Katie laughed. "I like that smell, too."

They rode up to a promontory where Sam sat with a couple of the puppies. "Howdy. Are you out enjoying the summer day?" he asked Jake and Katie.

"I've brought a picnic lunch." Katie indicated a bag tied to her saddle.

"This seems as good a place as any for lunch," Jake said. He dismounted from his stallion and held the reins to Katie's horse while she got off her mare. "I'll hobble the horses so they can graze," he said.

Katie spread the picnic fixings on a quilt, and the three sat down for lunch.

"Go on. Spit it out," Sam said to Jake. "I could see you were chewing on some news last night."

"I quit the Double D," he told his former riding partner.

"Did you, now? And why did Jake Riley, a cowboy from his hat to his boots, walk away from the biggest cattle ranch in the territory?" Sam queried.

"You heard talk of range wars before you left the Double D," Jake replied.

"I did. That's one of the reasons I left. I've been in enough battles."

"Well, there's another war coming whether we like it or not. This ain't my war – any more than the last one was. But if I have to choose sides, I'm choosing Katie." Jake shifted on the blanket. "So I quit."

"What's your next move, Riley?" Sam asked. "Ever since I've known you, you've planned two moves ahead."

Jake smiled. "I've staked a claim to the south. I checked out plats of land when we were in Twin Brooks last Christmas. This spring I rode down to see the lay of the land."

Sam grinned. "So, you're gonna run sheep, Jake?"

Jake snorted. "Nope. I'm a cowboy. I thought I'd talk with Tim Wright when Katie and I go for a visit."

Katie spoke up. "That's why we're here, Sam. I wanted to let you know that Jake and I are riding up to the Wright Ranch tomorrow. Jake thought Tim and Sarah should know about Dan Deacon's plans. And I want to talk with Sarah about sending sheep and wool to market."

"Makes sense," Sam agreed. "Maddie and me will just hunker down here with the woolies."

To punctuate his declaration, Maddie yipped at a wandering ewe.

Sitting outside that evening, Jake explained why he didn't tell Katie sooner about staking the claim. "After the flood, you talked about packing up and going 'home.' If you were really fixed on leaving, I didn't want to stand in your way. But Katie Rose, this is home." He gestured to the prairies and the night sky.

Katie leaned into Jake and kissed him. "You are right, mo chroí. This land is my home. And I am very happy you've decided to make your home here, too. So, when do I get to see the Riley Ranch?"

"Well, since I'm not punching cattle for Deacon anymore, I guess we can ride out and check out my claim later this week. Let's go after we get back from the Wrights."

It was a beautiful day to ride north to the Rocking W Ranch. Katie and Jake set out just as the sun's first pink rays were glowing in the eastern sky.

"As my nan would say, 'tis a grand day to be alive!'" Katie said.

"I want to meet your nan someday," said Jake. "You know, I have an Irish granny, too. The Riley clan came from Galway."

"I knew there was a bit o' the Irish in you." Katie's green eyes sparkled. "My nan would delight in meeting you, Jake Riley."

They chatted about inconsequential things. Katie realized that she and Patrick had never had this kind of easy friendship. She wondered why.

"You're deep in thought," Jake observed.

"I'm just remembering my life 'before.' Before I came to Dakota. Before I met you. Before I found my purpose."

"Ah, deep thoughts, indeed."

They rode over a hill, and Jake spotted the Wright cattle grazing in the valley beyond. "Finally, the sound of cattle."

Katie laughed. "I'd wager we'll be hearing the sound of sheep soon."

She was right. The pasture to the east held Sarah's flock of sheep. She could see that the Goyas had been hard at work, as a few sheep were freshly shorn. In the distance, Katie spotted Buddy, the Wright's border collie, herding a wandering sheep back to the flock. Watching over the flock were two of Sarah's children.

Katie waved to them and called out, "Is your mother at the house?" The older boy nodded and pointed toward the Wright soddy.

Sarah was tending a large pot over an open fire when Jake and Katie approached the house. In the distance, Katie could see Ben was hard at work shearing. One of the Wright girls was carrying a fleece to her mother for boiling.

"Katie! Jake! It's so good to see you. Tim is helping Ben with the shearing, and the kids are shuttling animals back and forth. And I'm on fleece-cleaning duty."

"You're lucky to have extra hands to help out," Katie said. "

"It's quite a process," Sarah agreed. "I'd ask if you're here to help, but I'm guessing something else is on your mind." She wiped her wet, lanolin-covered hands on her apron. "We were just about to have lunch. Help me move the table outside, and we can enjoy the summer sun."

The Goyas, Tim, and two of the four Wright children joined the group. "What's new at Shamrock Sheep Ranch, Katie?" Tim asked.

"I'll let Jake answer that," Katie replied.

Jake cleared his throat. "I've staked a claim to the south of Katie's land," he began. "Yep, I quit the Double D."

"Ready to be your own boss? I understand that," Tim said.

"That…and…there ain't no way to ease into this," Jake said with a grimace. "Dan Deacon and the other ranchers out west are gearing up for a range war."

The group was silent, taking in the gravity of that statement.

"I knew it would come to this," Tim said. "Deacon's a greedy bas…." He looked at his daughters and rephrased his statement, "…a greedy son of a gun. Those ranchers think the grazing land belongs to them by right."

Before Sarah could speak, Tim continued, "Don't get me wrong. I'm a cattleman, born and raised, but Sarah here showed me the error of my ways. Her critters can eat the stuff my cattle won't touch. And the sheep don't destroy grazing pastures, never mind what Deacon and the others say. This is a land-grab, pure and simple."

"What can we do?" Sarah asked.

"I've heard that Deacon is hiring outside guns," Jake answered. "Those drifters that Katie saw last winter? I think they've been scouting the sheep ranches and reporting back to Deacon. Just like further west and south, the cattle ranchers want to force sheep ranchers off the land. Then, with open-range laws, the ranchers move their herds onto those grazing lands.

"When I heard scuttlebutt about those plans, I started making my own plans. Last week I quit the Double D. Now, I'm a cattle rancher in search of cattle."

The four talked at length about what measures they could take to protect their sheep and their land. They agreed that Sheriff Brown needed to be alerted to the potential trouble.

"That brings me to the other reason we're here," Katie said. "Sarah, tell me about sending wool to market."

"It was tough in the beginning," Sarah began, "but I've made some contacts."

Sarah explained about the wool brokers who collect the fleeces each year.

"Now for my second question," Katie said. "How do I send my animals to market?"

"That isn't as easy as selling the wool," Sarah agreed. "We – the sheep ranchers around here – drive the sheep to Sioux City and on to Omaha. From there, the animals are shipped to packing plants in Chicago. Every rancher agrees to send at least one sheepherder with his or her flock." Sarah emphasized 'or her flock.'

Katie looked at Jake. "Do you think Sam would enjoy a trip to the big city?"

"If he doesn't want to go, I'll go. I need to buy cattle for my ranch. A lot of good livestock goes through Omaha."

Tim coughed, then said, "I can sell you a few head from my ranch if you're willing."

Jake shook Tim's hand. "It's a deal. Thanks, neighbor."

They spent the rest of the afternoon catching up on family news, local gossip, and plans for the future. Katie learned that Jimmy had, indeed, struck out for the gold and silver mines out west.

"Have you had any word from him since he left?"

"Not a peep," replied Sarah. "Of course, Jimmy never was much for writing. My sister – his mother – hasn't heard from him either. She's a bit peeved, but what can you do?" Sarah threw up her hands in a hopeless gesture.

"Speaking of letters, I'll write that letter to the wool broker now so you can post it in Twin Brooks. It's not exactly on the way home, but it will get to the brokers sooner."

"Jake," Katie said, "let's stop in Twin Brooks tonight. I need supplies, and I'm guessing you do, too."

"I think I just heard you say that Polly has cold beer on tap," Jake teased.

"That, too," Katie said with a laugh.

They all said their goodbyes. Katie and Jake headed toward Twin Brooks.

On the way to town, Katie read Sarah's letter to the wool brokers.

Dear Sirs,

This is to introduce you to Mrs. Katie Kelly. Mrs. Kelly recently established a successful sheep ranch in Dakota Territory. It is my understanding that your firm is interested in adding new suppliers. As this is her first year in business, she will require a supply of sacks, which she will fill when you visit her ranch, a half-day ride south of the Rocking W in Dakota Territory.

Best Regards,

Mrs. Timothy Wright

Chapter 28: 'Hoppers

June 29, 1867 – Twin Brooks

Katie

It was a hot, dusty ride to Twin Brooks. By the time they rode into town, Katie felt battered by the summer winds. They tied off their horses at the railing outside Polly's Place and entered the somewhat cooler saloon.

"Set 'em up, Polly! We're celebrating," Jake called to the barkeeper.

Polly poured two foamy draught beers and set them on the bar. "What are we celebrating, Jake?"

"My new claim! I quit the Double D and staked a claim," he replied.

"You're done cowboying?" Micah asked. He was standing at the far end of the polished bar. Katie thought of that spot as "Micah's Place at Polly's Place."

"Nope, I'm just done working for ranchers like Dan Deacon. I'm starting my own spread." Jake removed his black cowboy hat and ran his fingers through his hair. "Whew, it's a hot one out there."

Using her hat like a ladies' fan, Katie said, "Polly, I was as surprised as anyone when he told me about it." She watched Jake in amusement and continued, "I just hope he's a good neighbor."

Jake let out a whooping yell and swept Katie off her feet. "I'm feeling pretty neighborly right now."

"Down, boy," Polly said. "I run a respectable establishment here."

Jake soundly kissed Katie and then set her back on her feet.

"I told you it was worth celebrating," he said.

"That it is," Micah said. "What prompted your decision?"

"Hmmm, let's get a table, Sheriff," Jake replied.

The four of them – Jake, Katie, Micah, and Polly – found a table in a cool corner.

Jake began, "Things are heating up out there, Micah. And I'm not just talking about the weather. I'm talking about a range war. The boys in the bunkhouse heard tell the big ranchers are trying to push out the sheep ranchers along with the smaller cattle ranches."

"I've heard some rumblings about it," the sheriff said. "What else do you know?"

"There's talk that hired guns are coming to scare off the sheepherders," Jake said.

"They're doing that in Wyoming and down Texas way," said Micah. "A marshall came through town a couple of days ago. He said cattlemen were shooting and clubbing the sheep on the range. Somebody's gonna get killed sooner or later."

"If I have to choose sides, I choose Katie's side," Jake said. He tipped his nearly empty beer mug in Katie's direction.

"Dan Deacon made no secret about how feels about sheep and sheepherders, Micah," said Katie. "But raiding and killing is a far cry from name-calling. This is just plain evil fueled by greed. Sam and I can protect the sheep from coyotes and wolves, but this…" she shuttered.

"I'll ride out and have a talk with Deacon," Micah concluded.

"Enough of that," Polly declared. "So you finally made the jump from ranch hand to ranch owner? Good for you! That deserves a round on the house." She made a circling motion to the man behind the bar, and another round of beers soon arrived.

"What are you gonna name your place, Jake?" Polly asked.

"I have a couple of ideas, but I'm not ready to trot 'em out just so you all can shoot 'em down." He nodded. "I'll know when the right name hits me."

"Just like when Shamrock Sheep Ranch hit me," Katie said with a twinkle in her eye.

"How long are you in town?" Polly queried.

"Until tomorrow," Katie said.

"We both need supplies…and lumber," Jake cut in. "You heard about twister last month? Well, it hit Katie's barn – with Katie in it."

Polly gasped. "No!"

Katie filled in Polly and Micah on the tornado and her injuries. "But it's healed now," she concluded.

"My girl!" Polly exclaimed. "First a prairie fire, then a tornado. You're a tough one, Katie Rose Kelly!"

"You forgot the spring floods, Polly," Jake added. "But you're right. My girl is a tough one. She's a homesteader through and through." He patted Katie on the back.

"It's my Irish stubbornness," Katie said with a chuckle.

"Whatever you call it, I'm proud to call you a friend," Polly said. They all toasted Katie with the last of their beers.

Katie beamed at the compliments, and then she yawned. "I'm exhausted, but all I can think about is a cool bath. Do you have a room open?"

"I do, and it's all yours, Katie," Polly answered. "Why don't the two of you head to Emma's for dinner. Your rooms will be ready when you get back."

"You read my mind, Miss Polly," Jake said. "You read my mind."

Dinner at Emma's Diner did not disappoint, with fried chicken, mashed potatoes, and delicious chicken gravy. Emma enticed them to try her fresh strawberry pie. Katie finished every crumb even though she declared she didn't have room for dessert.

"Let's walk a bit," Jake suggested. He crooked his arm for her.

"Hmmm." Katie threaded her arm through his. Jake pulled her in closer.

"Remember the first time we walked out this way," he said.

"Of course, it was our first kiss."

"Nooooo, our first kiss was at Lone Tree," he corrected her. "You kissed me. What a bold colleen you are!"

Before Katie could protest, Jake turned her to him. Taking her face in his hands, he looked deeply into her eyes. "I love you, Katie Rose Kelly. I can't imagine life without you."

"And I love you, Jake Riley."

Their kisses were the promise of a deep and lasting love.

They walked back to Polly's Place, arm-in-arm.

In Katie's room, the tub was a welcoming sight. Lilac petals floated on the tepid water, and candles lit the small room.

"A real bath," she said, taking in the scene. "It's been too long!"

"Yes, it has." Jake shut Katie's door behind him.

They enjoyed the cool, fragrant bath water together – but not as much as they enjoyed making love.

Katie had coffee with Polly the next morning in the saloon's kitchen. She was no longer embarrassed by her nighttime activities with Jake. And Polly, as a good friend, never judged Katie's actions.

The two women chatted about their plans for the day. Katie listed the tasks ahead of her – the post office, the bank, the mercantile, and the lumber yard.

They made the rounds, stocking up on supplies. At the last stop, Jake made a deal for a used wagon. "I hate to hitch Finn to a wagon, but we all have to make sacrifices," he said as he attached the harness to his black stallion.

Katie tied her mare to the back of the wagon and climbed on board. "Giddy up, cowboy!"

"Very funny," he shot back with a crooked smile.

The ride back to Katie's ranch was just as hot and dusty as the ride into town, with one exception. To the north, they could see a dark cloud. At first, Katie thought it was a much-needed rain cloud. But it wasn't a rain cloud. It was a cloud of grasshoppers.

Soon, the flying insects were upon them. The grasshoppers were so thick that Jake covered his face with a neckerchief and handed Katie a handkerchief for her face.

Over the incessant buzzing, Katie called out, "Jake, I've never seen anything like this."

"I heard stories about 'em here in '64, during the War," he replied through his mask. "Soldiers in General Sully's outfit said the 'hoppers ate everything. When the crops were gone, they even ate holes in the wagon covers." He shook his head. "Looks like they're coming from the north. That means they've already had their fill of grasslands up there."

The grasshoppers swarmed around the heads of both horses. Jack stopped several times to swat them away and calm the animals.

From their vantage point on an eastern hill, they could see grasshoppers had covered the prairie grass. When they moved on, they left bare patches of dirt where they'd devoured the lush green grasses of the plains.

"We're almost home," Katie said with panic in her voice. "I'm worried about Sam."

When they found the sheepherder, he was lighting fires in the pastures where the sheep grazed. He saw the buckboard arrive and yelled to them, "Start making piles of wet moss and grass, then grab a torch and light those piles. The 'hoppers don't like the smoke. They might eat the grass, but they won't stick around to pester the sheep."

Katie jumped off the wagon and began collecting moss and reeds from the nearby creek.

Jake piled the fuel into pyramids and, using kindling, he joined Sam in creating a series of small, smoky fires that dotted the prairie.

In the meantime, Maddie and her brood continued to circle the sheep. The dogs were able to keep the flock together and, in doing so, keep the animals calmer. Everyone – people and dogs – worked through the night. While the fires crackled, Sam and Jake called on their experience herding cattle and began singing to the sheep.

Sam started, softly singing a song from his childhood:

Wade in the water, wade in the water, children, wade in the water,

God's gonna trouble the water.

Who's that yonder dressed in red?

Wade in the water, children. Must be the children that Moses led.

God's gonna trouble the water.

Wade in the water, wade in the water, children,
wade in the water,

God's gonna trouble the water.

When Sam finished, Jake began serenading the flock with the song he first sang to Katie.

Beautiful dreamer, wake unto me,

Starlight and dewdrops are waiting for thee;

Sounds of the rude world, heard in the day,

Lull'd by the moonlight have all passed away!

As the sun climbed on the eastern horizon, the three sheepherders found that the grasshoppers had departed. In their wake, they left not a green leaf or blade of grass. Sam shook his head as he surveyed the damage.

"They're like a plague of locusts out of the Bible," he said. "A plague." He tracked the insects' path and said, "Miss Katie, I'm gonna head over to the western pastures and see if there's any grass left over yonder." He saddled his horse and headed toward what he hoped would be greener pastures – literally.

Katie nodded sleepily. "Thank you, Sam."

"I'll stay here and keep an eye on the sheep while you get some rest, Katie," Jake suggested.

"I'll go," she said grudgingly, "but only so I can pack a lunch for all of us. We didn't get supper last night, and we skipped breakfast."

Jake grunted in agreement.

Katie and Sam returned to the flock about the same time. She had a lunch basket tied to her saddle, and Sam had a big grin on his face. On the way to find Jake, Sam filled in Katie on what he'd seen.

"The west pastures are good, Miss Katie. Plenty of grass on the western slope. Those devil insects passed right over that land. We'll get to herding the flock there directly."

"That's wonderful news, Sam." She paused and thought a moment. "The cloud came from the north, didn't it?"

He nodded.

"I wonder if the Wrights' land was in its path."

"Don't know, ma'am. Do you want me to ride up there?"

Katie weighed the choices. "If the grasshoppers hit their pastures, they'll need a place to graze their animals while the grass grows back. Let's talk with Jake about it."

Sam nodded in agreement.

They found the cowboy stretched out on the ground, asleep with his hat covering his face.

Katie kicked the bottom of his boots. "Some sheepherder you are, Riley."

He moved the cowboy hat just enough for one eye to peek out. "That's what the dogs are for. I'm here as a backup."

Katie and Sam both shook their heads in mock amazement.

"Lunch is served," Katie said after spreading the cold meal on a quilt. Jake whistled when he saw the three bottles of beer in the picnic basket. "You do know how to put on a picnic, Mrs. Kelly."

Over the meal, they decided that Jake should ride to the Rocking W to check on damage from the grasshoppers.

"I could clearly see that you're not a sheepherder," Katie said teasingly. "Sam actually *does* watch the sheep. Besides, you're a faster rider than I am.."

"I'll go tomorrow," Jake agreed. "I was hoping to take you for a ride on my new land today. It's not far."

"And I was hoping you'd ask me."

Jake

Spurring their horses, Katie and Jake surveyed the new claim. On the far south side of the claim, Katie noted, "You've got several creeks running through your land. It's good for the cattle but could be a problem in flooding season." She remembered how the early spring flood had frightened her so.

"I'll keep an eye on it. I'll keep the herd on higher ground in the rainy season."

They continued the inspection. "It looks like the 'hoppers came through the northeast corner of the section," Jake said. "But a lot of the pastures look pretty good. Now, I just need critters to put on the land. In the meantime, we can use my claim for the Wrights, if they need it."

They'd circled the claim, arriving at the northern edge of Jake's land, near the large cottonwood that bordered Katie's land. "My claim starts at Lone Tree, too." He pointed to the single tree that stood majestically on the wide-open prairie. Now, in late June, the tree was covered in fluffy, white cotton seeds. When wind blew through the tree, a wave of white cotton balls pulled loose and floated on the breeze.

"I love that tree," Katie said. "For me, it's a sign that I'm coming home. And now, it will be for you, too."

He dismounted, and she followed suit. "Let's sit a spell," he said as he took her hand. Together, they walked toward the cottonwood tree.

Under the tree's ceiling of green leaves and fluffy white cotton, Jake continued. "Choosing this claim wasn't a coincidence, Katie. I wanted to be near you." He paused, then said, "Forever and always."

Her head jerked up, and she looked into his dark blue eyes.

"I'm asking again, Katie Rose Kelly. Will you marry me?"

Katie was speechless. Her mouth opened and closed again before she could reply.

"I don't think I've ever seen you without words," he said. "Is this a good sign or a bad sign?"

He started to get up, embarrassed that he'd made this declaration.

"No, no, no. It's not that. I love you. I love you, Jake Riley." She gave a small, self-deprecating laugh. "And here it's me with the cold feet."

Again he started to rise, but she pulled him down.

"Jake, I want to marry you," she continued. "But I need time. I came west to prove to myself that I could make a life on the frontier. I also came west to put my marriage to Pat behind me. Nan always said I married Pat in haste.

She was right. I was a war bride. I've told you that it wasn't a joyful marriage. And, there are other complications."

"Such as?" he asked.

"When I marry, I'll lose the rights to my claim. That's the law." She raised her hands, "But the law doesn't govern my heart. I'm so confused." She kissed him.

"Your nan is right," Jake agreed. "We've got time, Katie Rose. Let's do some planning."

"You and your plans," Katie interjected.

He chuckled. "I'm not marrying you for your claim. But there would be some advantages to being next-door neighbors."

She gave him a side-eye look. "I know what advantages you're thinking about."

"No, no, no." Now it was Jake's turn to clarify the conversation. "You need to rebuild your barn. I need to build a new barn. Let's build on the property line."

"But it's not close to my dugout or well," she argued.

"Do you love that dirt dugout?"

"No. Even though it's warm in the winter and cool in the summer, it's buggy all year."

Jake smiled. "Then let's build frame houses next to the new double-barn…."

"…on the property line," she completed his sentence.

"Exactly. Then, Sam can live in the dugout when he's not in the sheep wagon."

"I think he'd appreciate that," Katie considered.

"When we tie the knot, we'll just connect the houses."

Katie

Katie noticed that Jake did not say 'if we tie the knot.' She was happy that she hadn't scared him away with her hesitancy.

"I think that's a good plan – or at least the start of a good plan," she agreed.

"Best of all," he said, "the plan gives you – gives us – time." He opened his arms, and she moved into his embrace. The kiss was a promise for their shared future.

They consummated their plans beneath the shelter of Lone Tree.

The sun was low on the horizon when Jake nudged Katie. "Mo chroí, we'd best be getting back."

"Let's just stay under this tree forever."

On the way back to Katie's claim, they continued planning for the future. As they neared the flock, Jake said, "I'll help Sam move the sheep to new pastures."

When Katie protested, he said, "I'll be gone for a few days. Let me give you a hand now. You can ride the flock tomorrow." He kissed her lightly, and she rode on to the dugout.

The peace and quiet of the dugout was a welcome reprieve for Katie. She hadn't realized how much she enjoyed the solitude. That evening, she retrieved the packet of letters from her family. Leaving Nan's letter for last, she opened the envelope from her father.

My dear girl,

I hope this letter finds you safe and well. I have a bit of news for you.

I have been without a wife for many years and have missed feminine companionship. You may remember Fiona Murphy. She is the widow of Seamus Murphy. Fiona and I were married this past May. It was a brief engagement since we're both widowed and don't know what the Lord has in store for us.

Fiona has moved into our home. The arrangement is agreeable with your nan and your brother. I hope that you will be able to meet Fiona when you visit us.

My love to you,

Da

The letter from her grandmother echoed her father's news, along with other news from home.

Mo stór,

If you have not read your father's letter yet, I will pause so you can learn his news. I am well pleased with our new family member. As I mentioned in earlier letters, your father was lonely, and Fiona is cheerful. I believe your brother may have a sweetheart, as well. But he has not shared that information with me or your da.

And how about you, my girl? You've not mentioned that cowboy, Mr. Riley, in recent letters. Do you see him often? Riley sounds like a good Irish name. Do you know where his people were from?

Your life on the frontier sounds very exciting! While I miss you terribly, I am proud you have the strength and optimism to succeed on that wild land.

I pray that the saints and your mother watch over you and keep you safe.

Be happy, my darling girl.

Nan

Katie thought about the news from her family. It seemed love was in the air. She was happy for her father, and she was excited to write to them about *her* news.

Chapter 29: Range War

Katie

Katie buttoned her pale green camisole and tucked it into the waistband of her trousers. The practicality of trousers appealed to her, especially when she was riding and herding sheep. Before she left the dugout, she wrapped a kerchief around her red curls. Sizing up herself in the mirror, she thought, "My work clothes on the ranch are a lot different from the blouses and skirts I wore in da's pub."

Her horse was saddled, and she'd packed extra supplies for a camp meal with Sam that evening. Even though he'd been on the ranch for only a few months, she had come to rely on Sam's steady hand and cool head. She couldn't imagine managing the flock without him. She wondered what his reaction had been to the news of her and Jake's marriage plans.

That thought left her head when, to the north, Katie spotted a group of riders headed east. She didn't recognize the riders and briefly wondered if they could be raiders that Jake warned her about.

There you go, worrying. Don't be looking for trouble, she said to herself. Still, she decided to mention the riders to Sam. They disappeared over the horizon as Katie trotted out to join Sam.

The lambs, now a couple of months old, were becoming braver and were leaving their mamas for longer periods of time. That made herding them more of a challenge, but she saw that her five border collies were up to the task.

She was watching Lorcan return a stray lamb to the flock when Sam approached. "Those pups are a sight to watch, aren't they, Miss Katie?"

"I love watching them work," she said. "It's like they're born knowing how to herd."

"I believe they are, Miss," he replied. "Lorcan takes after her mama. I've never seen a smarter dog than your Maddie. She's a keeper."

"And a life-saver," Katie said, remembering how the dog had discovered her in the rubble that had been her barn.

"That she is." He paused, then continued on a new topic. "So….Jake said you two are making plans."

"I wanted to talk with you about that, Sam," Katie began.

"If you can give me some notice, I'll start looking for a new place."

"Oh no, Sam. I was hoping you'd stay. This flock takes more than one sheepherder – and Jake will be running cattle. Between you and me, I think sheep make him a little uncomfortable."

The man's big, bright smile contrasted with his dark skin. "If you say so, Miss Katie. I do like it here." He continued in a secretive tone, "I know what you mean about Jake and sheep." They both laughed.

Katie remembered to mention the riders to Sam. He agreed it was probably nothing to worry about, but they'd keep an eye out just in case.

It was a peaceful day. But the oppressive July heat, which seemed to come in waves, drove Katie and Sam to find shade where possible.

After the noon meal, Sam had hunkered down next to a large boulder while Katie walked with her horse in a creek on the other side of the flock. All at once, she heard sheep bleating, men yelling, and gunfire. She mounted her horse and pulled out her rifle, checking to ensure it was loaded. Rather than heading directly into the line of fire, Katie skirted around the flock to determine what was happening.

What she saw was unbelievable. The group of riders she'd seen earlier were stampeding the flock. She saw more than a dozen sheep had been bludgeoned with clubs.

Sam had taken cover behind the boulder and was firing at the raiders. Before Katie could act, one of the four horsemen rode up behind Sam. With a mask to hide his identity, the rider took aim and shot. Sam dropped his rifle and slumped to the ground, motionless.

Katie nearly screamed but checked herself. She didn't want to give away her position. Instead, Katie circled behind the raiders. Picking out the nearest horseman in her rifle sights, she fired. The shot hit the rider in the shoulder. He dropped both weapons – the club and the rifle. Holding on to his horse with his uninjured arm, the man escaped to the north.

That left three raiders. Two of the men, on foot, continued to club sheep. Maddie charged one of the men, snarling as she attacked the man who was hurting her sheep. The raider swung at Maddie, then dropped his club and scrambled away, calling for his horse. Maddie bared her teeth and growled at the other club-wielding man. That was enough to convince him to abandon the raid.

The third man fired off a shot at Katie that went wide. Before he could aim and shoot again, one of the men on the ground yelled at the rider. "Billy! Come and get me!" The rider assessed the situation and decided the tide had turned against them. He wheeled his horse around, stopping to pull up his accomplice behind him. Together, they galloped away at full speed.

Katie rushed to Sam's side. His breathing was ragged, and there was blood everywhere. She listened to his heart and lungs. There was a bubbling sound that alarmed her.

"Oh, Sam! Oh, no!"

He opened his eyes. "Miss Katie. You've gotta stop the bleeding. I helped some in the medical tents. Check for a bullet." And then he was unconscious.

Katie ripped open his shirt and saw blood bubbling from a wound on the right side of his chest, close to his armpit. She raised a prayer that it wasn't near his heart. Carefully, she laid Sam flat on the ground. Next, she retrieved the medical kit from her saddle. Then she pulled the kerchief from her hair and poured cool water from the canteen onto the cloth. Katie cleaned the wound as best she could, wringing out the bloody cloth several times.

When she could see the wound clearly, Katie took a deep breath. She'd already checked for an exit wound, and finding none, she knew she needed to look for the bullet still in Sam's chest. Following his advice, she knew she must remove the shell.

She began probing the gunshot area with her fingers. It was a tricky procedure, something that she'd never done before – or thought she would ever *have* to do. Finally, after several minutes of tentative probing, Katie found a solid object that felt like a bullet. Sam moaned but still seemed to be unconscious.

But could she pull it out?

She worked the bullet toward the opening, and using her index fingers like a tweezer, Katie Rose extracted the bullet. She wanted to collapse but knew that her work was not over.

Katie threaded a needle from the medical kit and began stitching the wound closed. That completed, Katie put a compress over the wound and tightly wrapped Sam's chest with a long strip of cloth.

Thankfully, Sam remained unconscious for the procedure. Then Katie worried that might be a bad sign. Shaking her head, she sent another brief prayer to the heavens. Knowing that Sam was in God's hands now, Katie tried to decide what she should do next.

The sheep. She needed to see how many sheep were dead or injured. And what about the dogs? Had the raiders hurt her dogs, too?

With renewed determination, Katie Rose Kelly went to assess her flock. It was heartbreaking. More than a dozen ewes and several lambs had been clubbed to death. She checked Maddie and her litter. None of the border collies had severe injuries. Two pups were limping, but that might have happened during the stampede.

With the gruesome inventory complete, Katie returned to Sam. He was moaning and seemed flushed. She pulled him into a bit of shade from the boulder but realized the shade wouldn't last long.

Could she drag him to the sheep wagon? It was a long way off. Katie decided bringing the sheep wagon to Sam would be a better idea.

Sam's horse was hobbled in a nearby pasture, but Katie knew using her mare would be faster and easier. Katie hitched her horse to the home on wheels and drove the wagon over the rough pastures to where Sam was lying. Positioning the wagon for maximum shade, Katie unhitched her horse and let the mare graze.

Back with Sam, Katie spent the rest of the afternoon and evening applying cool, damp compresses to keep Sam as comfortable as possible. From time to time, he murmured a few words.

She had found some willow bark in the sheep wagon that she made into a tea to bring down the fever. Katie administered the tea and kept cool, damp cloths on Sam's forehead. In addition to the medicine, she'd found a scrap of paper and a pencil. She needed to write a letter.

Glimmers of pink and orange glowed on the western horizon as the sun began setting. Even after this horrific day, Katie smiled at the everyday beauty on the Dakota frontier.

Settling in next to Sam, Katie began her night-long vigil. As Sam slept fitfully, Katie wrote a letter to Jake.

Mo chroí,

We Irish, we love our land. We've fought for it. We've died for it. But I will not choose between you and my land. I choose you.

The fight today taught me that life is precious. I want to spend my life with you. I can think of nothing more important than joining our lives together. My claim will be your claim. My heart is already yours.

I love you. I want to be your wife and your partner in life.

Katie Rose

Chapter 30: The Second Attack

July 1867 – Shamrock Sheep Ranch

Katie

Katie welcomed the evening and its cooler temperatures. Until she heard the wolves.

The smell of blood from the dead or injured sheep drew them to the flock. Katie knew she must act quickly.

She reloaded Sam's gun and grabbed her own shotgun. But she couldn't leave Sam unprotected. She knew Maddie would be facing off against the predators, but the pups wouldn't be much help in a fight. They could, however, stand guard over Sam. She called and whistled to Lorcan and Colm. The four-month-old border collies came running.

Satisfied that was the right decision, Katie dashed toward the sounds of howling wolves, barking dogs, and panicking sheep. When she arrived, Katie took in the scene. Three grown wolves and two wolf pups were circling the flock. The border collies, Maddie, Donnie, and Conan, were between the wolves and the sheep, holding the attackers at bay.

The largest wolf peeled off from the pack. Katie followed him with her shotgun. When the animal was clear of the flock, she fired. Unlike the first time she used a shotgun on Hughes' ranch, Katie's aim was sure this time. The wolf went down with one blast.

A second wolf dragged one of the dead sheep carcasses away while the third adult took this opportunity to charge past Maddie. Maddie lunged at the wolf, biting into the beast's fleshy hind leg. Then it was a battle between two canine foes. But unlike Maddie's fight with the coyotes, the wolf and the dog were more evenly matched. Katie watched in horror as the wolf tore into Maddie's front shoulder.

A shot rang out, and the wolf dropped. The other wolves scattered into the darkness.

Katie looked behind her to see Jake lowering his rifle.

Jake jumped from his saddle and ran to Katie. "Are you all right? He took her into his arms. She buried her head in his chest.

"I'm not hurt, but…Sam…Sam was shot."

Micah Brown arrived in time to hear Katie's last words. "Was it those damn hired guns from Deacon's outfit?"

Katie shrugged. She was still trying to take in all that was happening. Then she remembered Maddie and tore herself from Jake's arms.

"Maddie! Maddie!"

Both of them, Katie and Jake, ran to the dog. Maddie's body was heaving. Katie could see the gash left by the wolf's teeth.

"It's deep, but it doesn't look like anything's broken," Jake assessed.

"Give me your neckerchief," Katie ordered. "I'll bind it for now."

The two male pups that had been in the fight tumbled onto their mother. Maddie's motherly instincts took over, and she began licking her babies.

Katie sighed in relief that the three border collies had survived the wolf attack.

"They're fine, Katie Rose. They're fine." He gently patted Katie's back. "Let's check on Sam." He looked for the other two pups. "The girls? Maddie's girls?"

"They're watching over Sam. I thought if a wolf tried anything, at least I'd hear them yipping."

"Smart," he said.

Jake, Katie, and Micah found Sam awake, petting one of the puppies.

"I think they want their mama," Sam said.

"Maddie might be laid up for a while," Jake said. "She gave as good as she got from that wolf, but she'll pull through. I can't say the same for the wolf."

"Wolf?" Sam said. "What wolf?"

"Seems you missed the wolves attacking while you were lying around," Jake teased, in an effort to lighten the mood.

Micah was no stranger to battlefield medicine and was already examining Sam's wound. "Looks like you did some fine doctoring, Katie. But we should get him into the wagon."

Jake and Micah carefully moved the injured man into his wagon. Sam sighed, "It's good to be home."

Next, Jake turned his attention to the dead sheep and wolves. "They'll just draw more predators. The quickest way to get rid of them is to burn them."

Katie agreed. She gathered dry brush and grass while Jake piled the dead animals. "We'll light it and keep watch that it doesn't spread. But stay back. It's gonna smell something awful."

Jake tied on a spare neckerchief and motioned for Katie to keep her distance. "Katie, why don't you take the wagon back to the dugout. Micah can stay with the flock, and I'll be there after a bit."

Katie was grateful for the excuse to leave the carnage from the night and the previous day. She slowly drove the wagon back home on the moonless night, carefully avoiding as many bumps as possible.

Once there, Katie checked on Sam. He was sleeping more comfortably now. She smiled when she saw the border collie pup nestled in his arms.

Quietly, she unharnessed her mare from the wagon and led the horse into the makeshift pen that Jake had built. She patted the mare. "We'll get that barn built before winter comes, I promise."

In her dugout, Katie stripped out of her bloody, smokey clothes and washed as best she could. Then, almost dead on her feet, she simply fell onto her bed in a stupor.

The light was streaming through the door to the dugout when she awoke. Jake was there, sleeping in a chair at the kitchen table. She pulled on a shawl over her nightgown, and trying not to disturb him, Katie went to check on Sam.

The sheepherder was also awake. He smiled when he saw Katie peek into the wagon. "Good mornin', Miss Katie. You did a mighty fine job of doctorin'. 'Course, it's gonna be a couple of days before I'm up and about."

"It's going to be more than a 'couple of days,' Sam Goodman!" Katie scolded him. "That was a nasty gunshot. You'll be treated to some good ol' Irish hospitality until I say you're fit for duty."

"If you say so, ma'am."

"I hope you're hungry. I know I am! Breakfast will be ready soon."

From the wagon, she went to the well for water to make coffee. By then, Jake had emerged from the dugout and stretched to work out the kinks from sleeping in a chair.

"Good morning," she said brightly.

"And top o' the morning to you, Sunshine." He kissed Katie on her forehead.

"I'll expect something better later."

"That's a promise, ma'am."

Inside, Katie began breakfast while Jake made coffee. "We make a good team," he said.

"Yes, we do." Her green eyes sparkled. "I've been thinking about your plans."

"And?"

Katie retrieved her trousers and pulled the letter from a pocket. "I wrote this to you last night – in case the wolves or the raiders returned. I wanted you to know how I felt…about you."

302

Jake scanned the letter and still clutching the note, he pulled Katie into an embrace. "This means you're saying 'yes'? You'll marry me even though the law says you'll lose the rights to your claim?"

"Yes, and yes, mo chroí."

"Katie Rose Kelly – soon to be Katie Rose Riley – I promise we'll be partners in love and in life. My land will be your land.

"Katie Rose Riley," he repeated her name. "That has a nice sound to it." He held her face in his big, calloused hands and kissed her.

Over a breakfast of eggs, bacon, and toast, Jake filled in Katie on his trip to the Wright Ranch.

"The 'hoppers cleaned out the Wrights' pastures – but not before the Deacon boys had paid a visit to Sarah's flock. The raiders killed about a quarter of her sheep. She was furious. Tim had already ridden into town to fetch Micah. I met up with the sheriff when I was at their ranch. We headed here as soon as we could."

"Oh my goodness, poor Sarah. What can we do to help?"

"I told them they could move their herds south to our land. They'll have to cross the river, but it's pretty low this time of year. Should be here in a week or so."

"She's helped me so much. I'm happy to offer her sheep a place to graze."

Sheepishly, Jake added, "I might have mentioned to Tim and Sarah that I popped the question. Don't be surprised if Sarah says something…"

After breakfast, Katie and Jake rode out to relieve Micah of his sheepherding duties.

"I haven't ridden herd on sheep or cattle for years," the lawman declared. "Truth be told, I kinda like it. It's a lot easier – and safer – than riding herd on folks. I'm not real eager to confront Dan Deacon and those ranchers up north. But that's the job."

"Do you need some backup, Sheriff?" Jake asked.

"I'm not going alone. Some of the other Territorial sheriffs and a marshall will be coming, too. We'll meet in Twin Brooks. Then, we'll have a talk with the cattle ranchers. I'll look for that raider you winged, Katie. And, if I find him, he's looking at jail time, depending on the courts."

He continued. "I've heard the cattle wars in Wyoming and Texas have been a lot bloodier. I want to stop that from happening here."

"Thank you, Micah," Katie said.

"Good luck," Jake added.

The Wrights arrived about a week later. Since Jake didn't have any animals yet, he helped settle the Wrights' cattle and sheep onto some of his pasture lands. Tim and his two boys stayed with the herds. Sarah didn't have a sheep wagon, so Katie loaned the Wrights her wagon. In the meantime, Sam moved into a lean-to by the dugout that Jake and Tim built.

"It's only temporary," Katie explained to Sam. "And if a storm comes up…"

Sam interrupted her. "It's just dandy, Miss Katie. I'll get the summer breezes, and I can watch the stars from my bed at night. Besides, I'm getting stronger every day. I'll be back with the flock lickety-split."

Katie wiped her hands on her apron and just nodded. "Uh-huh," she said dubiously.

As good as his word, Sam was back with the flock in a few days. But to appease Katie, Sam and Jake shared the sheepherding duties for several weeks.

By the end of July, Jake was getting restless and decided to make a trip south to buy cattle. After consulting with Sarah, Tim announced he'd accompany Jake on the trip. Sarah and the Wright offspring stayed behind to watch the cattle and sheep.

Sarah and Katie waved goodbye to their men early on a summer morning. "I thought they'd never leave," Sarah laughed. "Now, let's get to work. I brought several lengths of fabric and some trims for your dress."

"What dress?" Katie was confused.

"Your wedding dress, of course! Did you think Jake could keep it a secret? There are some Godey's Ladies Books in my satchel. Pick out a dress, and we'll get started."

Katie was overwhelmed – but delighted. "My last new clothes were trousers!"

"Practical for ranching, but not acceptable for a wedding."

One of the lengths of fabric was a soft pink. "I thought it was perfect for your coloring," Sarah commented.

"And perfect for my wedding dress." Katie started to tear up.

"Now, don't you start crying before the wedding day!"

With Sam and the Wright children watching the combined flocks as well as the Wright cattle, Katie and Sarah had time to work on her dress.

"Have you and Jake set a date?" Sarah asked. She snipped the thread on the fabric rose she'd just sewn on the dress skirt.

"Mmmm, sometime this fall, I guess. I should talk with the pastor."

Sarah looked down at her handwork with a smile. "Mmm, yes."

A couple of weeks later, Sally Wright, the youngest of the brood, galloped up to the dugout. "They're here! They're back! Pa and Jake are back – and they're driving a herd of cattle."

Katie and Sarah hurried to the top of a nearby hill. Looking to the southeast, they saw a cloud of dust. The dust was kicked up by about one hundred head of beef cattle. Jake, Tim, and two other riders were moving the herd along.

When Jake saw Katie on the hill, he spurred his horse toward her.

"Tim and me – we did some deals – and I'm now a real rancher." He gave a hoot of delight.

Tim rode up to the group. "We picked up a couple of cowboys at the stockyards to help move the herd," he told the women. Then, looking at Katie, he said, "They've agreed to stay on and build you a barn, Katie."

"And a house," Jake added. His eyes gleamed at the thought, and he gave another hoot. He leaned down from his saddle and gave Katie a quick kiss.

During lunch, Jake and Tim filled in Katie and Sarah on the cattle-buying trip. "I'm gonna head north to check on our pasture land, Sarah," said Tim. "If it's coming back – and I think it probably has – I'll be back to fetch you, the kids, and the herds."

Tim was correct. The Wrights' grazing land was recovering from the grasshoppers, enough so that Tim thought they could put animals back on the pastures. He returned the following day, and the Wrights began packing up to return home.

"Thank you so much for the hospitality, Katie," Sarah said.

"That's what neighbors are for. Besides, it was wonderful to have another woman to talk to. Not to mention the beautiful dress you sewed for me. I can't wait to wear it! Now I just need – we just need – to set a date."

Sarah hugged her friend and climbed onto the buckboard wagon. She made a clicking sound, and the team started moving. Tim and the children were already ahead of her. "I'd better catch up. I'll see you soon."

Jake and the two ranch hands spent the next few days with the new cattle. He explained that the herd needed to get used to the new pastures. "I'll be back in a couple of days," he promised.

While he was gone, Katie got down to the business of sheep ranching. Sarah and Tim said they would be herding part of their sheep to market in about a month, so Katie asked Sam to start culling animals to send to market.

Then the wool buyers arrived. They inspected the wool that Katie had bagged up and, much to Katie's surprise, offered her a very agreeable price for her first wool harvest.

She felt good about her ranch and her life and wanted to share that good news.

Dear Da, Nan and Ryan,

First of all, congratulations, Da! I am so happy that you've remarried. Nan and I agreed that you were a widower for much too long. But now you've found the right woman.

I have some wedding news, too. Jake Riley, the cowboy I've written about in earlier letters, has asked me to marry him. We have been keeping company for a while now. He has helped me through some tough times – the prairie fire, a tornado, a flood, and some trouble on the ranch.

He has staked a claim directly south of my land and will be running cattle. The two claims meet at a big cottonwood tree that everyone calls Lone Tree. We'll build our home and our lives on the combined claims.

Nan, I want you to know that I took my time getting to know Jake. We were friends for a long time before our friendship grew into something more. I know he's the right man for me. I hope that someday you'll get to meet him.

Da and Ryan, you'll be proud to know I've had my first "payday" from the sheep. The wool we sheared in the spring just sold to merchants for a nice profit. Soon, I'll be shipping part of my flock to market. Maybe you'll get to enjoy some of my mutton!

My friend Sarah says, "Cattle are for the prestige. Sheep are for the cash." I am very happy to say that's true – at least at the Shamrock Sheep Ranch!

My love to all,

Katie Rose

Chapter 31: Lone Tree Claim

Autumn 1867 - Lone Tree Claim

Katie

They settled into a comfortable routine. Jake staked out the walls for their new home and the new barn. Katie was surprised that the two ranch hands, Will and Rick, seemed adept at carpentry.

"It's not a big house," Jake cautioned. "But we can add on when we need to."

"How about a stone chimney?" Katie suggested. "I want to help, so I'll take the buckboard and collect rocks from the river bed."

The new house, built with lumber and river rock, began to take shape. Katie was looking forward to living in a home made of real lumber. While the dugout had been practical, she wouldn't miss the constant battle with bugs crawling out of the walls and ceiling.

"I heard Will and Rick talking about a cattle drive down south. Are we going to lose them before the barn is built?" Katie asked Jake one evening.

"Yep. That's the thing with cowboys – there's always another drive to join. But I was thinking we should have a barn raising. Invite the town. Make it a big party. What do you say, Katie Rose?"

"I think that's a grand idea! We have a lot to celebrate."

And so the preparations began. Jake and Sam moved the old cookstove and Katie's few pieces of furniture into the new house. She settled in while Sam and Jake camped with the sheep and cattle.

Jake arrived at the house one morning with Katie's horse saddled and ready to ride.

"Katie!" he called into the house. "I'm making a trip to town today. I expect you might be wanting a few things for the barn raising next Saturday?"

She took in the two horses and just laughed. "Let me get my list!"

Katie found autumn on the Dakota prairie to be breathtaking. The orange and golden prairie flowers. The leaves on the few trees along the way were starting to turn shades of yellow. Overhead, flocks of birds chattered as they gathered for their annual migration south.

"You know, I think I like autumn on the prairie best of all," Katie said. "The smells of the grasses and leaves are so rich and fragrant. The sound of the breeze rustling through the tall prairie grass is like a song."

They rode in silence, each enjoying the beauty of the frontier. Soon, too soon, in Jake's opinion, they arrived in Twin Brooks.

"The town's growing," Jake observed. "There's a new school house. And over there, that's a church."

"I'm sure Polly can fill us in on all the news."

Katie was right. Polly was cleaning glassware when they entered the saloon.

"Hey, strangers!" she called out.

"Polly, it's been too long! It's so good to see you," Katie answered.

"I heard there's a party out your way," the saloon-keeper said.

"Yes! That's one of the reasons we're in town. I wanted to invite you and Micah to the barn raising."

"Wouldn't miss it for the world!" Polly said.

"Miss what?" Micah said as he entered the saloon.

The three brought Micah up to speed on the barn raising. "I have news for you, too," he said. "The crew that attacked your sheep and Wright's flock, along with some others around here, are cooling their heels in the territorial jail in Yankton."

"What about the men who hired them?" Katie asked.

"I'm getting to that," Brown said. "Dan Deacon and his cronies will stand trial for breaking the law. If they're found guilty…"

At this, Polly snorted.

The sheriff continued, "If they're found guilty, they could serve time. But they'll probably plead out and then they'll pay fines to reimburse the sheepherders who lost livestock."

"Seems like they should be behind bars, too," Polly asserted.

"Maybe, but these are powerful men," Micah replied. "The law is sending a message. Let's hope we can avoid more trouble."

"I hope you're right, Micah," Katie said. "But I'm not going to think about those horrible men right now. I have a barn raising to host!"

"Katie's afraid she'll run out of food for the shindig," Jake explained.

"Oh, don't you worry about that, Katie," Polly said. "Everyone will bring goodies for a barn raising. It's the tradition."

"I know, but still…." Her voice trailed out.

"Well, go ahead and do your business, then come back for a beer," Polly instructed them.

The couple left to do as Polly commanded, each going their separate ways. Jake was already at Polly's Place when Katie re-entered the saloon. "The beers are on the house," Polly said. "I hear that congratulations are in order."

Katie just blushed. "We still need to set the date."

"That we do," Jake agreed.

After catching up on all the news of Twin Brooks, Katie and Jake headed back home. The sun was setting earlier in the evening. By the time they reached Lone Tree, Jake suggested they give the horses a rest. He helped Katie off her horse, and they sat down under the canopy of the big tree. She nestled into his chest, and he wrapped an arm around her.

"I've decided," he announced.

"Decided what?"

"What to call my ranch. There's the Double D, the Rocking W, the Shamrock. I'm calling the claim the 'Lone

313

Tree.' It has a good ring to it. Of course, the sheep will still be Shamrock Sheep."

Katie's face lit up. "The Lone Tree is perfect. It joins both our claims. I knew you'd find the right name."

Preparations for the barn raising heated up over the next few days. Katie made dozens of cookies and cakes. Jake decided they should have a barbecue 'just like down south,' but Katie convinced him to save his cattle for another time. "We have a lot more sheep. Ask Sam to pick out a likely animal for dinner."

"Yes, ma'am," he replied.

The morning of the barn raising, Sam and Jake had assembled the lumber and the hardware needed for the project. The Wrights were the first to arrive. Sarah hurried into the new house.

"Now, don't get upset, but you need to put on that new dress we made," Sarah said.

At first, Katie looked confused, but then it dawned on her. "This isn't just a barn raising, is it?"

Sarah's huge smile was all the answer that Katie needed.

The bride-to-be was nearly ready when Polly entered. "The pastor and the guests are all here. And I brought you a bouquet to carry." She handed Katie a bouquet of prairie wildflowers – black-eyed susans, golden rods, asters, and white boneset.

"They're beautiful," Katie said, overwhelmed. "And now, I'm going to cry." Tears welled up in Katie's eyes.

Polly pulled a lace hanky from her pocket and handed it to Katie. "Dry your eyes. This can be your 'something borrowed.'" Polly looked at Sarah, "Are we ready?"

Sarah nodded. Going to the door of the new house, Sarah nodded to a group of musicians on a platform.

On cue, the band began playing the *Wedding March*. Sarah and Polly hurried from the house, allowing Katie time for a grand entrance.

Wooden benches had been assembled, creating an aisle between the rows. At the end of the aisle stood Jake Riley and the town pastor.

Katie fleetingly thought back to her first wedding, when she married Patrick Kelly. *This is so much better,* she thought to herself.

Katie Rose Kelly stepped from the house, wearing the pale pink wedding dress and holding a bouquet of autumn flowers.

Jake Riley looked at her as if she was the only woman in the world. In fact, she was the only woman in *his* world.

They said their vows, and he placed a gold wedding band on her left hand.

"You may kiss the bride," the pastor intoned.

"I love you, Katie Rose Riley," Jake said to his new wife.

"And I love you, Jake Riley." She looked at their friends who had gathered. "Thank you for making this day so special."

Jake whistled. "Let's celebrate!"

The End

About the Author

Amazon best-selling author CK Van Dam is a daughter of the Dakota prairies. Lone Tree Claim is the second in her series of historical novels about the strong women who have built our nation and our world. Van Dam's first novel, Proving Her Claim, received two Spur Awards from Western Writers of America.

Learn more at ckvandam.com